I0733770

2

FEBRUARY:
CURIOUS

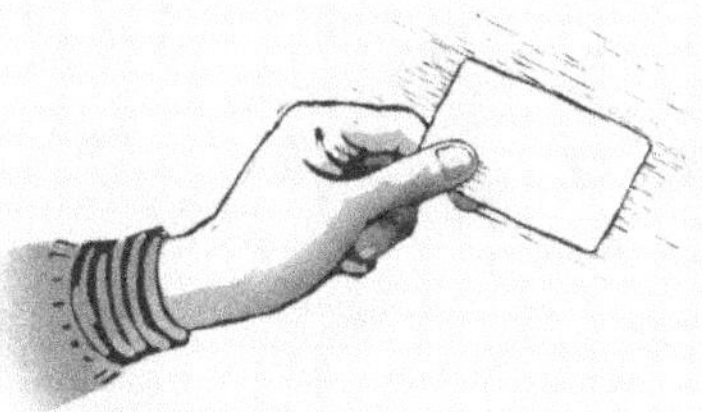

JAN FANCY HULL

A
TIM BROWN
MYSTERY

© 2022 Jan Fancy Hull

All rights reserved. No part of this book may be reproduced or transmitted in any form or by any means, electronic or mechanical, including photocopying, or by any information storage or retrieval system, without permission in writing from the publisher.

Cover image: Rebekah Wetmore
Editor: Andrew Wetmore

ISBN: 978-1-990187-33-9
First edition June 2022

2475 Perotte Road
Annapolis County, NS
B0S 1A0

moosehousepress.com
info@moosehousepress.com

We live and work in Mi'kma'ki, the ancestral and unceded territory of the Mi'kmaw people. This territory is covered by the "Treaties of Peace and Friendship" which Mi'kmaw and Wolastoqiyik (Maliseet) people first signed with the British Crown in 1725. The treaties did not deal with surrender of lands and resources but in fact recognized Mi'kmaq and Wolastoqiyik (Maliseet) title and established the rules for what was to be an ongoing relationship between nations. We are all Treaty people.

Books by Jan Fancy Hull

Non-fiction

Where's Home?

Short stories

The Church of Little Bo Peep and other stories

Inquire Within

The Tim Brown Mystery Series

January: Code

February: Curious

March: Enigma (coming in the fall of 2022)

The cure for boredom is curiosity.
There is no cure for curiosity.
—attributed to Dorothy Parker

This book is dedicated to the curious.
Uncover something good.

This is a work of fiction. The author has created the characters, conversations, interactions, and events; and any resemblance of any character to any real person is coincidental.

Contents

Jan Fancy Hull

February 1, 1999: Recalculating

Monday

Tim was starting a brand new chapter in his life—again. He expected some bumps along the way, especially after the month he'd gone through. Surely the bumps would be more manageable now —and more figurative than literal. He'd be pursuing his own interests, and he would be an easier boss to work for than his Aunt Stella had been.

Had she really changed? She did seem to be softening through the evening yesterday, but while top-shelf wine and a crackling fire were powerful change agents, the changes could be short-lived. He hoped for lasting improvements where relations with his aunt were concerned.

He had given Stella pretty much a whole month of his time, the first month of his treasured sabbatical year away from his work as editor and publisher of South River's weekly paper, *The Times*. In that month, he had more or less resolved his aunt's conundrum. He'd been eager to get started on his own quest to "delve" into issues around his hometown of South River, but he hadn't had a clue how to begin. That was embarrassing, so his aunt's quest had been a timely diversion and a learning opportunity. The road had not been smooth, but he felt he had learned a few things that might prove useful when delving into his own interests.

Of course, his report to Stella had been based on fibs. Maybe not the whole of it, but the file mix-up story was solidly in the white category of lies, a fabrication, a fiction. No harm done whether she found out or not. *Please don't let that happen before tomorrow night*, Tim begged the universe. *Get her surprise party over with, and then all the loose threads can unravel or be bound up, it won't matter which.*

The storm was not followed immediately by a sunny day, as sometimes happened. Today was overcast. The storm had altered the landscape outside. Snow banks made fortress walls fronting every property. He couldn't see the shops across the street, but he could see the peaks of a mountain range of snow the big bucket-loaders had scraped up from the parking lot. There was a trio of bagged newspapers on the porch, just the tops visible in the snow that had drifted in. He hadn't thought to collect the papers for a few days, he'd been so distracted, or focused, or both.

Driving around would be difficult, as the town would be scooping snow from the narrow streets. He knew what that back alley behind his office building would be like, drifts over top of that dumpster. No need to add to that congestion. He was content to work at home for the third day in a row.

He considered the rolled-up notes and notebooks and other assorted papers on which he had jotted thoughts and questions through January. He'd told Stella he was going to burn them, but he didn't like that idea this morning. All that work, up in smoke? Might it prove useful another day, for some other reason? Maybe to review his investigating methodology? There surely could be some efficiencies to be learned for another time. If one was supposed to be able to learn from one's mistakes, there was a lot of learning available there. He knew that repeating old mistakes stung like iodine in a fresh cut. He hoped for new mistakes.

This gave him a good question for future delving consideration, which he scribbled on a scrap of paper: *Do things have value just because we spend time on them?*

He started a new notebook, which he titled *DELVING TOPICS*. He tore out the first page, titled it *GET*, and wrote *Notebooks*. He had gone through a great many of them last month; not that he had written so much in them, but he had written a little in a lot of them, front and back and random pages in between, in the house and in his car. Evidence of a disorganized mind, he knew. No wonder he had found it such a struggle to solve that puzzle. He would try to use one notebook at a time from now on, one page after another.

Flipping through those notebooks, he saw delving ideas that had occurred to him on the fly last month. He copied them neatly into the new book, adding the one he had just thought of. These were exciting, and he was eager to pick one and get going on it. Or maybe he'd pick two, so if one lagged he'd be occupied with another. He could feel the potential.

> 1. *First, the evidence. Period.*
> 2. *Police: sidearm use, frequency, reports, protocols*
> 3. *Tow Away Zones: town bylaws? legal? Grey area?*
> 4. *Emergency Procedures: what businesses have them and are they observed?*
> 5. *Do we retain habits after the reason has gone, because they are habits, not reasons?*
> 6. *Do things have value just because we spend time on them?*

There was an empty accordion-style cardboard file in the back of a drawer in the tall cabinet next to the desk in the study. He folded or bent all the documents he had accumulated in the past month, including the multiple flip-chart pages he'd taped up all over the downstairs while he had worked to solve Stella's Mystery of the Code. He stuffed them all into the file, and looped the string in a figure-eight over the buttons on the front to keep it securely closed. With a black marker, he wrote *JANUARY* on the front flap and placed it back in the drawer.

A few minutes later, he took it out again. Lots of files were labelled *January*, here at home and in the newspaper office. He had recently learned what a colossal mess could result from look-alike file titles, so he added *CODE* to the flap.

JANUARY: CODE contained the elements of quite an entertaining account of his first month's attempt at delving, however thwarted it had become. Perhaps he'd write about those experiences sometime.

He wondered about the event planned for tomorrow, in celebration of Stella's birthday. Was it her sixtieth? It must be some milestone, to warrant such a lavish shindig.

He smiled at the thought, and then frowned at the elaborate measures that had been taken to cover it up. *Oh, what a tangled web we weave,* he reminded himself, *when first we practise to deceive.* Perhaps he would put that on the wall in the den, right under the plaque that urged him not to drift.

Robert phoned from the city, and they traded storm stories. He was surprised that Tim had ventured to entertain Stella on his own. She was his family and entitled to visit, of course, but what did he make for their dinner?

"She asked about you, almost didn't come when I told her you weren't here. But you know, burnt onions in beef drippings, accompanied by a good wine, is a pretty good meal, if I do say so myself."

"Mmmm. You must share your recipe."

February 2: Groundhog Day

Tuesday

When morning finally showed some light, it continued under overcast skies—typical February. The groundhog had no chance to be frightened by its own shadow today, so there would be only six more weeks of winter, according to folklore.

Inside Tim's kitchen, however, it felt like a sunny day, bright and cheerful. He read the morning paper while enjoying a cappuccino from the compliant European machine, dubbed "Gloria". He had found it so difficult to learn to operate it, so easy to do now. He wasn't certain what had contributed to the change, but she seemed to work best when he was assertive with humans, so maybe that carried over to machines that blew steam as well.

Tim continued plotting and planning, still trying to get his sail to catch a breeze and get moving, as the plaque in the study advised:

> To reach a port we must sail,
> Sometimes with the wind, and sometimes against it.
> But we must not drift or lie at anchor.
> - Oliver Wendell Holmes

"Not going to drift," he said to the plaque. "Going to sail. Going to delve into something interesting, something that will..." What was it, again? It was so easy to lose sight of what he hoped to achieve by delving, complicated by his reluctance to focus on an outcome. He just wanted to ask, ask, ask, and see where that would lead.

So, ask already, he chastised himself. *Or observe, at least.* That's what his mentor, Sherlock Holmes, no relation to Oliver Wendell, would advise.

He thought it would be helpful to start a notebook for each of the numbered topics, so he would be able to keep all the notes in one book for whichever of them might blossom—and maybe all of them would. There were no more fresh notebooks in the house. He could use scrap paper, but that didn't portray faith in his work, so he decided to make a quick trip to the office supplies store. He purchased a pack of ten spiral notebooks. That looked like business.

On the way home, he swung by the drive-thru coffee-shop for a large black, for old time's sake, and when the tinny voice asked if that would be all, he said "Two honey crullers, please." Blame it on habit.

He drove right home again, keeping his head in the cloud of destiny he had begun the day with, and took his purchases to the desk. Purposeful work, coffee, donuts—now that was a familiar and comforting scene. All that was missing from his years in the newspaper office was the clatter and constant interruptions. He didn't miss any of that. Last month, he had fallen asleep without those usual stimulants, but now he was acclimated to this new, quieter life.

Topic Number One: *First, the evidence. Period*. What did that mean? Was that actually a topic to be explored, or was it methodology? Should he devote a whole notebook to it?

"Don't think," he said aloud. "Just do." He wrote the topic on the first page inside the notebook and left it open for further developments.

Topic Number Two: *Police: sidearm use etc*. Now this was personal. No policeman had pointed a gun at Tim last month, but one nearly did, and that was close enough. He would definitely delve into that later.

Topic Number Three: *Tow-away zones*. This was more of a grey area than he had expected. Seeing his car on a tow truck hoist in the Loading Zone behind his office building had been a great surprise. He realized he didn't know who owned that precious strip of real estate, his business or the town. Who surveyed its dimensions, and who paid the taxes on it? Who had jurisdiction over the alley?

Lots of good questions to delve into there, though he put a red circle around the question about taxes: how deeply he delved might be determined by whether it was his land or not, and whether he had paid or owed taxes on it.

He took a big bite of the donut and considered the larger question raised by this question. Was it delving if he permitted personal matters to affect the course of his investigations? Wasn't that exactly and precisely what he was taking this sabbatical year to avoid? The rigours of a weekly community newspaper were tied quite closely to vested interests of all kinds, and he had wanted to step outside that trap, to see if—*if*—things appeared differently without those chains of assumptions and obligations. He couldn't erase the red circle, so he drew an "unhappy face" next to it to remind himself that he should keep an open mind.

This was going well. Coffee and donuts were soon gone, and he didn't recall how or when they went, a sign of deep concentration, he hoped, though not of good nutrition.

It was lunchtime. He wasn't hungry, but he folded a slice of bread around a piece of leftover roast beef, poured a tall glass of milk, and returned to the desk.

Topic Number Four: *Emergency procedures*. They had created such a document at *The Times*, with all tasks and processes assigned to staff, with one exception: nobody was in charge of keeping it up to date. Hence, when a case of mistaken identity resulted in a call to the police, the receptionist followed the written protocol, which said to notify Tim Brown. Trouble was, Mister Brown was on leave, so she'd phoned and left a message for him at home, while the interim editor, sitting in her office, remained unaware of any incident until the cops walked in.

Tim shook his head. That wasn't one of his happier memories, but—following yesterday's train of thought—at least it was a new mistake. He would see that the oversights were corrected at his own workplace, but there might be some value in delving into what other businesses had in place for emergencies, if anything.

Topic Number Five: *Habits vs Reasons*. What had he meant by this? Was this delvable? It might be a good dinner conversation, with the right people around the table. He'd give it a notebook and see about that later.

Topic Number Six: *Do things have value just because we spend time on them?* He didn't have a clear grasp of this concept, but he had the sense that delving into it might reveal the story of his life. Or his late mother's life. The newspaper enterprise which he now owned had been in his family for four generations, and he suspected that he spent a lot of time doing things because somebody had done them before him. Tim, and his Aunt Stella, who was preoccupied as the local MLA, not connected with the paper at all, were the only members of the Johnson dynasty left; even so, he would need to tread carefully if he were to pursue this topic. Many of his faithful subscribers felt they had ownership of the local paper, which was true in a way. His long-serving employees, too. Tim thought he should take care not to step on his own toes with this one. Self-knowledge was rare, and self-discovery could be bruising.

He finished labelling the notebooks and jotting his preliminary thoughts in each. This had been fruitful. He hadn't been able to accomplish this when 1999 began. He had been too eager to get go-go-going, while his ship was still at anchor, and that anchor was embedded deep in his career. Well, he could thank Stella for hoisting it out of the muck, though she tried to dictate where he should sail. No harm. He was now ready to roam. He had six more-or-less strong compass points to embark upon.

~

As the day grew dark again and it looked like life would resume normal operation, a tiny thought grew until he spoke out loud to the old kitchen clock.

"Six thirty-five, is it? Guess what's happening in half an hour."

He had promised himself to curb impetuous excursions, but before he could think better of it, he pulled on boots and jacket and carefully drove to the snowy road leading downriver to observe what might be happening at Stella's party. He was just curious, about how many cars would be there, where would they park with all the snow around, and how would the caterers be able to set up without spoiling the surprise? As much of a challenge as the planning had been, the actual carrying out of this party must have taken a ton of work without being discovered or rumoured around town.

He slowed as he approached Stella's driveway. Not a car in sight. It was nearly seven.

His heart sank. Something must have gone wrong. Had someone spilled the beans? Had Stella put the kibosh on the party? Had he been duped, and there was no party at all?

Her long, plowed driveway looked lonely. A dim light inside the house indicated that Stella was home, and a single light was on at the front door, but the house certainly didn't look like a party location.

There was no safe place to turn around there, with the twists in the narrow road, even narrower with snow piled up on either side, so he drove on by. A summer motel was around the turn, a couple hundred feet farther along. He would turn around there if the entrance was cleared enough.

Oh, it was cleared all right. The horseshoe-shaped driveway was plowed wide and clear of snow. Tiki lights were burning in the snow banks at the entrance. Cars of all kinds were parked around the whole driveway, along with a tour bus and a box van. The motel was dark, but people were milling about in front, heading toward the bus, boarding the bus. Tim pulled over on the narrow roadside and turned off the car.

What was going on? He quickly counted at least twenty cars parked in the semi-circle, and he knew that a passenger bus carried about forty-seven people.

Then the bus pulled out of the horseshoe and turned right, back toward South River, followed by the box van on which was painted the name of a caterer from the city. When they were nearly out of sight around the turn, Tim saw the bus and box van's brake lights and right turn signals flash before they disappeared into Stella's driveway.

Well, well, well! Some strategic ingenuity had gone into these arrangements. Stella's doorbell would be ringing right now, and what a spectacle would greet her! A huge bus, disgorging dozens of partiers calling out "Happy Birthday Stella! Surprise!" as they invaded her front entryway, followed by steam tables and trays of food, he imagined, carried by uniformed caterers.

Bravo to the army of conspirators who worked to pull this thing off!

Tim hoped that Sunday's gentler Stella would be the one who opened her door, not the control freak who would be mortified to find herself surrounded by her most fervent supporters when she was neither dressed nor made up. Surprises were not always happy events, despite intentions.

He was curious to see the party underway, but he couldn't just knock on her door uninvited. Maybe he could approach undetected along the riverbank. Because the motel and Stella's house were situated on a curve on the road, they were much closer together at the river than at the road. He could wear the barn boots, still in the trunk.

The boots turned out to be a good idea, as the snow was deep in drifts. He hadn't stopped to dress warmly when he left the house, as he'd expected to stay in the car, so now he also pulled on the plaid jacket and hat from the trunk. He took out his new backpack with the binoculars and the long silver flashlight in it.

It was dark out, though not pitch black. The clouds had parted, and the white snow reflected moonlight.

He trudged behind the motel and headed left along the river. It was harder going than he had anticipated as he encountered occasional invisible drifts.

He could already see the lights from the lower level of Stella's house, where her well-appointed and rarely-used entertainment room led through double doors to a sheltered patio, partly snow-covered. He could hear loud laughter, and live music. The instant party was underway.

He didn't plan to go closer, certainly didn't want to be recognized. He only wanted to satisfy his curiosity, to verify that there was a party after all, not a nomination, petition, or insurrection.

The guests were having too much fun for those.

He sat in a snow-drift, retrieved the binoculars from the back-pack, and focused them on the party windows. After a bit of fiddling to focus he could see clearly, and recognized several well-heeled South Riverites in the group. Servers dressed in black were circulating with trays of canapés and glasses of drinks.

Where was the guest of honour? *Don't tell me she's taken refuge in her room,* he thought. Then there was a commotion, applause, and whistles. Stella entered the room looking more elegant than any of her elegant guests.

"Brava, Stella," he said quietly. She certainly was a class act, ready or not.

He spied Stella's intern, Brittany, on the arm of a man who must be her fisherman husband, both looking handsome. And there was Garland Greene, Mayor of South River and instigator of this event, beaming, with his dowdy wife Patty at his elbow.

Tim saw enough to satisfy himself that all was on the up and up. It was time to go, and besides, it was darn cold sitting in a snow-drift. It was a beautiful night, though. He could see right across the river in the moonlight.

He giant-stepped back toward the motel. As he rounded the corner toward the semi-circle of parked vehicles, he saw the dome light of one of the cars come on. He stopped and watched from the shadows. He certainly didn't want to be discovered, not here, not now, not again.

Whoever was in the car got out and gently closed the door, and the dome light went off. Then another dome light came on. By the third time the pattern repeated, Tim realized he was watching a thief working the line of cars, most of which were unlocked because that was the South River way.

What to do? He could yell "Hey!" and the robber would likely run away. But perhaps he wouldn't. Maybe he'd come toward Tim, armed with a tire iron or worse. He couldn't just stand there in the cold until this fellow finished his pillaging, now could he? He wasn't going to watch him work his way to Tim's own car.

What was he looking for, anyway? Anything loose, he guessed.

Perhaps this crowd left better stuff in their vehicles than Tim did, unless empty coffee cups had a value. Whatever this creep was finding, Tim knew people didn't want it taken.

It was up to Tim to apprehend him.

He didn't like that at all.

Seeing no alternative, he began to work out a plan. The robber was spending about three minutes in each car, and while he was doing his work under the dome light, he'd be blinded to what was going on outside in the dark. Rookie mistake, Tim thought, feeling a little bit superior.

So he played hide and hide with this unknown petty thief until they were on opposite ends of a big silver SUV, which he immediately knew belonged to Mayor Garland Greene. The perp found Gar's door unlocked, pulled it open, stepped up on the running board, and leaned in. Tim rushed forward and pushed the door hard, pinning the thief against the door post.

"Hey, what the f—!" the fellow yelled.

The fellow sounded a lot like a girl, but no matter. Equal opportunity, still wrong.

"Stop right there," Tim ordered in a loud voice. "Drop your bag and put your hands up!"

What else would he say? Having said it, what should he do next?

The thief tried to push back against the car door. Tim leaned harder and said, "Don't even think about it, buster. Put your hands up, and I mean *now*!"

"I can't! You're crushing me!" The voice definitely belonged to a girl.

"Tell me what you're doing here," Tim said as gruffly as he could. "What're you after?"

"None of your business, you old fart! Let me go!"

"Oh, it's like that, is it? Okay then. I didn't want to do this, but you leave me no choice."

Tim pushed again on the door, then quickly reached in the gap and pulled the saucy robber out by the hair. He had squeezed the breath out of her and she was gasping.

Taking advantage of her momentary incapacity, he grabbed her parka hood, tugged it down over her face and pulled the dangling pom-pom ties. He crossed them under her chin and quickly tied them tightly behind her head.

"Help help!" she cried from inside the hood. "I'm suffocating! You're killing me, you bastard!"

"You're not dead yet, considering the noise you're making. Now shut up and settle down. Who are you and what are you doing here?"

"None of your damn business!" replied potty-mouth. "Let me go!"

They had already progressed very far along in a play Tim had never planned to act in. Why not let her go? She'd run off and he'd leave her bag of ill-gotten gains on the hood of Gar's SUV and high-tail it for home himself. Problem avoided, averted, solved. Right?

No.

"Listen, you little thief. I caught you red-handed stealing from these people's cars. I'm not letting you go. You—you've done wrong and you must pay."

He sounded a little like a country song. He was in it up to his ears now so he had to press on.

"You ain't a cop. You can't keep me here. Let me go!"

In broad daylight, Tim would be the first one to agree: he was not a cop. But in this moonlit night, he might impersonate some kind of law enforcement long enough to resolve this mess.

"You're wrong there, kiddo. I'm the security guard hired to protect these cars. Let's go."

He had the kid's hood and ties in his left hand. She was trying to strike out at him but her arm movements were restricted in the hunched-up parka. His long arm kept her away from landing most of the kicks, and the high green boots gave his shins some protection.

With his right hand, he retrieved the long-handled silver flashlight from his backpack. It was a multi-purpose weapon. He poked the butt end of the flashlight into the kid's back, hard. He put his mouth close to the parka hood.

"This is the business end of a sawed-off shotgun, kid. Now settle down or it might go off by accident. We're going to meet the people you've been stealing from."

Tim's two hands were more than full, but he looped his shotgun arm through the straps of the thief's backpack containing the stolen goods, as well as his own backpack straps.

"Now march!"

"Where? I can't see, you old—"

"That's enough from you!" he said, shaking the parka and its contents. "You just walk and I'll tell you where."

Off they went, the tall, thin man in the boots, checked jacket, and balaclava beneath a cap with lowered ear flaps, pushing and pulling a noisy girl trapped in her own parka.

They followed his tracks behind the motel and around the corner toward Stella's house. Her party was rocking. The double glass doors were open to the patio, smokers were outside, music was pouring out, and laughter continued inside. More tiki lights were stuck in the snow at the corners of the patio, which someone had cleared of snow. It looked like a fun time.

When Tim and his quarry stumbled into the outer reach of light from the patio, someone said, "Hey, who's that?"

He trudged a few steps closer to the crowd, perspiring and breathing heavily, pushing and dragging his uncooperative pris-oner. They presented the oddest sight to the partiers. It looked like a tall hunter had bagged some kind of game which was still very much alive and kicking.

A man in a tux stepped forward to the edge of the patio. "Hey, you," he called. "Beat it. This is a private party."

"Help! Help!" cried the thief. "Somebody help me!"

"Shut up, you rascal," Tim said, giving the parka a shake.

"What's going on?" asked several more celebrants as word of the ruckus outside spread inside. The band stopped playing. Every-thing went quiet.

Stella strode through the crowd, all five feet of her, plus heels. "What is the meaning of this?" she demanded from the flagstone edge of the patio.

Right then, Tim knew he should not identify himself as Stella's only living relative.

"I caught this person looting your guests' vehicles over at the motel," he said, gruffly. "Ma'am."

He held up both backpacks, which were on his right arm and secured there by the flashlight which he had been pointing like a weapon. He took a few more steps ahead with his prisoner.

"Stop right there, mister," said one of the male guests, a huge man with a shaved head. "Drop your weapon."

"Shut up, Marcus," Stella said sharply. "We're in no danger."

To Tim, she repeated, "What is the meaning of this? What is that? *Who* is that?"

Tim wondered what she must be thinking of this scene. His balaclava had partially unrolled over one eye under the woodsman's cap. He must look deranged. He was lucky his aunt recognized his voice, otherwise he might soon be whisked away in the back of a Mountie cruiser. Who knew, he might end up there anyway.

He let the two backpacks slide to the ground, and released his quarry's parka hood so her identity could be revealed.

"Marcy?"

Someone in the crowd knew the thief.

"Help! Help!" cried the thief. "He's abducting me! Stranger-danger! Help!"

"I'm not abducting you, you juvenile delinquent. If I were, I wouldn't have dragged you to this crowd, would I?" Tim gave the parka a shake. "Does someone here know this kid?"

"I don't know nobody here. Lemme go!"

"Marcy! Why are you here, dear?"

"Marcy, is it? Well, Marcy here has been visiting your unlocked vehicles over there, and she has a bag full of your possessions right here."

Tim tossed her loot-filled backpack toward the patio. "I suggest that whoever this kid belongs to can take over from here."

A couple came through the crowd and the girl's father stepped out into the snow. Tim backed away as the father grabbed his daughter's arm and roughly pulled her into Stella's house, where all three members of that unhappy family began shouting.

Stella paid no attention to them. She remained focused on Tim, who had still not been identified.

"My work here is done," Tim said, just loud enough that she could hear. He touched the brim of his cap and turned back toward the motel. Shouts commanded him to stop and come back, but he didn't acknowledge them.

When he reached darkness again, he turned to look back. Stella was still at the edge of the patio, watching him. Then she turned, raised her arms to usher her guests back inside, and soon he could hear the thump-thump of the band starting up again. *She'll handle it,* he said to himself. *A walk in the park for Stella.*

He stumbled through the trail he had broken behind the motel, and jogged back to his car on the side of the road. It wasn't locked either, but Marcy hadn't reached it. Lesson learned.

Gasping to catch his breath, he drove downriver, away from the parked cars, away from Stella's front driveway, away from the two adults holding a struggling youngster between them by the arms, coming along the edge of the road toward their vehicle in front of the motel. He prayed that nobody other than Stella had recognized his voice. Spencer might have but he was likely in the bus with the engine running, out of earshot of all the excitement.

Tim was soaked with perspiration from his exertions, and shaking with the adrenaline rush of what had happened. An icy drive in the dark on the circuitous route home was not what he wanted to do now.

Luck was with him. The South River cable ferry was still in. He checked the time on his dashboard clock: it was due to leave any minute. He drove on board, and the ferry immediately pulled away from the shore.

He had straightened the balaclava so he could see well enough to drive, but he knew he still looked freaky. The ferry attendant who came to the car window seemed startled. Tim paid the fare without saying a word and the attendant didn't speak either, possibly fearing he had an axe-murderer on board. Tim hoped to get home without being recognized or picked out of a police lineup, if those things really happened in South River.

Once safely parked in his own driveway, he rushed into the safety and anonymity of his own home, and shucked the cap, tuque, jacket and boots. He left them on the floor of the foyer and went directly to the shower to clean up and warm up.

After he dried off, he poured himself a snifter of courage from the liquor locker, and sat in front of the electric fire's heat to contemplate what had happened.

He had nearly ruined Stella's party, that's what had happened. What had he been thinking, abducting that juvenile delinquent? She'd have bruises. Why had he gotten involved at all? What else could he have done?

By the sound of the family row, this kind of altercation wasn't news to any of them. Perhaps that party crowd, power-brokers all, would find a way to see that the young lady got the right help. The belligerent father might be Marcy's problem more than the other way around. He would ask Stella about it.

Ah, yes, Stella. She'd no doubt be asking him some good questions of her own, and they would sting. The warmth they'd achieved on Sunday will have frozen solid, he expected. Crashing her party. Embarrassing her in front of her power-base. Over-stepping his boundaries. Rough-handling and threatening a minor.

Nothing to be done about it now. He wouldn't call her tonight. The party could still be going on. It had sounded like a good one.

He looked at the pile of clothes on the foyer floor. Were they a good kit? Did they come in handy when needed? Or did they enable his bad ideas? If he hadn't had the knee-high boots, would he've been tempted to trudge through deep snow to spy on the party, and what did he do that for anyway?

That was creepy, he confessed. A real security guard might have come behind him and dragged *him* to the edge of Stella's patio, accusing him of being a peeping Tom, and what defence would he have? "I was just curious" wouldn't do. Guilty as charged.

No, he had better dismantle that kit for his own safety. He would take it all to the hospital charity shop.

Tomorrow, he'd give himself another lecture about impulses

that involved hiding out to spy on people. Tonight, he would try to sleep.

His left shoulder was beginning to stiffen from hanging on to that remarkably active kid, and his shins were bruised despite the boots' protection. He warmed some milk and took it, with a couple of aspirins, to bed.

February 3: The day after that

Wednesday

Tim was leafing through one of several newspapers that had accumulated on the porch, not concentrating on anything, hardly noticing the beverage Gloria had yielded, when Stella phoned. He answered the call with dread.

"I'm sorry," he said preemptively.

"Good morning, Timothy," Stella said. "I hope it's not too early to call. I expected you might need to sleep in after your exertions of last night. I confess I'm a little slow getting underway myself, as the party went on quite late for a Tuesday night."

Was that laughter in her voice? "No, I'm up, thanks. How much trouble am I in?"

"You? You're not in trouble, not at all. My goodness, perhaps you didn't see the bounty that young person had gathered from the cars. Unbelievable what people leave in their unlocked vehicles. We had quite a lot of fun with it last night. Someone decided to empty it all out on the ping-pong table and make a game of it. They called it something like 'That's Not Mine, Must Be Yours'. Very funny when nobody claimed the condoms or the baggies—note the plural—*baggies* of marijuana. And papers. Even a pack of cigarettes went unclaimed. Presumably we have a clandestine smoker."

"Aunt Stella, what are you telling me? You had fun? You played *games*? Here I was dreading the long arm of the law, or your displeasure. Not sure which'd be worse."

"Well, dread no more. Neither will happen. I did wonder why you were there at all, of course, and in that backwoods outfit. Wherever did you get it, and why? Never mind. I quickly realized that you were looking out for me, in some ill-advised way perhaps, but with my interest at heart. Perhaps you were not certain if the story you told me about no one intending to harm me was actually true, so you came to see about that. Whatever it was, please don't tell me. It's over now. You were there, I'm safe, and you apprehended a child who may gain some kind of legal attention for her protection rather than for committing a gateway crime, so that is a very good thing for her. And you managed to keep your identity a secret from everyone but me, which will save both of us from gossip. All in all, I thought you did very well, and that's why I'm calling. To thank you."

He was floored.

"My goodness, you're certainly very welcome. I-I'll be glad if I don't have to explain what happened, because I'm not sure I can. Was it a good party, then?"

"Yes, it was. You were in on the secret, of course. I sensed that your story on Sunday about the code in the file was a bit of a stretch, but I knew you wouldn't cover up whatever it really was if it was harmful to me. Or embarrassing. And I had an inkling that I might have uninvited guests, so I kept my face on and had an outfit ready."

"Oh, you *are* good. What caused your inkling?"

"I didn't just fall off the turnip truck, you know. It was my birthday, a significant one, though they all are now, I suppose. I'd heard from absolutely nobody about it—other than you—a clear indication that something was up. So yes, it was a fabulous party, and your little interruption only added to the entertainment, once that unhappy family left."

"What will happen, I wonder? Marcy is quite a little fighter."

"They'll be seen to. I was pleased that nobody wanted to press charges. Social services will be there today to see what's behind it all. That kid's father is a brute, apparently, maybe to his wife also. Happens in the best of families. By the way, Timothy, do you recall that I warned you last month that you could get shot if your investigation on my behalf went wrong?"

"Yes, but I discounted that as hyperbole, with respect. Wasn't it?"

"Perhaps, considering how carefully you went about your inquiries. But last night there was a concealed firearm in the crowd. I had to stare him down."

"Oh, my goodness! I never thought I was putting you at risk!"

"Not me, Timothy. You. That's why I stood out there in the cold, between you and everyone else, so he wouldn't get all brave and shoot at an innocent man retreating in the dark. He might have hurt himself."

Stella actually laughed, an unusual sound. Tim loved it. "He only wants to protect me, as do you, but I like your unarmed method better."

"Why was he there, then? Is it even legal to carry a concealed weapon? He sounds dangerous."

"I didn't invite the guests, remember. He's a good man, harmless, really, and very generous." Stella hesitated, then added, "He's also very friendly to me."

"Sure, okay, but—wait, what do you mean, 'friendly to you'? Is there something I should know?"

"Just know that I'm not always alone, so be sure to use the front door next time you call after dark." Stella laughed again. "Until I can convince him to leave that stupid thing in the gun locker."

"My, my, Aunt Stella, you sound positively giddy this morning! Yes, I will be sure to give you and your gun-totin' fella lots of warning when I approach. But you can both rest easy. I'm going to stay right here and work on *my* first project in my sabbatical year of delving. It won't involve crashing parties or risking a shootout. That would've been so unfair, since I was armed only with a four-battery flashlight."

"Was that what it was? Don't ever do that again. That's what got him trigger-happy. He thought you had a sawed-off shotgun."

"He's not the only one."

Tim rotated his left shoulder and winced. He was very glad that was his only wound.

"I must let you go," Stella said. "I have scads of work to do. That darn party requires that I send dozens of thank-you notes, and they must be hand-written. Before I go, I'd like to offer you a feast you wouldn't normally get at this house. Last night's caterers were excellent. There's much more than I can eat still in the fridge. Would you like to come for a rare Tuesday dinner of appetizers and canapés?"

"Aunt Stella, I appreciate your invitation more than you can imagine, partly for the tasty bits, but more for the invitation to your house, which doesn't need catered delights. However, I will decline today, with regret. Can I take a rain-cheque, though? Not too far into the future?"

"All right then. You may have to bring the food, but it would make this place more welcoming to me if I had company in it from time to time. Your company, I mean."

~

Tim spent the rest of the morning deciding which notebooks to pursue first, two at a time to avoid becoming becalmed again. Or dead in the water.

Being becalmed had nothing to do with feeling calm, he had proven that to himself. He had seen it in real life, too. He'd gone sailing with a friend one calm day, which suited Tim just fine as it allowed the boat to remain more or less upright. But when the skipper attempted to "come about" to change direction, the boat stopped moving entirely when it was pointing directly into the light wind, and it couldn't be steered to port or starboard. Worse, to the skipper's vocal consternation, it began drifting backwards. They were "in irons", he said. Everyone on board was obliged to rock the boat and flap the sails until they got underway again. Nothing calm about that.

Not the fault of the boat, thought Tim. *We must not drift nor lie at anchor, but a steady breeze would help a lot.* Two delving topics on the go would keep things moving forward, like having a motor as well as a sail.

Having made his selection, Tim began to make a schedule for the rest of the week, and was a bit surprised to find that today was

Wednesday already. Oh well, there were two good delving days left. That would be a nice start.

He would make phone calls to arrange appointments. He was looking forward to them. He had spent most of January working alone, because his work was supposed to be secret and he hadn't a clue about how to go about it. And whenever he involved real people it had been close to disastrous.

This time, he knew the what, where, who, when, and why of his topics, or three of the five, at least, and he would fill in the missing bits for the sheer pleasure of finding out. That would involve wide-ranging conversations, familiar turf for Tim the newspaper man. No secrets, just delving.

Ten o'clock seemed like a good appointment time. He'd start the day however he wanted, sometimes going downtown to the Daisy Café for breakfast, then proceeding to discover whatever was before him. He'd go home for lunch, then transcribe his notes in the afternoons.

He chose Topic Number Four to start, as it had a practical interest: Emergency Procedures. A visit to his workplace was long overdue anyway. This time, he'd go in the front door and be expected, not the back door like the last time, which had resulted in the call to the police that triggered the emergency procedures.

"Hello, Rachael, it's Tim Brown. May I speak to Miss Fong, please?"

"Good afternoon, this is Elaine Fong, Editor at the Times. How may I help you?"

"Elaine, it's Tim. You're still managing that long greeting. How are you?"

"Hello, Tim. Yes, people seem to like it. What can I do for you today?"

"Couple things. May I have an hour of your time, tomorrow or Friday, preferably around ten?"

"Let me check. Nothing wrong, is there?"

"Nothing I'm aware of, ha-ha. No, I'm looking into something which involves *The Times,* peripherally or maybe tangentially, so I just have a few questions. Besides, we haven't had a chat since the

New Year began, and that seems delinquent of me. Just an hour and we'll see what gets covered."

"Ah, sorry, Tim, I'm booked solid tomorrow."

Darn it. His plan to meet with people would have to be adjusted to accommodate their schedules.

"When, then? You say."

"May I put you on hold a moment?" Elaine didn't wait for him to agree, but she was back quickly.

"Nothing until late Friday, I'm afraid, Tim. Four o'clock?"

"I'll take it. Friday at four. Thanks, Elaine."

He called the front desk again, this time to speak with Rachael, the receptionist. He made his request and hung up. He wasn't going to wait until Friday afternoon to get momentum, no sir.

He phoned Marlene Wentzell, the head librarian, and then the safety manager of the town's biggest industrial plant. They would have Emergency Procedures where they worked. They might be quite different, might be interesting, he'd find out. Both were out, so he left messages asking them to call him back.

Now, with whom would he start the day tomorrow? He didn't have an answer to that question until after lunch. When the mental light bulb flashed, he made the call. His target greeted him warmly, and he didn't have to explain anything. Sure, ten the next morning was fine.

~

Stella's intern, Brittany, called Tim. She had been pivotal in his detective work for Stella. "The party went off without a hitch. I thought you'd like to know."

"I did—do! Thanks for calling to tell me."

"She was totally surprised. All the work that everyone put into it paid off, big time. Thanks for keeping it a secret."

"You're very welcome, Brittany."

"She seemed very relaxed. No suspicions."

"Did she really? That makes me happy. Everything went well, then?"

"Yes. Very."

"No upsets?"

"No, none."

He accepted Brittany's story without comment. No amount of grilling would force her to reveal that there had been a disturbance at Stella's party, and he didn't want to hear about himself in the third person.

"Did you have to be her eyes and ears last night, or was it a party for you, too?"

"Oh, I'm never off-duty. It's just how I'm wired, I think."

"I'm sure she appreciates all you do for her."

"I know she does. She said so last night, several times, in front of many people."

~

Tim spent the rest of the afternoon with mundane chores like laundry and widening the narrow pathways in the snow. His housekeeper, Mrs Aquino, would arrive early tomorrow morning, and she wanted access to front and back doors, winter and summer. No problem, he needed the exercise, though he favoured his tender left shoulder. He felt energized, and flung the snow far and wide.

He had just come back in the house when the doorbell rang.

"Oh, hi, Spencer. Nice to see you. What brings you here this afternoon?"

"Hello Tim—I mean—Mister Brown. Miss Johnson has sent you this package."

"You don't have to be formal with me, Spencer. You can call me Tim. I won't tell."

"If—if it's all right with you, I'd rather keep it businesslike when I'm on business for Miss Johnson. It helps me remember."

"Really? Are you having memory problems, Spence?"

"No, not memory problems. But she asked me to make sure I remember that I'm working for her, and to keep things confidential. Being formal helps me, I think. It's hard. I'm a friendly guy."

"Yes you are. We all know that. Call me Mister whenever it suits you. So what's in the box?"

Tim knew at a glance—or hoped he knew—what Stella had sent. The thin, white cardboard box was stamped with the same name and logo that was on the van heading to Stella's house the night before, that of the catering company from the city. This would be the tasty leftover canapés she had invited him to share. Maybe Stella used Spencer to deliver all sorts of things to constituents in her riding, not only to drive her around. That hadn't occurred to him before. She did have luxuries, contrary to what she had stated, but perhaps she shared them more than anyone knew.

"I think it's from the—there was a—gosh, Mister Brown, I can't say. Sorry. But she said you'd know what's in it."

"That's all right, Spencer. Pretty sure I do know. Please tell Miss Johnson that Mister Brown says thank you very much. It's almost like being there. Will we see you at choir on Thursday, Spence?"

"Sure hope so."

Tim had declined Stella's invitation so he could remain engaged in the task at hand. And so, he had. His ship was neither adrift nor in irons, and he had creative hors d'oeuvres as his reward. Things were looking up.

February 4: Embarking

Thursday

Tim's sabbatical year wasn't entirely a decision of privilege. He had worked at *The Times* in positions of increasing responsibility since he was in junior high, and he'd be turning forty this year. He had never taken more than a few days off at a time, ever. He said he didn't mind, and he mostly didn't. He couldn't miss what he had never known.

But in recent years, he had begun to notice that some parts of him did mind. He worked hard, did a good job, but the job seemed to follow him home more and more—he couldn't put a finger on when it had started—until it was always on his mind. He was anxious, irritable, headachy, and had indigestion.

His physician, Dr Muhammed, had run the usual tests, and warned Tim about his blood pressure, but said there wasn't anything he could point to that was wrong. "But there could be if you don't make some changes, and the sooner the better," he told Tim. "Some conditions are cumulative, after continued stresses over time, and then it's hard to fix without intervention. Make changes now. Take some time off."

Tim hadn't liked the sound of "intervention" so he began to take steps to take a break. A big break. The more he thought about it, the more he knew a week or fortnight or month would not accomplish the change he knew he needed. He wouldn't be able to hire a competent editor to replace him for only a few weeks, so he developed a plan to take a whole year, and found the uber-competent Elaine Fong to sit behind his desk.

So it was with a sense of irony that Tim found himself going to

The Times to begin—re-start, actually—his sabbatical year of delving.

"Good morning, Raquel. I'm here to see GB. He's expecting me."

"It's Rachael, Mister Brown. Wasn't that an awful storm on the weekend? I hope everything was all right up on the hill?"

"Uh, yes, it was, and yes, it was, thanks for asking. How about you?"

"Oh, we were fine, thanks. We have cross-country skis, but it was too stormy to take them out. This weekend, though, for sure. Oh, and here's the document you asked for yesterday. I put it in an envelope for you. I think it may be out of date." She handed him a copy of the newspaper's Emergency Procedures.

"Oh right, I'd forgotten. Yes, I believe you're right about 'out of date'. Do you have your copy handy?"

"Oh yes, it's right here." Rachael pointed to the wall behind her desk.

"Good. Can you tell me if it still says to notify me if there's an emergency?"

"Oh yes, Mister Brown. Right here." She pointed to the top of the list.

"No other name is there?"

"Gosh no, Mister Brown. You're still the owner, aren't you?"

"Yes, I am, Rachael, but you know I'm on leave this year. I'm not glued to my office as I often was before. Would you please add Elaine Fong to that list?"

"Sure, Mister Brown, but I'm really not supposed to."

"And why is that?"

"Well, it says right here"—she pointed to a line at the bottom of the page—"that nobody is authorized to make changes without your approval."

Tim's body tensed a little bit, all over. He hadn't been able to identify what the particular sources of his stresses were, but perhaps he was in front of one now. He abandoned the conversation with Rachael and went to GB's corner of the office.

GB was Gregory Barss, but nobody ever called him that. He was the newspaper's librarian and archivist, and had been filing details of every article and photograph in the paper since long before Tim had arrived. GB was past retirement age, but he seemed to like to come to work, and Tim would never be the one to "let him go". He was too fond of GB to ever do that.

"Pleasure to see you in person, Tim," GB wheezed. "Big storm. You okay?"

"The storm. Yes, it was quite a big one, wasn't it. I enjoyed it, to tell the truth, GB. I had a—a project to work on, so I happily stayed inside and listened to the wind suck all the heat out of my house. You?"

"Warm enough. House is small, makes it easy to heat. Missus doesn't like the wind whistling."

"I suppose not." Tim didn't really want to delve into the winter storm cares of old folks. "How's work?"

"Different here these days. Steady enough. Not many chats."

"Different stories need different research, I suppose. But this is your lucky day, GB, because I'm here for a chat. Or a general kind of question, anyway. You may know I'm hoping to spend some of this year looking behind the curtains in South River, to see if there might be a connection between this and that, more than meets the eye, y'know? Our paper lines litter-boxes every week and we move on to whatever's next. It seems somewhat superficial. So, I'm just wondering, do you ever find yourself putting two and two together back here, and getting a sense that there's more than four? While you're sorting and filing?"

Tim had envisioned GB tapping his finger on his temple, or some similar gesture, and then saying, "Sure do, right over here." He imagined GB taking him to a dusty filing cabinet and pulling out a fat file from the back of a drawer, saying, "Here's a juicy one for you."

That didn't happen.

"No," GB said. "Don't recall, anyway. Got a name? Or a date? Deal a lot in those." He gestured toward the banks of file cabinets. "Decades of names and dates here. You're welcome to look in them. They're yours anyway, of course. But don't take things out or put things in without asking. Might get misplaced."

It was all Tim could do not to roll his eyes—not at GB, but at his own fortune, his fate. Early last month he had been stymied because he didn't know what to delve into. Here he was again, no clear path forward. "Well maybe something will occur to you, GB. Keep me in mind. What's the most interesting thing you've been asked to dig up for our staff lately?"

"Someone wanted to know when the new waste treatment facility was built. That took a few minutes. Name of the hurricane that took out the old bridge. That sort of thing. Keeps us busy. Slower now."

"That's okay, GB. Being busy is overrated. It can wear you out. You know, I never really asked, because I didn't need to, but what's your system here anyway? Do you file pictures one place and columns another, and then have a master file? How many entries do you make when you file one article?"

"Miss Fong came back here asking the same type questions. Fixing to put in computers, maybe. Can't see it myself. Up to you, Tim. Can't work forever anyway."

"Now don't you worry about that, GB. Not one bit. It's Elaine's job to know who does what here, but there is absolutely no plan to move you aside. How's your wife doing, by the way?"

"Not good, Tim. Breathing's bad. Worries a lot. Not good."

"I'm so sorry, GB. She's a nice lady. Please tell her I asked about her. Now remember, if something occurs to you, something that should have been in our paper but never was because it was overlooked, please let me know, okay?"

"Will do. Thanks, Tim."

Tim waved at staff who nodded hello to him as he strode past their desks, but he didn't stop to chat. He didn't want Elaine Fong to emerge from her office and chase them back to work. He'd see her tomorrow.

It wasn't even eleven o'clock when he left the building. He didn't know if Marlene Wentzell, the Head Librarian, might have returned his call yet. He had left his home phone number, not his mobile, but the library was next door, so he headed there to see if he could have a quick word with her about Emergency Procedures.

He met James Olsen on the sidewalk, coming to work. James was a reporter for *The Times*, Tim's last hire and Elaine Fong's first. He replaced a man who had been with the paper for three or four years, whose work was passable but had never really caught fire. When Elaine arrived to start her fifteen-month tenure, that reporter had begun pulling his eyes up in the corners when Elaine's back was turned. If staff found that funny they didn't dare show it. The first time Tim saw him do it, he frowned and shook his head slowly. The second time, Tim fired him on the spot.

Then they hired James Olsen. He was teased about his name in the newsroom, because Jimmy Olsen was the name of the junior reporter in the Superman comics. Elaine let it be known that teasing anyone for any reason at work was grounds for dismissal. His by-line in the paper was James Olsen, and nobody said any more about it.

"Hi, Mister Brown. Wasn't that a great blizzard?"

"Hi, James. Yes, I guess it was. I was preoccupied, didn't have to pay much attention to it. Everything okay where you were?"

"Oh, for sure. I have a four-wheel drive with knobby tires. It's made for that kinda weather. Gotta be able to get out and bring in the story in all kinds of weather. So, what brings you to the mean streets of downtown South River?"

"Oh, y'know, heading to the library. I hear there are some good stories in there. What are you working on?"

"Not much of interest, I'm afraid. Complaints about road clearing, town and county. School science projects. Somebody was cross-country skiing last week and fell through the ice somewhere. Snow over ice is like a blanket. It doesn't freeze solid. It leaves traps."

"Yes, it's been an up and down winter. You're right, James, those stories aren't big news, but it's our news, eh? Do your best with it. Nice to see you."

"You too. Drop into the newsroom sometime, why don't you? They talk about you a lot. Nicely, I mean."

"That's very kind of you to say. Bye for now."

Marlene Wentzell was not available. Tim could have asked

someone else for a copy of the library's Emergency Procedures, but he didn't want to have to go through a lot of fol-de-rol, especially if he'd meet a stone wall like his own receptionist was capable of putting up. Anyway, he really liked Marlene and always welcomed a chance to exchange a few words with her.

On the other hand, he still had the copy of *The Adventures of Sherlock Holmes* she had given him last month "on extended loan", and he hadn't checked what "extended" meant. He had intended to purchase his own copy, but the bookstore in Mahone Bay hadn't been open on the day he went there. Their sign said they'd be open on weekends during the winter. Today was Thursday, not weekend. Was Friday part of the weekend? Would they be open on Sundays? No, they weren't allowed, though the topic of Sunday shopping was bandied about in the Legislature and Stella was in the thick of it.

Tim wondered if he should delve into how hard it is to get anything done. Wrong day. Not in. Forgot it at home. Can't remember. Last month he tried to shop for a new dishwasher, but the only clerk in the empty store couldn't be bothered to greet him. His receptionist couldn't make a notation on a piece of paper because she was missing a few links of logic.

It was lunchtime. He was on the sidewalk mere steps away from the Daisy Café, but he wasn't in the mood to navigate around whomever he might encounter there. The diners sitting at the front tables rapped on the window as he walked by and waved. Nice people. Tim waved back, but didn't go in.

~

Mrs Aquino was still in the house. The back door was propped open, though the temperature was close to freezing outside. Tim could hear her vacuum cleaner running somewhere.

He began to close the door just as Mrs A appeared with his duvet in her arms. She was of a very short stature, and the duvet was queen-size.

"What you do?" she said from inside the duvet.

"Oh, sorry, Mrs A. I thought you forgot the door was open."

Mrs A somehow balanced the bedding on the doorstep railing and began to shake each corner in the cold air. No wonder his bed smelled fresh on Thursday nights. No wonder his furnace oil bill was high. The vacuum was still running upstairs.

Tim wrote a cheque for her pay and left it on the kitchen island. He was in no mood to flee from room to room to avoid her cleaning tools. Her crashing around the house was already getting on his nerves and he had just arrived.

He needed to lose this mood. Tonight was choir practice, and Robert would arrive in time for a light supper before they went to the church. Robert often brought his own cloud, depending on his workload at the university or his organ-playing responsibilities, so starting off cranky was not a good strategy.

He went to the supermarket to look for something for supper and to replenish some staples. He had been preoccupied with solving his aunt's puzzle during the days leading up to last weekend, and then there had been The Blizzard that everybody seemed compelled to talk about, so he needed to spend some time—and money—in the store until he knew Mrs A would be done.

~

"It smells good in here," Robert said as he came in the front door.

"Praise be to Mrs A," Tim said. "But does it ever not smell good? Like bad?"

"Truth?"

"Yes, please. Always."

"There's a basement smell sometimes. Dampish. Not so much now, but in the summer. When the ground thaws out, I suppose. Mouldy."

"You're right, now that you mention it. Perhaps one of the crypts has broken open. I'll get the gravediggers on it. The fresh-air smell today comes from having all doors and windows open to the winter winds. They're closed now, and soon it will smell like broiled pork chops."

Robert and Tim had precious little time together due to Robert's busy teaching load, so they took comfort in routine. Robert arrived on Thursday afternoon, attended to a few phone calls while Tim prepared their dinner, during which they shared stories of what they had been doing since their last time together, usually early Monday morning. While both enjoyed a glass of wine—or two, or sometimes three—Thursday dinner was normally dry, as it was followed by choir practice at Saint John's United Church, where Robert was the talented and well-loved organist and choir director.

As one of the few tenors in the choir, Tim rarely consumed alcohol or garlic before singing. Robert had taught the choristers to sing from their diaphragms, which fanned the fumes of whatever they'd eaten for supper. Robert would never permit an alcoholic beverage to touch his lips if he was going to touch the organ manuals later that same day. After practice was over and they were home again, that was a different story.

Practice went well enough, but several choir members were absent. The absentees were required to phone the choir president, who placed the list on the organ console for Robert to consider while he practiced in the church sanctuary. When he buzzed for the choir to come in, he had amended his rehearsal plan for the evening to accommodate any holes in the sections.

While the choir members waited to be summoned, they reviewed every flake of snow that fell, blew around, and fell again. Tim practised deep diaphragmatic breathing. He'd had enough of talking about that blizzard and did not wish to delve into it anymore, but he tried to look interested.

While the choir sang through the music for Sunday and beyond, Tim tried to analyze his grumpy mood. Thinking over the day, he saw that he had expected everyone he met to behave in a way that was very different from how they had always behaved—except for James, whom he hadn't known long enough to be able to judge his *modus operandi*. He was relying on others around him to make his delving dream come true, even to do the spadework for him. That wasn't fair to anyone and would not achieve anything new and valuable, which Tim sincerely hoped he would do.

He thought of dusty old GB amongst his dusty old files. He had been doing the same thing for the same purpose for decades, and while he had a prodigious memory, it wasn't fair to assume he had been harbouring brilliant side-ideas. If he'd had them, surely he would have shared them long ago.

A vision of GB steepling his fingers in deep contemplation came to mind, inspired by illustrations in the heavy book of Sherlock Holmes capers. The mental juxtaposition of the old clerk with the great detective was amusing and Tim snorted aloud. He had not been paying attention. The snort was ill-timed, earning a frown from Robert for his indiscretion. He wouldn't explain what had been on his mind, but he might have to atone somehow.

~

They stayed up late with a bottle of port and a bowl of spiced nuts, with stories to share from the past week. Both had taken advantage of blizzard-cancellations to do other things. Tim heavily edited his "other things", not wanting to even hint that he had gone to observe his aunt's surprise birthday party and apprehended a juvenile delinquent. Robert would've taken it as spying, and Tim wouldn't have been able to dissuade him, partly because he thought of it that way himself.

Robert's storm-enforced accomplishments were more sedentary than Tim's had been, but they had implications for both of them. He had used the time to plot out his schedule to the end of the current university term, and then summer opportunities for workshops, concert tours, time to design a new course he hoped to teach.

Tim followed every detail with interest and a growing sense of foreboding. Robert had filled in most of every week for the next six months. Tim had hoped for a little holiday trip, maybe to Prince Edward Island, just the two of them and a big, wide, red sand beach. He had to say something.

"What about summer?"

"Summer? You mean a holiday, time off? Not much there, I'm

afraid. I have to accept all concert offers right now, and enter that competition, which will take a hellish amount of work. Until I get tenure, in Halifax or elsewhere, I have to work all the time, not that I won't when I do get it, I suppose."

"I know you're building your career, Rob, and you know I support you in that. But I worked eight days a week since I was a child, and I nearly lost my grip. Can't you insert some relief into your schedule here and there, to allow you to rest and get refreshed? I think you'd be the better musician and teacher for it."

They tossed the debate back and forth, both managing to keep it light, at least for this first round. Tim mentioned his PEI dream.

"I do have a concert booked over there, in Indian River. July. You could come."

Robert's notorious high-tension approach to organ recitals did not fit in the same frame as a bucolic holiday on the Island, and Tim ventured to say so. Then he had an idea. "What about after? What's planned for the following week?"

"I was going to do some writing for the new course...but...what if I did it over there, would that work?"

"Could you? Would you? Oh, I know just the place, Rob, a gorgeous inn with a wonderful chef, beaches nearby, quiet..."

"How do you know that? I thought you never took holidays."

"I didn't. But I did attend the odd conference, and one of them was at this place. Leave it with me. I'll get a brochure. Thanks, Rob. I guarantee this will be good for you and for me. For us, too."

"Can't argue with that," Robert said. "Can we sing Amen now? It's tomorrow already."

February 5: Yes, no, maybe

Friday

The alarm clock woke them just five hours later. Their eyes were gritty from the late night, but their minds were focused on tasks in the near and far future, which propelled them into the day. Now that Tim had learned how to get a decent coffee out of Gloria's spouts, he was trying to make the pretty patterns in the foam like baristas did in the city cafés. His results were drinkable but far from artistic. At half-past five in the morning, it was amusing.

Only one of his Wednesday calls had left a message, which he had retrieved on Thursday. And now it was Friday. Good thing he wasn't trying to earn a living by delving. At this rate, he'd—never mind. Yesterday had ended well, and he was hoping to keep a thread of good attitude going. That took constant attention.

The safety manager at the plant had said he wasn't sure what Tim was looking for, but he could call again if he had concerns. The man had sounded very guarded. Of course he would. A nobody by name of Tim Brown had called to ask if he could review the plant's emergency procedures. No receptionist at a business took the return call; it had gone to voice mail on the phone in Tim Brown's kitchen. What was the recorded greeting on it, anyway? He couldn't remember what it said or when he had set it up.

He made toast and a pot of regular coffee, and began to update the greetings on his home phone, and then the mobile phone. He wrote out multiple versions of what he wanted to say, recorded multiple versions of how he wanted to say it—trying not to say "Hello, this is, *uhhh*, Tim Brown"—and was finally satisfied an hour later, having acquired a new appreciation for those on his staff to whom he had simply handed such chores, saying, "Here, do this for me, please."

He didn't have a business name to lend credence to his telephone presence, but his announcements now sounded like he thought he was important, and the caller should, too.

~

The safety manager answered when Tim called him back. He was concerned that Tim might be suggesting something was unsafe, a touchy topic in a union shop. Tim assured him he was looking for some general information which, if he used it at all, would not appear with the plant's name without his permission. Could he drop in and have a quick chat, maybe have a copy of anything helpful that wasn't classified? How about right now? Sure, he said, now's good.

When Tim arrived at the plant, the receptionist said the safety manager had been called away. He said he was sorry, but that was the way his job worked. He had left a booklet for Tim and hoped it would help.

Tim thanked the receptionist, took the booklet, and drove home again. It had the plant's name and logo on the front cover, but it seemed to be boiler-plate inside, mostly about general safety not pertaining to the plant itself.

What did he expect? His newspaper office didn't have pipes filled with scalding steam nor sharp blades whirling, so this booklet didn't relate. What about paper cuts? Seriously, was there an up-to-date First Aid kit at *The Times*, and was anyone certified to give First Aid, or that other thing where you pumped a person's chest or breathed for them if they had a heart attack or drowned?

Tim saw this topic was unlikely to be fruitful for delving. Still, he reminded himself not to pre-judge. Delving was to delve, not to identify a preferred conclusion and then chase it down. That was investigating, and he was sure there was a difference.

He kept himself occupied for most of the day by trying to devise a list of good questions about emergencies until it was time to go to the newspaper office to meet with Elaine Fong.

She was ready for him, even had a pitcher of cold water and two glasses on a tray on her desk. A notepad and pen were the only other items on the desk. Other office essentials, like a computer and phone, were on the credenza behind her. Tim had rarely seen the surface of the desk when it had been his.

Elaine had an agenda of her own, hand-written on the notepad. "Come on in. Tim. May I take your coat?"

Tim felt out of place, sitting in the guest chairs in the office he had occupied for so many years. He placed his jacket on the spare chair and took out his own foolscap list of questions.

"Duelling agendas, I see. Why don't you go first, Elaine?"

Elaine got up and closed the office door. "Thanks, I will. Just a few things, really, and I know I could have called you about these, but I was saving them for a time like now. I've been trying to stay out of your hair and resolve any issues that may arise on my own, or with appropriate staff. I must say, they are a great bunch, very willing to share their knowledge of who does what and when. You trained them well."

"Glad to hear it, Elaine. Some of us grew up together in this of-fice, and I do miss them. But I don't miss working, if you follow. Not yet, anyway. I hope I will, by the end of this year."

"I do follow. And I do like working here, so take your time."

Elaine Fong was a serious woman most times, but she smiled warmly at this, and Tim felt comforted, reassured, and something else which he couldn't identify. *Don't think now*, he told himself.

"First question: what do you think of my editorials? Not the con-tent, though you can comment anytime. I mean the new format, running them along the bottom of every page."

"Ah, yes, I saw that. It encourages the reader to read each page. The advertisers must appreciate it, yes?"

"I'm not so sure. That was my intent, but from what I hear, the readers aren't following the trail of breadcrumbs. It's too much work. They read what they can see on the first two-page spread and then give up."

"Hmm, yes, our Dear Reader is a lazy oaf, and please don't quote me. I must confess, Elaine, I haven't even opened *The Times* recently. January ended with a blizzard of activity as well as snow, so I have some catching up to do. I forget: do you say 'continued on next page'?"

"No, but it's in a shaded box along the bottom, surely they can figure it out?"

"Don't overestimate our readers. They're not stupid, but they're not committed to reading us, either. We're on trial with each issue, and they will condemn us at the slightest provocation. They will threaten to cancel their subscription, and some do, of course, though less often than you'd expect. But they stick with us for two main reasons."

Elaine's pen was poised. "And what are they?"

"One, photographs of them or their family or neighbours doing whatever they do. Two, the television schedules."

Elaine put down her pen. "That's disappointing, isn't it?"

"Oh, I wouldn't say so. If we had competition, we'd have to be a lot sharper about what we write. But since we're pretty much a monopoly—ignoring the Halifax daily paper which ignores us—we just have to give them what they want and sell enough ads to pay for it."

"Is there no hope?"

"Sure. I let things slide in the last couple of years because I was tiring of the game, but you can try lots of things to see if you can increase subscriptions, or reduce cancellations, or gain respect as a journalist."

"Any suggestions?"

"I'd start by putting your editorial back in one block. Make it short and pithy. Risk getting a few letters arguing with you, and print those. Hey, maybe put a border of boxing ring ropes around it and invite people to join you 'in the ring'. And expand what's familiar: more and better photos. Bigger photos with punchy five-line captions instead of a flabby article that is bound to repeat or misspell something."

Elaine was busily writing notes.

"Get James Olsen on it. He seems like he'd enjoy chasing down a good photo and making a story about it."

Elaine sat back in her chair. "I thought you said you were getting away from the business. This is great stuff. You have a lot to contribute."

"I didn't know I did until you asked," Tim said. "I've always been the one who proposes changes, but I was making the suggestions to myself, often, without outside input. When you asked me about your editorial, I was commenting on *your* work, answering *your* questions, and apparently I had lots of ideas ready blah-blah. I hope they're helpful."

"Me, too. Let's do this again, shall we? I'd sure like to have your guidance from time to time. Maybe monthly?"

"I'd enjoy that, Elaine, as long as I don't get dragged back into work. We can try it."

"Good. Now, you have a list of questions for me?" Elaine glanced at her watch. "I don't mean to rush you, but—"

There was a knock on the office door behind Tim.

"Excuse me a moment." She beckoned to the knocker to enter.

"Sorry to interrupt, Miss Fong—oh, hi, Mister Brown, I didn't recognize you from the back, and you're not in shirt and tie! Great to see you! Um, just to remind you that the party starts at five, Miss Fong, so we're all leaving in ten minutes."

Elaine seemed doubtful.

"You will come, won't you, Miss Fong? You too, Mister Brown?"

"What's this, now?"

"Don't you remember? We have two staff birthdays in the first week of February, so we're all going to the bar at the new hotel. Oh, please come, Mister Brown, they'd be so pleased! Just one and done, right?"

"Thank you, we'll consider it," Elaine said, and the staffer, whose name Tim found he could not recall, closed the door again. "Did you go to these?"

"Sometimes," Tim said. "I preferred to make it occasional, not regular. 'One and done' is the agreed plan. You can drop in, have a glass of wine—or a soft drink—and be on your way in half an hour. I'm glad they're still doing it. Staff that like to socialize together work well together, I think. I didn't realize that this was Friday afternoon—that's what being on leave has done to me."

"Well, you can go. I'm not really comfortable in social situations like that."

"Oh, come on, Elaine, let's go together. I'll protect you. We'll give them ten minutes to get there and settled, then we'll pop in for twenty minutes, and then vanish. I'd like to go, but not if you won't; that might upset some power balance perception that isn't worth delving into."

"Okay, fine. But what did you want to see me about today? Something about the Emergency Procedures list, I think?"

"Yes," Tim said. "Update it. And check on First Aid training and supplies. And that other thing, three letters."

"CPR?"

"Yes, that's it. There, now, we're done. Let's go."

~

The dozen or so newspaper staff in the bar cheered when Tim and Elaine entered. It felt like a standing ovation, and was, technically, since they were all standing around a high table in the room. Tim ordered ginger ales for himself and Elaine, which arrived quickly and cost too much. A server brought out two cupcakes with sparklers for the birthday celebrants and the group loudly sang "Happy Birthday". They made a lot of happy noise, and their party was soon over.

"One and done" had been the pledge for some time, and they kept to it so it would be safe and repeatable. If anyone wanted to stay afterwards, they were on their own time and not part of "the paper gang". Tim was pleased to see today's organizers visiting the booths and other tables, undoubtedly to beg forgiveness from the other patrons for their boisterous noise.

Elaine seemed to enjoy herself, chatting and smiling with her staff. Tim appeared at her elbow to ask if she'd like him to leave her there. She said she would rather follow him out.

In the parking lot, Elaine thanked Tim for encouraging her to go to the bar.

"And thanks for your great ideas. I'm going back to the office right now to re-work my editorial for the next edition."

Back to work on Friday night. Tim remembered all too well what that was like. At the time, it was just what he did. Now, from the distance of less than two months, it seemed like crawling back on top of a lit funeral pyre. He liked the newspaper business, but he certainly didn't miss that.

At home, Tim burped the ginger ale's sharp bubbles as he poured a generous glass of *Vendredi Soir*. He had asked the hotel bar to wrap up their daily special for him to take home for his supper, which he happily warmed in the oven.

Through the evening, he half-heartedly made entries in the notebook assigned to Emergency Procedures, but there was little to add. When the time arrived to engage with Elaine on the topic, he had lost interest in delving into it. He asked her to update it, and he knew she'd do it immediately or sooner, probably this evening. He didn't have to point out the oversights in its present form; she would see them.

He didn't care, either, what they did at the plant. If their procedures were lacking, resulting in risk to life, limb, or property, one of *The Times'* intrepid reporters would report on the deficiencies after they happened, which was the weekly newspaper reporter's job. Nobody was going to be interested in Tim Brown's philosophical musings, least of all Tim Brown.

This was a somewhat harsh assessment, but he acknowledged it with a bit of relief, assuaged by the wine and distracted by the hotel's meatballs and rice in an uncertain sauce. When his aunt had mocked his determination to delve into things, it had stung. As long as he was the one judging his priorities, Tim believed he would find his way.

He turned the Emergency Procedures notebook over and entitled the new first page *PERSPECTIVES*. Below that he wrote a short account of his visit to the office today. The conversation was easy, his counsel was sought, his advice was valued—even he was impressed with his suggestions. New and old staff had greeted him warmly, and he had even welcomed a social outing, brief though it was.

Had this happened in the past? Yes, No, and Somewhat. He hadn't been asked for editorial advice in the past because *he* had been the Editor, and before that, his mother had never asked his opinion on anything. He was particularly pleased to note how easily he came up with what he hoped were good ideas for Elaine, yet every darn question he asked himself so far in this Year of Delving was a dud, yielding not one good idea.

He also noted that all the good things that transpired today had been *with other people*. Was this significant? He had never worked solo as he was trying to do now. This very morning he'd been frustrated at how long it took him to change the message on his voice mail. Not that he couldn't learn—he got it eventually—but the learning curve is not only steep but constant when one is a Unit of One. If he'd had an assistant or a sidekick this morning, he might've done the chore all the same, but his outlook might have been better if there was someone around who would say, "You can do it, I know you can, I find it frustrating, too."

He tried to read a bit of Sherlock Holmes, but his eyes were heavier than the book, so he went to bed. Before he drifted off, still thinking about the Great Detective, Tim felt a new appreciation for the sidekick. *I wish I had a Doctor Watson,* he thought.

February 6: Rescue

Saturday

Of course. That's it!

Tim threw off the bedclothes and got out of bed with a spring in his step. He had slept well on his last waking thought—the one that came after his wish for a Doctor Watson.

Last month, he had explored the upper level of the old building the newspaper occupied, looking for an unused room he could work in undisturbed, where he could leave his notes without having to put them away if anyone like Mrs Aquino came along. Indeed, there were empty rooms on the second floor, dusty and cobwebby but eminently suitable for his purposes.

He'd been put off the idea because of a case of mistaken identity resulting in a small tangle with the town police. He needn't have been so sensitive.

At the time he was just looking for a private work-space. Now, he realized, he needed a private space that was near people. People sparked questions. He had been avoiding people's questions because he was afraid they'd ask him what he was doing with his year off, and he didn't have a good answer. "Delving," he'd say, and they looked at him like he'd made a bad smell. Who cared? Good answer or bad, nobody ever paid real close attention to what he did, so he would simply have to make up a stock answer.

"Oh, I'm looking into various things," he said to Gloria, his pre-breakfast companion, and she showed her approval with a frothy latté. The plan was so elegant, so simple. He would try it out today.

He knew Elaine Fong would be at her desk, though it was barely daylight. He knew her direct number, as it had been his for so long.

"Hello?"

"Good morning, Elaine. What happened to the formal greeting?"

"Well, I can see it's you, Tim, and you surprised me, calling on this line so early in the morning. How may I help?"

"Ah, that's more like it. I had to make certain you weren't an imposter, ha-ha. The reason I'm calling—"

"Excuse me, Tim, before you start, I want to tell you how much I appreciated your visit and counsel yesterday. I hope you'll like the new editorial page. Can't wait to get the creative department on it."

"Oh, I'm glad, Elaine. Don't you worry, Helen will make it work. I'll be sure to watch for that."

He made a mental note to bring in the accumulated weekly papers from the box on his front porch. Such neglect.

"And thanks for making me go to the drop-in party, too. It was easy and a nice break. Not knowing anyone around here, I guess I've been considering my work time as people-time."

"That's not good, Elaine. Oh, speaking of people-time, will you be joining the choir? It sure was great to have you drop in the alto section that time."

"I haven't heard yet. I think the decision will be made next month."

"Ah, right. So, the reason I called is that I would like to set myself up in one of the unused rooms upstairs. That's what I was looking at a few weeks ago when the police got involved, when I thought I'd cause less disruption if I came in the loading door, silly me. So here's what I propose: I'll come in every day next week, through the front door, and just walk to the back hallway and up the stairs. Then I'll walk out again. There might be a little disruption for the first day or two, but the staff will soon get used to seeing me come and go and they won't be distracted. I think last night helped with that, anyway. What do you think?"

"It's your building, Tim."

"Yes, it is, but it's your office to manage and I don't want to be a disruption. Can we try it?"

"Of course. Good luck training them, though. They're more like a litter of cats than a herd."

"True that. Okay, so, the upstairs is a dusty mess. I'll call a cleaning company, rather than involve our caretaker, I think. They'll have the equipment and the staff to get it done quickly. Then, a fresh coat of paint would be nice. What paint hasn't flaked up there appears to have once been Bilious Green. I think an off-white would brighten it up, don't you?"

"I haven't seen it. But while we're talking paint, have you looked around our offices on the main floor lately? What shade do you think is on these walls?"

"Uh-oh. Have I opened a can of worms?"

"Maybe. A fresh coat of paint would look nice, and do good."

"I hear ya. Okay, let's do this: the job upstairs is important but small, so I'll get a guy up there as soon as the cleaners are done. I'll ask him to see you about the downstairs. He'll give you a quote, and then we'll discuss. How's that sound?"

"That sounds really good, Tim, thanks!"

"Oh, and there's more. I'll need a phone up there, so—"

"Why?"

"Beg pardon?"

"Why do you need a phone installed upstairs? Will you be working up there a lot?"

"Not a lot, no. Sometimes."

"You have a cell-phone. Why not use that? Then you'll always be 'in', no matter where you are. My advice? Upgrade your package, buy a new phone if you need to. That'll serve you better than a phone on a desk, recording messages because you're not there. The twenty-first century is nipping at our heels, Tim, and whatever it brings, it won't bring phones wired on desks."

"I think you just called me an old fogey, Elaine, and thanks for that." He laughed. "I suppose you will have some advice about installing a computer there, too?

"We can hook you up to the internet, certainly. No desktop computer, though. A new portable laptop. One for me, too, please. Then we could both work from home sometimes."

"Yikes. What a concept. Can you get prices on those, too, please?"

"In a flash."

"Okay, I'd better hang up now. A simple idea to use an empty room for free has turned into a major re-decorating and electronics upgrade, and I haven't had my breakfast yet! This has been fun, I think. Listen, don't stay at work all day, Elaine. It looks like it's warming up and the sun's out. But one more thing before you go, can you ask Raquel to add my name back to the In/Out board? It might help the staff know whose boots are walking around overhead, without getting the police to check."

"Her name is Rachael. Will do. Thanks for calling, Tim."

~

Tim was delighted. He was right: people could be helpful. Well, some people, anyway, like Elaine Fong. She was smart, and while she was respectful of him—he owned the business and she was his temporary replacement—she wasn't reticent about making suggestions, even if they were contrary to his ideas or cost the company money.

He decided to drive to the bakery down along the South River and have one of their delicious scones for breakfast. It was a beautiful February day, and the sun sparkled on all the snow that had fallen last week. He might find a place to go for a walk, since the temperature was above freezing.

He dressed in his sporty outdoor jacket and pants and hiking boots, recently purchased and still feeling new to him. They were so different from his business-wear of long coat and leather shoes that he still felt like he was somebody else when he wore them.

He looked like somebody else, too, and not in a good way, when he put on the balaclava/tuque, so he chose ear-muffs, also new, and hoped they'd keep his head warm enough.

~

A trail ran all along the south shore, using the right-of-way of an abandoned railway line. Various community groups had taken responsibility for the upkeep of sections of it, making great recreational opportunities.

Following breakfast, Tim caught the cable ferry across the river and drove away from the coast to Blockhouse, a tiny hamlet near Mahone Bay, where he knew the trail passed near the village. A few cars were parked at the entrance, a hopeful sign that the trail was walkable. He wanted a pleasant stroll through the woods, not a trudge through deep snowdrifts. He'd had enough of that to last a long time.

He wished he'd thought to buy sunglasses. The sun was brilliant on the snow. But as he began walking along the trail, following snowmobile tracks that had flattened the drifts, he moved into shade from the trees that grew close to the trail on both sides. The shade reduced the sun's warmth, but he was keen to get some fresh air, so he walked on. The exercise would soon warm him.

Tim found it hard to judge where he was on the trail in relation to the surrounding area, hemmed in as it was by the trees. He lost sight of any houses as the trail plunged into the woods.

It was so quiet there. The snow muffled traffic sounds, and there were no leaves to rattle on the trees, just bare branches and the evergreens. A saucy chickadee called to him from a nearby branch. Tim whistled a hymn tune back to the bird:

> I feel the winds of God today,
> Today my sail I lift...

Because the trail followed the old train route there were no sharp turns, just a long curve. He saw a cluster of people on the trail ahead. *Nice to see other people enjoying the day*, he thought. As he came closer to them, one left the group and ran fast toward him, calling out something Tim couldn't make out. He removed his ear muffs.

"Help!" the runner cried, a teenage boy. "Help! Do you have a phone? Call 9-1-1!"

"Not with me, no," Tim answered. Elaine told him to use it, but he hadn't thought of taking it on a Saturday morning nature walk.

"What's the matter?"

The boy ran on toward the trail entrance. Tim walked quickly toward the other two people, who were bending over someone on the ground.

"What's wrong? What's the matter?"

"Do you have a phone?" the woman asked.

"No. What happened?"

"Do you know CPR?" she asked. She was kneeling over a woman lying on the snowy trail, barely moving.

"No, sorry."

The man said, "She-she-she musta fell in. She's froze."

"Fell in?" Tim looked around. "In where?"

"There," the man said, waving vaguely toward the thick undergrowth. Tim didn't see anything but trees and snow.

"We need help here!" the woman called, on her knees.

Tim leaned over to look at the victim, if that's what she was. Her lips were blue and her face was scratched. She was shivering uncontrollably, and trying to talk. She was wearing only tights and a tank top with a torn light blouse. Her feet were bare. The woman was rubbing the victim's hands.

"I don't think you're supposed to do that," Tim said to her. "Or chest compressions either. She's still conscious."

Tim had no idea what were the right procedures for this person, but he was pretty sure she needed expert attention immediately. He knew there was a volunteer fire department in Blockhouse. Somebody needed to take charge of this scene or it could turn out very badly for the woman on the ground, if it wasn't already bad.

"Okay, listen. Take off your jacket right now. We need to get her warm."

The kneeling woman quickly took off her jacket, and they both put it on the victim and zipped it up. The man had vanished.

Tim took the car keys and wallet from his pockets, then took off his trousers. The woman helped him pull them, still warm with Tim's body heat, on the victim. The pant legs were long enough that they could tuck her bare feet inside them.

Tim removed his jacket and placed it on top of the other one. He folded the victim's arms across her chest, put his arms around her from behind in a bear-hug, and lifted her up, holding her tight against his chest for warmth. The woman took her feet, and they both hobbled as quickly as they could with their precious burden toward where Tim had parked.

As they rounded the long curve they could see the trail entrance —not as far away as it felt at this moment—and they heard sirens. Neither Tim nor the woman said a word, as they were both gasping with the effort, but their silent prayers went up that the siren was on an ambulance coming to the rescue.

It was. The boy had told the first people he saw that someone had fallen into water, and word travelled fast.

The paramedics arrived from Mahone Bay, ready to treat hypothermia, and quickly took the victim into the back of the ambulance.

"I need my jacket," the woman said. "It's got my wallet and everything."

The paramedics handed both jackets out the back of the ambulance and Tim and the woman quickly put them on.

Sirens wailed again and the ambulance began to move out.

"Which hospital?" Tim called out.

"South River Memorial," the driver said.

She looked down at Tim, raised her eyebrows, and Tim looked down at his legs, which were not wearing pants. He pointed toward the back of the ambulance, and she nodded as though she saw this sort of thing every day. Perhaps she did, but she didn't pause to discuss Tim's clothing choices.

The ambulance sped away, with his trousers in the back.

As the siren noise faded in the distance, the woman and the boy who had run for help looked to Tim for further instructions.

"Hang on," he said.

Tim was grateful for the relatively new and warm boxer shorts he had put on that morning, but he didn't want any social engagement until he covered up. His bony legs were very cold. He ran to his car and retrieved a dusty old plaid blanket from the back seat, which he quickly wrapped around his legs and tied in a bulky knot at his waist.

"Do you guys know her?" he asked when he returned.

They shook their heads. "No, we were just out for a walk—this is my son—and heard someone calling for help."

"Was she just lying on the trail like that?"

"Yeah," the teen said, "and that guy was just standing there. He looked like—he looked odd."

"Well, she was very lucky that you came along to run for help. I don't know what we do next."

A rescue vehicle from the local volunteer fire department rounded the corner and pulled up beside them. An RCMP cruiser arrived right behind, followed by a contingent of neighbours. The firefighters directed the traffic.

"Are you the victim?"

The Mountie seemed amused as he gestured toward the blanket covering Tim's lower half.

"No, I'm not. The victim went in the ambulance. I'm—I'm the—a —I helped carry her from the trail."

"Why did you carry her from the trail? Why were you there? Was she injured?"

"I was walking on the trail. Those two were already there when I came along. She was on the ground and close to unconscious. There was another guy who said she had fallen in the water but he disappeared. I didn't see any water, but I knew we needed to get her to help urgently, so this woman and I portaged her here. This young man ran ahead to raise the alarm."

"Can you show me where it happened? Is it far?"

"Not far at all," the woman said. "My son and I have to go that way because our car is parked farther along. We can show you where we found her."

"All right. Wait over there, please."

The Mountie beckoned to Tim to follow him a few steps away from the others.

"Sir, why were you on the trail wearing a blanket? Are you fully clothed underneath that?"

"No, I'm not!"

He began to lift the blanket to show that he had lost his pants, but the Mountie stepped back and held out his hand.

"Stop, please, sir! Just tell me, why are you dressed in that fashion, and what were you intending to do on the trail?"

"What? What do you think? I was out for a nice walk on the trail, dressed as normal people dress, when I came upon the scene as described. The victim appeared to be hypothermic, and was lightly clothed, so that woman over there put her jacket on her, and I pulled off my pants—which I had been wearing as normal people do—to cover her legs. The paramedics returned the jacket but drove away with my pants, so, to protect my modesty, I retrieved this blanket from my car."

Tim's voice was rising. "Don't even think about what you were thinking about, Constable. Your implications are bordering on offensive. That woman can verify everything I've said."

"Lower your voice, sir. I'll need your name and phone number in case we need additional information later."

Tim gave his name and home phone number. In spite of his rising temper, his body was cooling down from his exertions on the trail, and the blanket ended mid-calf.

"Are you finished with me now, Constable? This blanket isn't half the fun you seem to think it is, so I'd like to go home to get another pair of pants."

He turned the heat on full blast and drove straight home, taking care not to do anything that could necessitate him getting out of the car again until he was safely in the privacy of his own driveway.

~

Tim warmed up with a long, hot shower. He wondered about the young woman who was clearly in grave danger. He wondered if they had done the right thing, carrying her. He wondered what would have happened to her if that mother and son hadn't been there. He wondered how he knew that rubbing hands was not to be done for hypothermia, and he wondered if he was right about that. He wondered why he seemed to run into some kind of drama every time he went outdoors.

Well, that wasn't quite true. He had run into drama last week because he snooped on his aunt's surprise party, with the purest of motives, of course.

He re-examined, with a pang of guilt, his decision not to mention that episode to Robert when they were re-hashing their pre- and post-blizzard experiences. *Was it a lie if I didn't even tell it?* There could be moral consequences there, but he felt it was better to wait and see than to tell a story that really had no basis in reason, no excuse, no defence.

Today, he had gone out, heart full of hope and happiness after his chat with Elaine, to have a coffee and scone and then to enjoy a short walk in the beautiful day. On a public trail. Whistling a hymn. He hadn't spied on anyone.

He did wish he'd taken his mobile phone with him. If anyone quizzed him about that omission, he'd say he hadn't expected any calls, and wouldn't have wanted to disturb the peace and quiet. In hindsight, going alone into a trail in the woods was a good reason to take a phone, not to receive calls but to call out—if there even was a signal there. Lesson learned.

One thing he was very glad about, he thought as he towelled himself dry, was that he'd worn good underwear. What was that old joke about not wearing torn underoos in case you got into an accident? Based on today's experience, it didn't have to be your own accident that might cause the revelation of your underwear.

He was disappointed in one thing. The paramedic had found the blanket funny, which it was, but the smirking Mountie seemed to think he was up to something deviant with it. He was glad he'd pushed back this time.

Tim searched the closets for a pair of Saturday pants to replace the ones that had gone with the victim—wouldn't she be surprised to see herself wearing his long-legged pants when she came to! He sincerely hoped she would live to be surprised.

It was disconcerting to find that the only pair of what he would call casual pants suitable for winter, an old pair of blue jeans, was quite snug around his waist. Had he gained weight? He thought he was taking in fewer calories since he wasn't eating donuts every day, but perhaps he wasn't burning as many calories when working at home.

He'd think about that later. Right now, he needed something to wear. He'd rather go out wrapped in the plaid blanket again than wear sweat-pants in public, so he pulled the jeans on and managed to close the waistband.

He was suddenly very hungry. No wonder. He had carried more than half of that unfortunate woman's weight for what had seemed like miles. He scrambled a few eggs for lunch, and followed up with a couple wrapped chocolates someone had given him at choir practice. It seemed like a balanced diet for current conditions.

~

At the sporting goods store, Tim chose two more pairs of the pants he had just donated to the ambulance, six more pairs of the fabulous wicking boxers, and a tuque that would not unroll into a balaclava at the most inopportune moments. He didn't know what else to buy for future challenges, so he wandered around the store awhile before going to the cash register.

He had spent so much of his life indoors, seven days a week, that he felt more unprepared for the great outdoors than he had expected. Things happened outside the familiar walls of his home and office, and not all the happenings were his fault.

At the cash counter, where the impulse-buy trinkets were on display, he picked up a highly-overpriced pair of sunglasses. Then he tossed a combination compass and whistle on the pile.

"Does it work?" he asked the clerk.

"The compass works all the time," she said. "But you have to blow the whistle yourself."

~

Home again, Tim sat in his study and stared at a blank page on the desk. What had he learned that he could make useful notes about?

He felt he was in shock a little bit from the surprises of the morning. The morning had started long before his trail walk. He'd almost forgotten about the early-morning phone call with Elaine Fong. What had they discussed, and was he supposed to do anything?

The life-or-death situation on the trail made it hard to concentrate.

Tim put down the pencil and picked up the phone. He called the South River Memorial Hospital and identified himself as one of the people who had rescued a woman on the trail at Blockhouse this morning, who was brought in by ambulance. He'd like to know how she was doing. Yes, he knew that there were privacy concerns, he didn't need to know her name or anything that would identify her, but he was very concerned about her and would appreciate some information. Also, she would've been wearing his pants when she was brought in, which he'd like to get back if that wasn't too much trouble.

He called the RCMP depot with the same message, adding that the constable had asked him to stand by to give a statement, which he was very willing to do, but mostly he just wanted to know how she was doing.

Who could tell him?

Maybe James Olsen? He was a likely ambulance chaser. If the Mounties, fire department, and ambulance were all called to attend a scene, James would know about it. He probably had a police scanner in his off-road vehicle. He might be at the hospital now.

Tim didn't have his mobile number. He called the newspaper and left a message.

His head was still spinning, but more slowly now, and memories of his conversation with Elaine returned. Indeed, there was a good list of Things to Do. He would go to the office once each day, go upstairs, walk around, and come back down, so that the staff would get used to seeing him there. He had told Elaine that he would come in and leave without disturbing anyone, but he did hope to add a little human contact to his days, so he might stop at a different desk each time, say hello, ask how they were, what they were working on.

On Monday, he would contact a cleaning company to come and chase the spiders out of the room he wanted to set up in. He might as well get them to clean all the rooms up there so the neighbouring spiders wouldn't feel welcome to visit.

And painters to brighten those rooms. It'd be quite nice up there, with the sun shining in those tall, freshly-cleaned windows. He should have a look at new window blinds or drapes, in case the sun was too bright, or if he was working at night.

Oh yes, things were looking up again, as his thoughts righted themselves from the roly-poly punch they'd received earlier.

Tim would never confess this, but he'd been lost in these thoughts so far that he forgot this was Saturday afternoon, close to suppertime now, when Robert was due to return for a relaxing evening. What reminded him was the sound of Robert's car in the driveway. He speed-dialed the pizzeria to order their favourite, and managed to hang up just before Robert came in the door. He pulled a goodish wine from the cupboard, and set out two balloon glasses.

"Gee, what are we celebrating?" Robert examined the label.

"Being alive, I think. I've had a day and a half. I didn't rent a movie for tonight. Thought maybe we could just spend time together, maybe talk for a while, if that's okay? Supper will arrive soon."

That was fine by Robert. It was fine by Tim, too, as he could finally tell Robert about an escapade in which he didn't star as an inept, or nosy, gumshoe.

In fact, as he related the events on the Blockhouse trail, Robert kept interrupting for clarification.

"Who did that? You said what? Wow, you carried her all that way?"

When Tim told the part about his trousers going away in the ambulance, leaving him in his boxers, Robert was in hysterics, and so was Tim. It sure felt good to laugh, and Robert clearly saw him as the hero in the story, though the anonymous teenager who ran for help surely was as well.

Then Tim told about his call to Elaine before all that had

happened, and his elation at obtaining this new work-space, painting the walls, getting a new phone and everything. And being around people socially and casually.

Robert nodded along, smiling as Tim recounted positive after positive. Then he looked serious.

"What?"

"Do you know, Timo, I just realized something. You have never, ever, worked on your own. You grew up in the newspaper office, with your dear dragon mother directing your every move and choice. You didn't even get to go away to university, where you'd have to make new friends, make choices, shop for clothes. You never had to apply for a job or start a business. No wonder you're struggling with what to do now that you have a whole year to do what you want: you're not accustomed to it. It's quite a culture shock, in fact, like getting out of prison."

He folded up a final piece of the pizza and put it in his mouth. When he finished it, he said, "If I had a whole year to do whatever I want, I'd go crazy trying to choose only one or two things. You don't have any dreams in reserve because all you've known is the same one job. Cut yourself some slack, Tim. If you don't discover some great thing this year, at least you will have acquired a healthier way of living, a worthy accomplishment in itself. You're getting it, and you'll get it."

He raised his glass. "Meanwhile, let's finish this fine wine with a toast to today's hero!"

February 7: Excused

Sunday

It's amazing how a few well-chosen words can change so much so quickly, was Tim's waking thought. He had hoped that his conversation with Robert last evening, rehashing his long and over-full day, would help him understand everything that had happened while maybe getting a little sympathy, a little support. Not that Robert wasn't always supportive.

He was more. Robert had summed up his whole life in a few sentences—a summary that Tim understood instantly. No wonder he'd struggled to get his feet under himself in January, the first month of his year-long sabbatical. No wonder he hadn't gained traction until yesterday morning.

Robert hadn't told him last night what to do or how to do it. No, and thank goodness for that, because that might have sparked an argument. The miraculous thing Robert had done was to give Tim *permission* to drift about as he was doing, without pressure. He'd removed the requirement—Tim's *need*—to accomplish something wonderful, while leaving the door open to the possibility that he might.

No wonder he loved this man.

Tim felt like bounding around the house, as he had yesterday morning. His mind was free, light.

His body, though, was stiff and heavy today. Bounding might result in considerably more back pain than he already had. Carrying a near-unconscious woman along a bumpy hiking trail will do that.

Tim swallowed two extra-strength painkillers before gingerly descending the stairs to put his order in with Gloria. He wasn't at all confident that he could carry the two demi-tasses upstairs. The pain he felt came from having done a good deed, so there was some emotional comfort in that. The elation he felt came from all of yesterday, and he was determined to enjoy every moment of joy coming to him, even through gritted teeth.

Robert was highly impressed to have espresso delivered in lieu of the alarm clock. When it was really time to get up and prepare for church, Tim knew he couldn't go. The painkillers helped a little, but not enough yet. He wouldn't be able to stand and sit as the service required without a lot of groaning, as he was doing now.

"Sorry, Rob, I think I'll have to stay home with an ice pack this morning. I sure hope at least Spencer comes. What if there's no tenor in the choir today?"

"Yeah, what if? I do hope the Music Committee will approve section leads next month so we're not hung up when this sort of thing happens. But when it does, your highly-skilled Music Director will play the accompaniment with the extra Tim Brown Tenor stop, and nobody will notice the gap. Or not much."

"Gee, I should go so I could hear that."

"If you went, you wouldn't."

"Hmm. At least if you're playing the tenor part, all the notes'll be right. Have fun. Pray for me. I'll have lunch ready for your return. Oh, and Rob? My excuse is that I slipped on ice in the driveway, okay? No heroic stories."

"You know me."

~

Tim took a cold pack from the freezer to the den, turned the electric fireplace to medium-high, and pushed back in his recliner chair. He was beginning to doze under a cosy throw when the phone rang. He moved too slowly to answer before it went to voicemail, but the message light was flashing. He took the phone back to the den, re-arranged the comforts, and punched the buttons to retrieve the message.

It was James Olsen. He wasn't familiar with the incident Tim had called about, but his sources said the girl was okay, might be going home today.

That she was alive and would recover, praises be! That Tim had not hastened her death, hallelujah! He pushed back in the recliner and fell fast asleep.

~

He was still asleep when Robert returned from church and rummaged in the pantry for a light lunch. Tim awoke feeling groggy but the pressure in his lower back was considerably better.

"She's alive," he said to Robert.

He allowed Robert to serve lunch to him on a lap tray in the recliner. His head cleared significantly after Robert turned down the heater and opened the den door wide to permit cooler, fresher air in the small room.

"How'd it go?"

"Oh, you know. I was great. You were awful."

"Me? I wasn't there!"

"Exactly."

"Oh. Was Spencer?"

"Yes, though you'd hardly know it. That man is so insecure without you, and he doesn't need to be. I had to add strings to the tenor line so he would have something to follow. He's no leader, our Spencer."

Robert searched the freezer for something to turn into dinner. Tim took another pain pill and ventured upstairs to shower and dress. He deemed sweatpants to be acceptable dress today. For a fleeting moment he wondered if the back pain had come from wrestling with his tight jeans yesterday, but knew it hadn't. He wouldn't admit it, anyway.

The aromas that began to waft through the house were certainly encouraging. Tim felt flexible enough to carefully bend to light a real fire in the parlour.

He stared into the fire for most of the afternoon, thinking and thinking, occasionally chatting with Robert, until it was time to

dine.
    It was nice to do nothing.

February 8: Decorating

Monday

After Robert's early-morning departure for the city, Tim considered his plans for the week, following up on his conversation with Elaine on Saturday morning. His spine was still telling him that he should move carefully. He took more pills and strapped an ice-pack around his waist.

He wanted to go to the office today to put in an appearance, but he could wait until the afternoon when he might be less stiff. Some people might go for sympathy, but he didn't want to call attention to his injury, especially with reporters on staff who might—no guarantee—ask questions.

He made some calls to find a cleaning service for the long-empty offices. He found one, but they couldn't get there before next Tuesday, sorry. Oh well, that would bring structure to next Tuesday.

He called painters, painting services, anything with the word paint in the Yellow Pages listing. None were available before March. That was not enough present structure. Tim wanted to occupy his new office space by the end of next week, whether he had work to do in it or not.

Well, then, he would just have to go places and ask people. Oh sure, people could mean trouble and distractions, when he wanted peace and concentration, but surely the simple act of walking through the newspaper office to his upstairs office wouldn't derail his mental attitude. Any human encounters there would be brief, but might also bring new ideas or concepts, you never know. He'd stroll through the office, check out the upstairs rooms again, say hello, maybe ask if anyone knew of a painter for a reasonable price, and call it a day.

~

"Hi, Mister Brown. Say, are you all right? Did you hurt your back?"

So much for flying under the radar. "Uh, yeah. Lifted something I shouldn't have. Just a little stiff."

Tim leaned into Elaine Fong's office. "Sorry to bother you, but about the painters—"

"Hi, Tim. Yes, their estimator will be here tomorrow at, lemme check, eleven. Did you want to be here to show them around upstairs?"

"You—you found painters already? I was going to ask around if anyone knew of anyone to do it."

"Oh, maybe for upstairs, but I think a professional company is better for the offices, don't you? They have all the gear and insurance, and it will be a team doing it, not just one guy who might take forever. And what if he's pals with someone on staff but doesn't work out? That would be awkward."

"Elaine, everything you say makes sense. Yes, I'll be here tomorrow at eleven to show them around. When do you think they can start?"

"Not sure. You in a rush?"

"Sorta kinda. I have cleaners coming in next Tuesday to exorcise whatever is crawling around up there, and then I was hoping to get the painting done before the end of the week."

"Done? As in 'finished'?"

"Yup."

Elaine stood up. "Let's go see."

They both laughed as they climbed the stairs. Elaine found the steps high for her short legs, and Tim found them narrow for his large feet. He winced as he reached the second floor.

"Hurt yourself?"

"Just, uh, twisted my back, shovelling. It's easy enough to do." He made a mental note to keep his story straight, in case people compared notes about his back later.

"So here we are." He gestured to the rooms at the front of the building. "I plan to use only one room, but we might as well clean up the whole floor at the same time."

"Do you think?" Elaine looked doubtful. "I mean, why spend the money now if you don't intend to use the space, or not for some time? If I were you, I'd just get one room cleaned and painted and get on with whatever you're doing in it. These rooms look like they haven't been used in years, and may not be for more years. Unless you want staff working up here."

"Oh, good heavens, no! I want peace and quiet, and privacy. That's what attracted me up here. I can't leave any notes lying around at home because my housekeeper will stuff them in a bag and leave them outside the back door. I was working on a—on something last month that required me to use large flip-chart papers, and I had to keep taking them down. So that's why I came down here that day—to see if there was a suitable room I could use undisturbed. When I leave it, I'll lock the door and nobody will mess with it. No staff up here."

"In that case, I suggest you get this room thoroughly cleaned and painted. And you'll want a new blind, right? The painter can put that up for you. That won't take long. You should give me the details about the cleaners so I can let the staff know who is coming and going. When those jobs are done, you'll want a chair, a desk, a filing cabinet, maybe? Let me know when these things will be delivered. Then you should get a locksmith to change the lock so you'll be sure to have the place to yourself."

"Elaine, I knew you were a good newspaperwoman, but you make good renovating sense, too. I like your suggestions. I think there are bits of furniture up here that I can use, though. I'll have a look around. I don't need much."

"Suit yourself," Elaine said, "but don't try moving anything yourself. Look after your back. The caretaker can do it. He has the handcart and straps."

After they made their way down the awkward stairs, Elaine returned directly to her office. Tim strolled slowly, looking around for someone with whom he might have an impromptu conversation, but everyone appeared busy.

Several of the staff were marked OUT on the IN/OUT board in the reception area. His name was back on the board, and he noted that he was IN, so he moved the marker to OUT, and bade the receptionist a good day. He didn't feel terribly cheated that idle chit-chat was not available, given his productive walk-about with Elaine.

At the door, Tim turned around and went back to Elaine's office. Her door was closed now, but he saw through the window that she was alone. He tapped and put his head in.

"I have one more task for you, Elaine. I want you to go to the office supplies store and pick out a new office chair—for yourself. When it's delivered, we'll have this old one moved upstairs. It knows me."

As he drove to the hospital, Tim hummed a hymn, as he often did, often unaware of what hymn it was unless he added words. Today's selection, he discovered, was *It Came Upon the Midnight Clear*, a Christmas hymn, but his enjoyment of hymns was not restricted to the liturgical seasons.

> For, lo! The days are hastening on,
> By prophet bards foretold.
> La-la the ever-circling years
> Da-dum the age of gold...

He didn't know why this tune had come to mind. He wondered what form the 'age of gold' might take, in this 'ever-circling year'. Sometimes it was interesting to slow a verse down and sing it over and over until it made no sense at all.

At the hospital, Tim asked at Reception if "an item of clothing" had been brought into the ER by ambulance with a patient on Saturday morning. As she picked up a phone, the receptionist directed him to take a seat in the waiting area

After about fifteen minutes, a hospital porter carrying a plastic bag approached the receptionist, who gestured toward Tim.

"Are you the owner of these pants?"

Tim looked inside the bag. "Yes, these are mine, thanks. Can I ask—do you know how she is? Is she still in the hospital?"

"Sorry, sir, I don't know anything about that. I was asked to give this bag to you. Just sign here to signify that you received it."

This was frustrating. Who did Tim know in the hospital who could relieve his mind about the young woman he'd rescued? Nobody he could think of. He knew a number of the medical and nursing staff, he had grown up with many of them, but knowing that the woman's identity was protected—as it should be—he couldn't come up with a convincing way to ask how she was. And he didn't want to place himself at the scene of her rescue, either.

He was a little disappointed that he couldn't get a tid-bit of information on his own. As Editor of *The Times*—which he usually was, but not right now—he could've stuck the PRESS badge in the virtual brim of his virtual fedora and asked all sorts of impertinent questions. But he didn't want to impersonate himself, however convoluted that thought might be.

As Tim left the hospital, a paramedic was replacing a gurney in the back of an ambulance. She was one of the crew who had attended the scene on Saturday. Tim walked toward the ambulance.

"Excuse me," he said. The attendant turned.

"Oh, hi!" She smiled broadly. "Nice to see you wearing pants. How are you?"

Tim held up the bag. "Just got the others back. I'm fine, thanks; a bit stiff. Listen, I wonder if you could do me a favour. I don't want any private information, but do you know or can you ask about the woman we, uh, carried out on the trail? How she is? I've been very concerned about her, wondering..."

The paramedic raised a finger and walked through the sliding glass doors into the Emergency Department, leaving Tim standing at the back of the ambulance. She came out a few minutes later. "Fully recovered. Went home this morning."

"Oh, thank you so much. Fully recovered, you say? That's wonderful! Does anyone know what happened to her or how it happened?"

"I don't, sorry. We just pick up and deliver. You know more than I do. You did a good job of keeping her warm, by the way. Sorry I teased you about your trousers."

"Oh, that's no problem. I get that reaction every time I go out without them, ha-ha."

"I bet you do. Try the Mounties? Maybe they were in to see her."

~

Tim's day had wobbled a bit at times, but, looking back at it in the evening, he thought it had gone fairly well. Being out amongst people had resulted in gains, though not from the sources he'd expected.

While savouring the remnants of his after-supper wine, he entered his thoughts in the *PERSPECTIVES* notebook, writing sentences instead of making lists and grids.

Expect the unexpected, he wrote.

No, that wasn't what he learned today. He drew a line through that phrase, but just a thin one so he could read it again if he needed to. He thought a while, and tried again.

Be clear about what you want, but be open to it coming from unexpected sources.

February 9: Curiosity

Tuesday

Tim retrieved the morning paper, placed carefully next to the storm door. That reminded him to see about *New Door* today.

He had a new appreciation for having things to do, at least as an alternative to not knowing what to do. How many times had he joined in the water-cooler chat about how nice it would be to have an extended vacation, not having to come to work every day? Because the others at the water-cooler were his employees, they usually hastened to impress upon him how much they really, really liked their jobs and how this was just silly talk, though if they won the big lottery jackpot they might have to give notice.

"Yes, of course, I understand completely," he would say. "Me, too."

Tim didn't have to win the lottery. He didn't even buy lottery tickets. He was the one with the option to take a year off with pay, and here he was, in Month Two of an extended leave. And here he was, looking for structure, and finding it back at his office.

"Office *building*," he said aloud. "I am going to the building, not to work at my job, the ball and chain."

There were some components of his former workday that still appealed, including the occasional breakfast at the Daisy Café, next door to the newspaper office. Since he was going to that office to meet with the painting contractor this morning, it seemed convenient to stop in for a light breakfast. Normally it wasn't their light menu that appealed to him, but he remembered those snug jeans.

Last month he had worried about cholesterol, but his doctor had told him he was healthy, so he'd allowed himself some big greasy breakfasts. Now he was gaining weight. It was hard to win.

No, that wasn't quite right; he was neither winning nor losing. That wasn't his intent. His aim for the year—other than wanting to delve, however that might be defined—was to be comfortable, maybe even healthy. He was not unhealthy according to medical tests, but he hadn't really felt well in recent years, often anxious and stressed. He was glad he'd had the sense and the great good fortune to be able to step away from his lifelong career to give his body and mind this chance to re-stock.

As he dressed, he looked at himself in the full-length mirror in his bedroom. He didn't see any fat. Perhaps the jeans had shrunk in the wash.

The Daisy wasn't very busy by the time he arrived, as the morning crowd had moved on to work. The table in the front window was available so he sat there, instead of the usual booth where the soft bench might aggravate his sore back. It felt much better, thank heavens, but he didn't want to call attention to it.

He could almost see *The Times* office from this vantage point. He wasn't looking for anyone in particular, just noticing the different view.

"What's wrong, honey?" The effusive waitress, Evelyn, seemed genuinely concerned. "You don't like your booth any more, after all these years?" She poured him a cup of coffee, which Tim considered 'bad since 1967'.

"Good morning, Evelyn. Nothing wrong at all. I thought I'd try a new table, a new view. Is that okay?"

She frowned and took his modest order.

Thanks to the new view, he recognized someone walking by. He rapped on the glass and beckoned to James Olsen, who turned around and came inside.

"Got a minute, James? Can I buy you a coffee?"

James sat at the table. Evelyn brought a menu and poured him a coffee. "I see you found some company," she said to Tim, and then said to James, "He's my favourite customer."

"Thanks, Evelyn. This is on my tab, James. Everything's good here."

"Really? Gee, in that case…I didn't have breakfast yet, so…"

He ordered the South River Log-Jam. Tim was envious, but he didn't change his toasted English muffin order.

"So, James, how's it going? Working on anything interesting this week?"

"Well, between you and me, Mister Brown, no—but I can't tell the boss that, can I? I mean, I'm doing my best, but what's interesting around here? I keep on the lookout for stories about the local economy and such, but that's interesting to exactly nobody except the people involved."

"Really? We've been publishing stories about the local economy, as you call it, for decades, and subscriptions are steady."

"Yeah, steady, but not growing, I bet. Am I right? Okay, I shouldn't have said that. I'm not criticizing you or *The Times*. It's this town, this region."

"In what way. James?"

"It's so, I dunno, so *safe*!"

"We're safe? Is that a problem?"

"Not if you want to raise a family here. South River is the safest place to live of anywhere. You could let your puppy-dog play in the street and send your toddler out to bring it home. Nothing would happen, except that all the cars would stop and three drivers would get out to make sure dog and kid were okay. Don't get me wrong. People will buy the paper for a photo of the empty street with a riveting caption that says, *Something almost happened here*!"

James tucked into his breakfast platter. Tim accepted a coffee top-up from Evelyn.

"What you say is most interesting, James. I won't argue with you about the safety of traffic in these communities, though the police do make arrests for speeding from time to time. Doesn't that add a little zing?"

"Sure, and a few drug busts, lots and lots of drunk driving, domestic abuse, littering, things like that. But what I mean is *crime*, man! Bank robberies! Gunfire! Arson! Abductions! Action! Mystery!"

"Ohh, I see. Action. Mystery. I agree, these are mostly absent from our pages. D'you think there is such a thing as a real mystery?"

"Sure, there's lots of mysteries. Television is full of mysteries. People are hooked on them. Books, too, I guess."

"Yes, of course, but those are mostly fiction. What happens out there on the street, in real life, is just grunt work, most of the time. Life is ordinary. Go ahead and ask the law enforcement people. In fact, I recommend that to you as an article."

"Okay," James said without enthusiasm.

"But I ask again, do mysteries actually happen, or is it all in how we tell the story? Could you write your story of the puppy and the toddler with a little suspense, turn it into a mystery?"

"Yeah, maybe." James looked a little uneasy now. "Thanks for breakfast, that hit the spot. I better get in there or Miss Fong will be giving me dirty looks. Thanks for the talk, too."

"You're welcome, James. We'll do this again."

Tim wished the café served decent coffee so he could stay and mull over what James had said. He sensed a nugget of insight hiding in there somewhere. But there was just enough time for him to go to the coffee drive-thru by the highway before he was due back to meet with Elaine and the painting contractor.

He brought the large coffee and cruller back to the office, signalled to Evelyn that he would be upstairs, and went up to his new old office. There was a straight-backed chair and a heavy oak table in the room, and hooks on the wall behind the door, where he hung his jacket. With a handful of napkins he brought from his stash in the car, he wiped the dust from the table and sat to record his thoughts from breakfast with James.

There *was* a nugget. Two, in fact. One, James had stated what Tim himself felt in recent years, about the paucity of newsworthy happenings in the greater South River region that readers of *The Times* would be eager to learn about. They might be interested in a lukewarm way, willing to suspend judgment for seven days until the next issue came out. Two, James' narrow view reminded him of Stella.

He sipped the coffee, took a big bite of the totally unnecessary donut, and gazed across the river through the dirty window. James and Stella were both wrong, he was certain. A quiet community was worth celebrating. And nobody, anywhere, was far from crime, if that's what the people wanted to read about. Or danger.

There was a knock at the bottom of the stairs. Tim inhaled to call "Come in!" but sneezed a great sneeze instead.

Elaine Fong appeared at the top of the stairs with a man in tow. "Are you all right? Or was that your door alarm?"

"Excuse me, please. Doh, if I sdeeze like that all the time I'll hurt byself. Please come in, and pardon the dust."

Elaine introduced the contractor, Rory O'Dowd, a stocky young man with a bushy red beard. He looked like a weightlifter to Tim.

Rory shook Tim's hand with a weightlifter's grip, and took out his measuring tape. "Just this room?"

"Yes, that'll do for now," Elaine said before Tim could speak. "Oh, and I think you'd better include that stairway? It's awfully dark. A bit of white paint there would help a lot. Is that all right with you, Tim?"

"Sure. Good suggestion. I'll get the cleaners to wipe that down, too."

"Oh, no need," Rory said. "Our crew will do that."

"You have cleaners? I called all over and couldn't get anyone to even look at the job until next week."

"You can't get 'em because we have 'em," he replied. "We ran into the same trouble, getting hung up on jobs 'cause we couldn't get cleaners, and the customers weren't happy when we painted over dirt, so we hired our own. These guys know how to prepare a surface for painting, let me tell you. They remove dust and grease and stuff like that, even fill holes and cracks, so the painters just come in and paint. Sometimes saves our customers a whole coat, and that saves you a lot of money."

Elaine was pleased. Tim was astonished.

"Wow," he said. "So when can you do this job?"

"We'll need the estimate first." Elaine was in charge, no doubt about that. "We're including the downstairs, remember, and that's a much bigger consideration."

"Oh, right," Tim said. "Well, soon, I hope—*if* we go ahead, of course, ha-ha. It's hard for me to play hardball when I'm so eager to get in here—and get this dust out. By the way, Rory, can you supply a blind for the window, along with everything else you do?"

"Sure can. Do you have a preference?"

"Gosh, I have a choice? Um, white, not dark green. I dunno, a roller blind, I guess? Like what's there, only without cracks?"

"Oh, do you think?" Elaine sounded like she had bitten off the greater piece of what she might have said and had swallowed it instead.

"I have a book with samples in my truck," Rory said.

"Why don't I leave it up to Elaine, then? As long as you don't have to order something in from Montreal. I think a blind that prevents people seeing in if I'm working here at night is what I want, more than one that keeps sunlight out."

"Okay, sir, we'll get right on it. I'll have our quotation to you by this time tomorrow, maybe sooner. And it will be a quote, not an estimate. We don't dicker, we just get the job done."

"I like the sound of that. Let's hope we like the price."

Elaine and the contractor made their way down the stairs.

Tim sat again at the old table. He was trying on the room, and it felt like a good fit. He wouldn't need much added. He'd bring his old chair up when Elaine got her new one. This table would suit just fine for a desk; he'd pick up a blotter to cover the ink stains and gouges. There was an old file cabinet down the hall if he needed one.

He just wanted space to think, and walls where he could post his thoughts on large sheets of paper if he chose to use them again. The thoughts that often seemed to elude him at home might arrive fully-formed here.

He opened his notebook to where he had left off musing about Stella and James. Stella could do whatever she wanted as the MLA for South River and the Harbours, and she took instruction from no one. But James was a reporter, and the "five Ws" were the tools of his trade. Was he asking who-what-when-where-why when he took his notebook to a story? Or was he just recording whatever he was told? He hadn't seemed very curious at breakfast.

That's what connected these two very different people, one who made the news and one who reported it. Both had reached the same conclusion about South River's lack of depth, and were convinced of their rightness *because they were not curious.* Surely, curiosity was the sharpest tool in the delver's toolbox.

Tim Brown was curious. Sherlock Holmes, his fictional mentor, was curious—didn't he often say the word? Sure, Sherlock noticed things that mere mortals overlooked, but even that famous detective would have failed to use his vaunted powers of observation if he hadn't allowed himself to be curious.

Tim quickly clattered down the steps, then realized he had left his jacket behind the office door upstairs. So he clattered up and down again. He found Elaine back in her office.

"Call me as soon as you hear from that guy," he said. "I want to buy what he's selling."

"On your cell-phone?"

"But of course!"

Tim was eager for his next stop. The Library was right next door, and the Head Librarian was behind the desk.

"Marlene, do you have—I mean, good morning, Marlene."

"Good morning, Tim. How goes it?"

"Portentously, if bumpily."

"Interesting! A portent could be auspicious or calamitous. Bumpily leans toward the latter."

"It could go either way, Marlene, given that I'm the one doing the doing. However, I live in hope."

"Good for you, Tim. I hear that's a great place to live. You were going to ask me about a book?"

"Yes. Is there a book about curiosity?"

"Oh now, that's a good question. I can think of several, but they're for children. Not what you seek, I think?"

"Yeah, no. Something about the—what would you call it—the practice of curiosity, the quality of curiosity, that sort of thing? An inquiring mind, perhaps? For adults?"

"I'll have to research that for you. Just write your name and phone number on this card and I'll call you when I find something suitable. There must be one. Now you've made me curious!"

"Good for me! It must take a lot to stump you, Marlene. By the way, I'm trying to get to a bookstore to order my own copy of *The Adventures of Sherlock Holmes*. Am I still okay to hang on to the copy you loaned me?"

"Yes, of course. Nobody has requested it, oddly." She smiled. "If someone does, I'll call it in. You know, you could always phone your order in to the bookstore."

"I could, but I'd like to go in and browse anyway. I suppose I could order it and browse when it comes in. Maybe I'll do that. Thank you, Marlene. I look forward to hearing from you."

"Stay curious, Tim. It looks good on you."

~

Tim *was* curious. He felt as though he had discovered a new word, and that word was indeed portentous. He would be a curious delver.

His curiosity took him to the RCMP Depot across the highway from the Town of South River, into the municipal district where the Mounties had jurisdiction. He went to the counter and stated the circumstances about which he was curious: he had assisted with rescuing a woman with alleged hypothermia, on Saturday morning, on a trail, in Blockhouse, and the constable had asked if he'd be prepared to give a statement, and he had said he would.

"Did someone call you to make a statement?" the civilian clerk behind the counter asked.

"No, nobody called, but I was going by so I thought I'd come in and offer my services. And I have some questions as well."

The clerk asked Tim to have a seat. She disappeared down a corridor to speak to someone Tim couldn't see. When she returned she beckoned him to approach the counter.

"We don't need a statement, but we do thank you for offering. We have your contact information if it's needed."

"Well, okay. But can I just speak to the constable for a moment? Or have his name so I can call him about it? I do have a rather important question about what happened there, and I think I have a right to know."

"Was—is the person a relative of yours?"

"No, that shouldn't matter. Listen—"

"Write your name and phone number here and I'll pass it on to the constable when he comes in. That's all I can do. It's up to him."

There's a curiosity-killer. Stonewalling. You'd think the Mountie would at least want to come out and shake his hand to thank him for helping to save the woman's life. She'd been in pretty bad shape, and her first helpers hadn't been helping in the right way. And Tim suffered a back injury in the process, not to mention a slight injury to his dignity.

But none of that mattered. He was curious and he wanted to ask his question.

Curiosity, he was discovering, was not only an openness to discovery. It contained a certain degree of urgency. "Perhaps that's what killed the cat," he mumbled as he returned to his car. "Kitty was impatient."

He knew he would hear from the Mountie eventually, because he would keep asking until he did. Curiosity could also be persistent. That cheered him somewhat.

At the electronics store, he asked a clerk to tell him about the newest, best cellular phone. His flip-phone, which he believed looked pretty nifty though it was too tiny in his hands, was no longer the hot ticket. The clerk produced a new model that was in one piece, no flip cover, no tiny antenna to get caught in his pocket.

"How hard would it be for you to transfer my current number to this new phone?"

"Not hard at all. I can do it for you right now if you like. Let's get you started."

Tim produced his credit card, setting wheels in motion. Well, there might have been wheels at one time, like a rotary dial. Nowadays everything was solid state, no moving parts, yet amazing things got done, post-wheel. Computers seemed to have changed the world.

That reminded him of Elaine's suggestion that he get a laptop computer so his work could be portable. He decided to put it off for now. He didn't see himself using a computer this year. He liked the old-fashioned act of jotting thoughts in a coil-bound notebook. With a pencil. Seated at an old oak table with a view across the river. Those seemed like the right tools for a curious delver. A notebook was very portable.

Besides, he had spent enough money for one day, or soon would. Rory O'Dowd's company's work would not be cheap, but who could argue with efficiency?

The new cell-phone was ready. The phone numbers—the few he'd bothered to put in the old one—were all transferred. The voice mail greeting he had struggled to record on Friday was there. The clerk offered to help him choose a ringtone, and after auditing all the beeps and bloops, he settled on the one that sounded like an old-fashioned telephone ringer.

"I'm going to stay in the twentieth century a bit longer," he said to the clerk.

Tim drove home feeling quite happy with the day. Last month, he had felt good if he'd done anything at all, as action—however misguided—felt better than inaction. Today, he'd had a list of things to attend to, some of which had worked out and some of which hadn't, and one had opened up a whole new thought process.

He uncorked a bottle of *Mardi Ordinaire* and poured a generous glass.

Robert had told him to go easy on himself, and talking with James had led him to be curious. Surely something good would come of both of these.

February 10: Speed of light

Wednesday

Retrieving the newspapers in the morning, Tim remembered he had intended to find out about getting a new storm door. Yesterday's events had distracted him from this, being far more interesting.

He noted that the thought had returned to him while he was on the cold porch. This reinforced his theory that some thoughts exist in specific times and places. Writing them down helped to move them to where they could be worked on. If he failed to do that, he might not remember them until he returned to where they hung in the air.

He hadn't been reading his own weekly paper first thing when it arrived, and sometimes it sat around for days before he got to it. Perhaps this confirmed the irrelevance of the paper. Much of it was irrelevant if you weren't involved in any of the so-called news stories that reporters like James found or followed, or if you weren't looking to buy things on sale from the advertisers, or watch something on television.

But a newspaper didn't have to be relevant to be of interest, did it? He thought he should explore that sometime.

But this morning, he was interested to read the paper, and last week's, too. He wanted to see what James had done with the hiker incidents.

He started with last week's account of someone on cross-country skis who had fallen into a pond. The ice had been thin when the recent blizzard covered it in snow. The skier had managed to get himself out of the pond and back on the trail. There was a warning to stay off ponds.

In this week's section of the paper that grouped together short "Community Notes", there was a mention of a similar incident:

> **Ponds Claim Second Victim**.
> Hikers who depart from established trails are courting calamity. We reported last week that one person skied cross-country from a trail and sank into a hidden pond that had not frozen solid. This past weekend another hiker reportedly broke through ice into deep water. Local Fire Departments remind the public to stay on groomed trails, and never to go on the ice without testing it first.

Tim read this with dismay. It was so ho-hum it was ridiculous. He had been at one of these so-called pond incidents, and it had been far from ho-hum. That woman had been in grave danger. Three emergency services attended the scene. How could James have overlooked the significance of two similar events happening on the trail—a coincidence that Tim himself hadn't known about? James seemed to pass these events off as silly accidents. Tim was also very curious about what had caused two adult hikers to wander into the woods and risk hypothermia or drowning.

To be fair—and Tim was fair to a fault—he hadn't told James what he knew about the incident he'd been involved in, because he wanted to stay on the down-low himself, and he had been curious to see what James would dig up on his own.

Well, he was seeing now: James had dug up nothing, and following yesterday morning's breakfast chat, Tim could see why. But there was a difference between lacking curiosity and turning a blind eye, surely? Assuming there's no story is a career-limiting mind-set for a reporter, no matter how irrelevant the publication.

He wondered what *would* attract James' attention. This warranted further attention.

Now Tim had a dilemma: as editor, this would be his responsibility. But he was on leave, and Elaine Fong was interim editor. He wouldn't go behind her back, but neither did he want to get into the weeds of telling her all about his rescue caper either, at least not yet.

Speaking of Elaine, he knew she'd be looking for his comments on her new approach to her editorials.

He flipped to the editorial page and there it was: *Get "In The Ring" with Elaine Fong*, with boxing-ring graphics. She invited readers to comment by phone or by e-mail. Her topic was about a forestry issue currently being debated in the Legislature, and she appeared to be leaning toward the governing Liberal party's position.

"Uh-oh," Tim said aloud.

Almost on cue, his home phone rang.

"Good morning, Aunt Stella. It's been a long time—well, a week, anyway. How've you been?"

"What are you up to now?"

"Me? Nice of you to ask. I'm getting a vacant room downtown cleaned and painted so I can—"

"Not that. You know what I mean. This editorial. Whatever possessed you to write this?"

"Aunt Stella, you know my name is Tim, right? I'm not Elaine Fong. Elaine Fong wrote the editorial. And before you tell me I should have stopped her, I remind you that I am on leave this year, and I therefore do not edit the editor."

"That's claptrap. You still have the responsibility to operate the newspaper in a professional manner."

"Oh, it's very professional, just not toeing the Conservative party line."

"You told me clearly that you would never support either side, as that would jeopardize your impartiality."

"Precisely. I'm glad you remember. But you're missing the point, Aunt Stella. See the invitation to 'get in the ring' with her? That's open to anyone, including you. We seldom publish your publicity-seeking press releases on their own merits, but now the gauntlet has been thrown down, and the door and telephone and e-mail are wide open. This is exciting! Call Elaine! I look forward to seeing your rebuttal published in next week's paper. I really do."

"It better be." She abruptly hung up, as was her usual style.

Tim had hoped the recent thawing of relations between them, achieved after much hard work, would continue. Perhaps it would, but where politics was concerned, especially her politics, Stella would never warm to disloyalty, especially from her nephew who had professed neither loyalty nor opposition.

He sighed. All this on one tiny espresso, and it was barely daylight yet.

He brewed a pot of regular coffee, put two slices of bread in the toaster, and made a To Do list for the day.

He had one constant for each day this week: go downtown, walk through the front door of *The Times*, clatter upstairs to his office-in-waiting, and leave again. He was tempted to take things to leave in the room, but since cleaners and painters would be there in all corners first, he'd wait, and set aside the notebooks and pencils on the floor in his study.

He made a note to tell Elaine not to have an internet cable extended to his office. He wanted original thinking to go on up there, not fooling around with a connection to the world-wide web. He wouldn't purchase a new laptop so he could carry his burdens home, either. The new mobile phone was his only concession to modernity.

The damaged front door: where do you go for those and who installs them? Tim's mother had known every handyman in town, and had made good use of them. They seemed to be grateful that she allowed them to perform their services for her. Bragging rights, perhaps.

In the years since her death, Tim had made a stab at keeping up with repairs, but mostly ignored whatever wasn't urgent. He knew that wasn't good, but he also knew he didn't know how to approach these people. His mother always told her chosen victim what was to be done and how much she would pay for it. Tim hadn't inherited this trait, and he doubted that his kinder, gentler approach would be effective.

He wished for someone to whom he could delegate tasks, a sort of house-Watson, as Elaine was turning out to be at the business:

she listened to him, then told him what was best for him to do, and praised him for doing it.

He shook his head. Dreaming wasn't doing. He added *Door* to the list and resolved to make the rounds of building supplies stores. They must know.

Desk blotter was in his comfort zone. He knew how to shop for office supplies.

Elaine had suggested a *Locksmith*. There was only one around, and it was rumoured that there was a long waiting period, so he'd better make the call now.

For a fleeting moment, he considered learning the trade. Wouldn't it be fun to be able to pick locks? That reminded him that the old file cabinet would need keys, so the locksmith could do that, too.

While he was down at the newspaper office, he'd tell Elaine that he liked her editorial, and alert her to an incoming response from Stella Johnson, MLA.

Tim knew that a short *To Do* list could take all day, especially with interruptions. Time seemed to pass at a different speed when roaming around versus staying in one place. Einstein had discovered that, hadn't he? People at home grew old and died, while those who whizzed through the universe at the speed of light hardly aged...he thought both might apply in his case, but he was moving only at the posted speed limit so the difference would be noticeable to only him.

~

Elaine had heard from Stella by the time Tim arrived for his walk-through.

"Oh, dear," he said. "Should I apologize?"

"Why?" Elaine was beaming. "Sure, she was crackling with indignation, but she knows her stuff, too. I asked her to put her comments in writing rather than have me try to transcribe from a telephone message. And I encouraged her to speak to the issue rather than chew me out, which is where she began. I didn't expect to hook such a big fish on the first cast, so to speak. Brilliant suggestion, Tim. Thanks very much for that."

"Oh, don't thank me. She's a formidable one, our Stella, but she has a great following hereabouts, so to have her appearing in your 'ring' can only be good. Float like a butterfly, though. She can sting like a bee. Now, lemme see, I had a couple other things. Oh yes, I won't need the internet cable upstairs. But I did upgrade my mobile phone." He held it up for her to see. "Now all that has to happen is for the signal to be mobile, too. It's a dead zone as soon as you head inland."

"I know, reception's awful around here. But you have voice mail, right?"

Tim was prouder to say yup than the answer warranted. Little victories.

"So, we have the quote from the painting contractor," Elaine turned her computer screen toward Tim. "Can you read it?"

He squinted. "Um, can you get a print-out?"

She did, and handed the pages to Tim. While he looked them over, she laid out an array of paint colour chips in shades of white, ranging from cool to warm. He scanned the quote details and arrived at the figure at the bottom of the second page. And whistled.

"I know," Elaine sighed. "Me, too."

"It's a lot," Tim said.

"Yes."

"Maybe we should put brighter bulbs in the lights?"

Elaine smiled, and gathered up the colour chips. "Come with me."

They walked out into the reception area, where Elaine taped the sample shades in a row on the wall. Tim had thought the walls were white, but they were some kind of pale green, once thought to be restful on the eyes, now seeming in need of rest themselves. The chips looked brilliant by comparison.

Then they found a blank wall space in the inner office, above a bank of storage cabinets, and stuck the colours up there. "I think you can keep your light bulbs as they are," Elaine said. "No need to pay a higher electricity bill every year when a nice coat of paint will do the job and won't cause headaches."

Back in her office, Tim asked, "This includes upstairs, too? My office and stairway?"

"It does. Plus your blinds and a few other bits. You won't know the place."

"I'll have to authorize this," Tim said. "The accountants won't let this go through without knowing that I saw it."

When he had decided to take a year's leave, Tim wanted full freedom from editing the newspaper and financial management of the business. He told his lawyer and accountant to set it up as though he was going to climb Mount Everest, meaning that he would not be reviewing expenses nor signing cheques. He trusted that Elaine would keep extras to a minimum—she had a discretionary amount—but here they were, not even at the middle of February, discussing major extra expenses already.

The company had enviable assets, but even though Tim was taking a reduced sabbatical-year income, he was paying Elaine's full salary, so he had to watch it. Advertising sales had better be good.

The walls wouldn't paint themselves, though. He wanted his hideout upstairs done. There wasn't a good fiscal reason for it, maybe, but it was what he wanted, so he wrote a note to the accountant on the invoice and signed his name.

"When can they start?"

"Their prep team, also known as cleaners, can be in tonight—" Elaine glanced at her watch "—if I call him right away. I'll get our caretaker to stay for security."

"Will he do that?"

"Sure. He owes me."

Tim decided not to ask the nature of that transaction. Elaine had her ways, and nobody seemed unhappy with her. Perhaps she used a touch of his mother's strategy.

"I'll check on the painting, but I think he said they could start Friday at five. They work all night."

"I never heard of painters doing that."

"They do. Perhaps I neglected to mention, they work for all the banks, and you never see tarps and stepladders in banks. When they renovate, the work is done instantly and invisibly. These are that crew. And since Sunday is Valentine's Day, he said they'd like to be finished by early Sunday morning so they can clean up, get some sleep, and be home with their sweethearts."

"Really?"

"That's what he said."

"Astounding."

"You won't regret it, Tim. You might be able to get a cheaper estimate, but I'm doubtful you'd be more satisfied."

Tim noted that he had forgotten to mark himself IN on the IN/OUT board, so he slid the little white disc to IN and back to OUT on his way out. "I'm out, Raquel," he said to the receptionist.

"Oh, hi, Mister Brown. It's Rachael. I didn't notice that you were in. But, goodbye."

Mission accomplished, he thought. It was only Wednesday and his presence was not attracting notice.

He drove to the office supplies store with just a little less eagerness than he'd anticipated. He was one of those who liked to stroll the aisles and admire the reams of paper and styles of pens and try to think up reasons to buy them—but not right now. He had authorized thousands of dollars to be spent on paint, so a little frugality was in order. A lot of frugality.

Fancy laptop computers were on display on special counters under special lighting. A clunky older model was on sale for almost as much as the paint job. This cheered him up. If he twisted his logic hard enough he could say he paid for the painting by declining the computer.

On the other hand, these devices, which he knew all sorts of businesses were buying and using, would become ubiquitous in his business, and how would they be paid for?

That line of thinking made him nervous, so he moved along to the display of low-tech desk blotters. There were some handsome embossed ones, suitable for desks of people who charged big fees for their services. Tim selected the lowest-priced one, without embossing.

Finally, he examined the office chairs, and hoped Elaine

wouldn't choose the fancy leather number for herself. Of course she wouldn't. It was too big for her, like the one she was using now, which is why he'd suggested she select something new. He was sure she'd be reasonable.

Tim put the blotter in the trunk of his car, to wait until the office was ready. That might be as soon as next week, a very exciting thought.

It was past lunchtime, so he went home to have a bite and take stock of what he was accomplishing. Elaine had given him one other major thing to consider in addition to cleaners and paint: Sunday would be Valentine's Day. What would he do about that? He dialed Robert's mobile and left a message for him to call.

~

While the kettle was boiling for lunchtime tea, Tim found the locksmith in the Yellow Pages and left a message for him to call. No telling when he'd hear back. It wasn't urgent, but there'd come a day when there'd be things in the office that he didn't want disturbed. Like thoughts.

He was satisfied with the morning's decisions and accomplishments, and didn't feel like going out again to see about replacing the damaged front door. Saturday's warm, sunny day had turned into February's worst behaviour: temperature above freezing by day to make lots of slush, freezing at night to turn slushy bootprints into obstacle courses waiting to twist ankles. It was raining now, so all those frozen holes were slick as, well, as ice. And even though the temperature was relatively mild, it was damp, and it penetrated into one's bones.

So he stayed in. Thinking about money this morning reminded him that he had not paid last month's house bills yet, so he went to the desk in the study to catch up on the mail.

Robert called back.

"So, guess what day is Sunday?"

"Oh, you don't have to remind me. This is a university, remember? University students are like children when it comes to special events, especially if there's candy. Or romance. They are children, anyway. What's in your mind? Not dinner out, I hope?"

Robert and Tim were as much a couple as they could be without being married. They were not 'out', but not closeted either. They knew well that people had opinions on their relationship, but neither man was interested in others' opinions on their private life. An event that encouraged public demonstrations of affection was far outside their comfort zone. So, while they'd be happy to dine out at a restaurant—if it was a good one—they wouldn't be caught dead in one on Valentine's Day.

"Don't worry, Rob, I wasn't thinking of going out. We couldn't get a reservation anywhere good now, anyway. But the main dining room in the Johnson Mansion is quite good, depending on which chef's in charge. We don't have to celebrate the bloody martyrdom of poor Valentine, but it *is* mid-February, as gloomy a time of year as any, and I thought maybe a little attention to Sunday dinner might be fun."

"That sounds like a good idea—maybe. What did you have in mind for fun? Inviting Stella?"

Both men laughed at this. Stella Johnson was always a welcome guest at Sunday dinner, but she had rarely been invited more frequently than quarterly, though she had been there twice in January for enjoyable visits. They didn't use 'fun' in regard to Stella.

"Perhaps not Stella. I think she may be snuggling at home, anyway."

"What? Seriously? Stella snuggling—I'm not sure I want to think about that, though I bet she could bring a lot of energy to it."

"Okay, stop. I'll send her some flowers and an enigmatic card that will make her beau pay attention. So, what do you think about inviting Elaine Fong? I don't think she has much of a social circle. She'd likely spend Sunday afternoon in the office eating pizza. I say that because I usually did that. Before you."

"Poor you. Yes, sure! I liked Elaine. Great voice. Hey, why don't I bring some music and we'll sing some *tafelmusik*? Great idea, me! We'll need a soprano, one who can sight-read, of course. This could be fun. I haven't sung for pleasure in a while. I have lots of great scores."

"Wow, I didn't see this coming, but sure, yes, let's. Who for the soprano? That gal who came to church, what about her? She sure can sing."

"Mmm, maybe not. She has a big vibrato, not sure if she knows how to control it yet. Let me think about that. Oh, I know: remember my organ student, Helen, whose car broke down last month? She has a lovely clear voice, and I know she can sight-read like the dickens."

"Would she be able to come down from the city for dinner? I mean, would her car be reliable?"

"Good point. I can ask her. Would you mind—can I offer her the spare bedroom if she would prefer not to travel back after dinner? We never know about the roads, and of course, there might be wine."

"Of course she can stay. Good timing: Mrs A comes tomorrow, so I'll get her to freshen the guest room. This is shaping up to be a nice party. I hope they'll agree to join us. Oh, I must warn you, though, the piano is very out of tune. I've booked the tuner for March, the earliest I could get."

"I know. I tapped the ivories last Sunday when you were sleeping off your sore back. How is it, by the way? Your back, I mean?"

"Much better, thanks. So, what about a menu? It needn't be elaborate."

"I'll devise one and bring it with me tomorrow, okay? You can do the shopping?"

"You betcha. We'll have a rollicking celebration—without the Valentine *schmaltz*! Do either of these ladies know about us?"

"They will if they don't. Don't care. It'll work."

February 11: Tafelmusik

Thursday

The painting crew was finished already. They had replaced the old, cracked, green blind with flouncy drapes. The walls were streaked, and the floor was covered in paint splatters. They had moved the old filing cabinet into the room, and had pried the drawers open with a tire iron, which was lying on top.

All the money was gone.

Tim's grandfather had hidden thousands and thousands of dollars in that drawer. Now there was none, and the cabinet was ruined.

Tim was devastated. How could everything have gone so wrong?

He pulled the cheap drapes aside and looked out the streaked window. Elaine was getting into the painting contractor's fancy little roadster. The top was down. They both looked up, and smiled, and waved.

He rapped on the window. "Stop! Stop! Stop!"

They drove off, paper money blowing out of the car. They didn't care. They had lots now.

~

Tim's shouting woke only him. Oh, how absolutely awful he felt. He got up to pee and heard the alarm go off while he was in the bathroom. Yes, it was a nightmare, only a dream, but the emotions felt real. Total fiction, of course.

He was surprised at how hard it seemed to be to convince his subconscious that none of it was true. The painting job could not and would not have been finished yet. There was zero money in the old file cabinet: he had pulled the drawers open when he'd been there and knew each was empty. Elaine and the contractor—well, he wouldn't judge, but that seemed highly unlikely. And those drapes! He laughed at that detail. His imagination was evidently trying to see how far it could stray from the realm of possibilities.

He made a double espresso to start the day, and brewed a half-pot of regular coffee right after. The coffee-jitters would give his nerves something real to jangle about.

He checked the calendar: Thursday, a busy day, starting with Mrs Aquino and her air-exchange services, and ending with Robert's arrival and choir practice. In between, he would make his daily visit to the office, which wouldn't take long, and search for a new front door and someone to install it, which might take all day. He would try not to be in a hurry, as he preferred not to be home while Mrs A was charging around the house.

He wrote a cheque for her regular fee and placed it on the kitchen island, hoping she'd be finished before he returned. When she arrived at seven-thirty sharp, he asked her to freshen the guest room upstairs.

He realized that Thursday's regular events should include breakfast at the Daisy Café. He didn't have to order the Log-Jam each time. Neither he nor Mrs A liked to share the house with the other. He didn't want to see her propping the doors open while the furnace ran constantly, and she didn't want to see him closing them.

Tim took the Yellow Pages book with him. He wasn't in a great rush today, but he didn't want to get frustrated driving around looking for aluminum doors in all the wrong places.

At the café, he found the ads to be interesting reading. He learned that a lot of places offered doors, including a building supplies store in Blockhouse. Well, wasn't that convenient? He could go there and ask about doors, and then maybe go for a little stroll along the trail where he had encountered so much drama last Saturday.

But not today. He didn't want to take any chances today. It

seemed that every time he put boots on to go outdoors, something unexpected happened. Yes, he endorsed curiosity, but one could surely choose which days were best for satisfying it, couldn't one? Uncurious Thursday sounded right.

He knew Robert would have a grocery list for him to work on tomorrow or Saturday for Sunday's musical dinner, and he still wanted to visit the bookstore in Mahone Bay to order his own Sherlock copy, so he could do all that on the same trip. Another day planned. Anyway, today was still unpleasant outside, damp and sloppy. Perhaps the sun would come out again by Saturday.

At the office, Tim made a point of marking himself IN, and greeting Rachael by her correct name, assisted by her name plaque on the counter.

He tapped on Elaine's door. "Sorry to hassle you, Elaine. I won't bother you every time I come in. Today, though, I come with an invitation. May I?"

Elaine waved him in, and he closed the door behind him. "Sunday dinner at my house, with Robert. Can you come?"

"Oh! How nice of you to think of me..." Elaine looked over Tim's shoulder, so he turned to see what was there.

On the wall was a large white-board featuring a weekly grid. Each block was filled in.

"I'm not sure I can, Tim. I was planning to work on—"

"Don't do it, Elaine." Tim moved to block Elaine's view of the board. "That looks like the schedule I left behind. Give yourself Sunday afternoons off once in a while. This Sunday, anyway. Robert is a fabulous cook. Come at four. Yes?"

"You are very persuasive, Tim. Sure, I'd be happy to come. Thank-you. Can I bring something?"

"Well, actually, you can."

"What is it? I'm not much of a cook."

"Your voice. Robert intends that we will have *tafelmusik*, meaning that we will sing at the table, before, between, and after courses. We're inviting a soprano as well. Should be fun!"

"Oh, that does sound delightful. Not sure about my sight-reading if he brings ancient square-note manuscripts, but it's fun to try. I haven't done any of that since university."

"Gee, if there are square-note manuscripts, I'll just pour drinks. Oh, do you have any food allergies or preferences or other habits we should know about?"

"My tastes are pretty ordinary. I was raised on northern Ontario cuisine, ranging between hot turkey sandwiches and road kill. I'm omnivorous, though I usually skip sweets."

"I'll tell Robert. I'm sure he can work with that. I'm really looking forward to it. We'll have fun. And there will be wine."

"Maybe a glass. Thanks, Tim. Oh, by the way, the cleaners will be here tonight, and the painters will start tomorrow night. Make sure you leave the doors unlocked upstairs."

Time ascended the stairs with a happy heart. He couldn't help looking for the scene of his nightmare, but the old blind was still at the window, the file cabinet was not in the room, the walls were not painted, badly or otherwise, the dust was still undisturbed.

He walked down the hall to a small room where several file cabinets stood. None had been pried open. He didn't bother looking for bundles of cash he knew weren't there. That nightmare was hanging on too long.

He sat at the table, took the cell-phone from his pocket and left another message with the locksmith. What if he was locked out? He'd be standing out in the cold for days.

He supposed that if he'd said he was locked out, the locksmith would've called back. Changing locks wasn't the emergency that lost keys could be, but still.

He had no reason to stay in the room today, so he went down to the main floor and strolled past GB's corner. "Hi, GB, finding things to keep you interested, are you?"

"Hi, Tim, nice to see you. Oh, you know, the same. Fresh issue, need to get it sorted."

"Say, GB, I have a question for you."

He picked up a copy of this week's newspaper, of which GB had a stack for clipping and filing. He flipped to the Community Notes item and pointed to the short bit about the hikers who had fallen through the ice. "How would you file this, GB?"

Tim noticed GB's hands shaking as he held the paper. He hoped his old friend wasn't ill, as well as his wife.

"Several places," GB finally said. "Blockhouse. Old Train Line Trail. Blockhouse Fire Department. That'll do it."

"Interesting. Next question: does that little clipping raise any questions for you? Does it make you curious about anything?"

GB scanned the item again. "'Fraid not, Tim. Not curious very often. Got enough on my mind."

"Of course you do. How's Mrs Barss today?"

"Not good. Will tell her you inquired. Good of you."

~

Tim made the rounds of stores offering screen doors, learning a lot more than he wanted to know about a subject that didn't interest him. The door he had was perfectly good, except for a huge dent in the lower panel made by a copy of *The Daily* which someone who must be a football quarterback had thrown at it. He intended to submit the bill to the newspaper, and expected full restitution. If the side door had been dented he might have overlooked it, but this was on the front of the house and gave it a dilapidated appearance—or exacerbated it, more accurately.

He supposed the house was due for painting, another huge outlay of money. Maybe he'd invite Mister Instant Contractor to give him a quote. But not today. He didn't want to trigger another nightmare.

He had neglected to add them to his To Do list, but luckily he remembered flowers for his aunt as he drove past the florist. He hoped it wasn't too late to get some, given the nature of the day coming up.

"Sorry, roses of all colours are spoken for," the florist told him. "Mostly all we have left are these daisies. See here." She went to the cooler and brought out a bucket of huge, flat flowers in all colours. "Gerberas."

"Perfect. Just perfect. No complicated message implied with these, is there?"

"Not that I'm aware. Friendship, maybe? But they're pretty. I would dress them up for you, of course, with greens, baby's breath, some ferns, a ribbon."

"Sold. Can you deliver them on Sunday?"

"What's the address?"

Tim wrote Stella's address on a sticky note and the florist consulted her order book. "You're in luck. Our driver is going down that way on Sunday afternoon. Will that be okay?"

"Sure will. I guess I should get something for my own table, too. More of these will be nice, without the fluff."

He waited while his flowers were wrapped, paid the charges, and headed home. Mrs A was loading her cleaning implements in her car as he returned. He thanked her for her excellence and presented her with a big yellow daisy from his bouquet.

He was surprised to see how genuinely pleased she was at this simple gesture. Her cheeks dimpled as she smiled. *Don't judge*, he said to himself. *You never know.*

Tim prepared supper, and was skimming storm door brochures when Robert arrived. They reviewed plans for Sunday's musical dinner. Rather than sticking to their usual low profile on Valentine's Day, they enjoyed planning this event. Robert's organ student, Helen, had confirmed her attendance, so they had their quartet.

"I mentioned the piano to her," Robert said. "She said she would try to get here early on Sunday and bring her hammer and sickle to see what she could do."

"What?"

"Her tuning tools. Hammer and tuning fork, to tune the worst of the strings. You'll think she's a mouse when you meet her, but she'll tackle anything. She's a mighty mouse."

"I'm looking forward to meeting her—to this whole event, really. What'll we sing?"

"I'm having a hard time cutting down the list, there are so many lovely motets and madrigals."

"Go easy, now. Remember I'm your tenor. You know my skills."

"Yes, I do, and they are better than you give yourself credit for. A little practice and you'd enjoy the improvements. Maybe you'll make some time for voice lessons in the spring. Not before Sunday, though. Don't wear out your voice, and don't worry. We'll start with some rounds to tune our ears. I'm more concerned about the menu. It has to be tasty, but light. We don't want to burp our way through the music."

February 12: With the wind

Friday

In the early morning, Robert browsed the assorted storm door brochures.

"This one," he said, and pushed the others aside.

"How do you know? How can you tell so quickly?"

"I saw you looking at it a few times last night. I like it, too."

"But you don't know how much it costs, or the warranty—"

"So what? If the newspaper pays you for it—which I sincerely doubt—then cost is no issue. If you get a door that dents as easily as this one did, you won't like it. Paying for quality is not being wasteful. Quite the opposite, in fact."

"Hmm. You sound like Elaine. I must keep you two apart on Sunday. Oh, speaking of which, have you got your menu settled so I can pick up supplies?"

~

Tim left the house soon after Robert departed for the city. He picked up a large coffee and two sour cream donuts at the drive-thru, and took them to the offices of *The Times*.

A panel van with the name of the painting contractor was parked in front of the building. It was not yet seven o'clock, few vehicles on the street, slim chance they would collect a ticket from the town police.

Inside, the cleaners were folding the drop-cloths they had laid over the desks to protect them from drips as they worked overnight to prepare for the painters. The place smelled fresh, Tim noticed, and inhaled deeply for the second time in sixteen hours.

It didn't look all that great, though. The walls and ceiling were spotted with white patches where cracks and holes had been repaired. Light fixtures were hanging loose to permit the painters to reach behind them. All work charts, safety notices, bulletin boards, calendars, cartoons, paintings, and photographs were off the walls, including a faded portrait of Tim's grandfather. On closer inspection, it wasn't faded, but the glass was very dirty.

One of the cleaners saw him looking at it and came over with a cloth. "I was saving that until I could ask someone," she said. "Some customers don't want us to touch artworks. Is it okay to clean the glass?"

Tim gave his approval and headed toward the back stairs. On the way, he saw Elaine in a back corner, examining something. "Good morning, Elaine! You're in early. Whatcha think?"

"Good morning, Tim. Yes, I couldn't stay away. You either, I see. Sure is clean in here. I think they got down to the dust of ancient civilizations. Part of your heritage, I suppose. A lot of old printing ink was embedded in the walls from prehistoric times. They had to scrub hard to neutralize that."

"Amazing. Have you been upstairs?"

"Sure have. Let me know what you think."

Tim bounded up the stairs and entered his hideaway office. The old blind was gone and the old glass cleaned, so the window let in considerably more light than before. Ceiling, walls, and floor were scrubbed, and patches were still drying. The table and side chair appeared to have been washed and oiled.

He was happier about this simple job than he had expected to be. He sat at the table, which smelled citrusy, and took out his notebook. While he wondered what to write down as his impressions, he consumed the coffee and donut.

What is so special about having the cleaners in? he wrote. He listed what might've happened if Elaine hadn't secured these crackerjack workers:

A. Wait for days or weeks

B. Use our own custodian (not the best)
C. Do it myself.

He laughed at this, and was still smiling when Elaine came up the stairs.

"You look happy," she said. "All good?"

"Better than. I was just thinking what my options were had you not found these people. I thought that I would've had to do this myself, and that struck me funny."

"I agree, hilarious. Okay, I must get back down there. Everyone's coming in early and working through lunch so we can clear out by four, when the painters will arrive and cover everything with tarps. They'll do ceilings, window and door trim, then walls. I'm waiting to see if they think we'll get away with one coat, or need two. There's a top-quality paint that he thinks can do it in one coat, but it's more expensive. Or cheaper paint, more labour costs. Do you want to help decide?"

"I don't know what kind of pressure it puts on you, Elaine, but the fewer such decisions I have to make this year, the happier I will be. You've steered us well so far. Carry on, okay?"

He gazed out the washed window. The old glass had bumps and whorls in it which made objects in view move around as he moved his head. It held his conscious attention while his sub-conscious mind wandered back to his earlier question.

What *was* so special about having the cleaners in, followed by the painters? They were essential preliminary steps, he saw, ones that needed to be done *before* he could do whatever he was going to do in here. Everything starts somewhere, but rarely at the starting line. Many things had to be in place before they fired the gun to start the race.

What had Robert said to him last Saturday? *You never had to apply for a job or start a business.* He hadn't said it to imply that Tim lived a life of privilege—though maybe that was inherent in it. What he meant was that Tim had no experience with starting things. The beginnings he needed in his job were already there, long-established, and he caught flak if he wanted to omit or deviate from them. He was expert in continuing, not in creating from scratch.

So here he was, sitting in his little sailing ship of dreams, seeking relief from the pressures of that inherited continuum, hoping to gain satisfaction from his nebulous intention to delve, more than a little frustrated that he was getting nowhere. Even though he seemed to be moving a bit, he was not yet underway. He was drifting in and out with the tide.

So, yes, a thorough scrubbing was a sign that things were Getting Ready. No successful army had ever gone into battle without a lot of preparations first, and it wasn't the generals who shod the horses or hammered the swords. If they had, the battles might never have been waged...not a bad idea, but that idea didn't fit the current situation, so Tim discarded it. The battle he wanted to wage was to discover delving this year, and furniture polish seemed like an essential catalyst.

He turned back to the notebook and had to blink a few times to focus; the bubbles in the window had held his gaze unfocused for some time. He jotted down his great insights and finished the coffee and donut.

He called the cleaning company he'd booked for next Tuesday, and cheerfully cancelled the booking. He tried the locksmith once more, and was surprised to get the man himself. He was happy that he was in the office when that happened, as he wanted to know what kind of locks were there, which Tim could tell him by looking right at them. He said he would come in on Tuesday unless he had a lot of emergency calls.

He didn't stop on the way out to look for any chance encounters from the newspaper staff this morning. All heads were down, everyone hastening to get their work done so they could stay home on the weekend and let the painters do their work. He wondered why they couldn't do that every week, but he supposed the pace might not be sustainable.

He did admire how the staff seemed to respond to Elaine, though. He would discuss that with her sometime, but not now. It was working, all he needed to know. When her contract ended and he returned to the Editor's office, he'd deal with that then.

Elaine walked past as he was moving the white button to OUT.

"I saw a nice selection of office chairs in the store yesterday, Elaine. Looked like there were a few in your size." Some were on sale, too, but he wasn't going to emphasize price. It didn't seem right.

~

He had Robert's grocery list in his pocket, so he went to the supermarket. From the list of items he couldn't guess what the menu would be, but he had complete confidence in Robert's food sense.

Nothing looked like dessert so he picked up a Valentine's tray of strawberries dipped in chocolate. These imported berries would be tasteless, but they'd look nice on a plate.

He thought everyone might appreciate something to soothe their throats after singing, or even between songs, so he added some sorbet to the cart, and took it all home to put away. As usual, he noted on the list where he put the things so Robert could locate the ingredients when he needed them.

Timing would be tight on Sunday. Church sometimes ran late if the Reverend Doctor was preaching, as he often had difficulty arriving at a conclusion, and would circle around doggedly until he found it. They'd have a light lunch, and then Rob's student Helen would arrive, as quickly as the highway would permit, to tune the worst of the piano strings. She'd need lunch, too.

He had taken the flowers to the cool cellar to preserve them, and to keep them a surprise. He went down to check, and they looked as good as they had at the flower shop.

He wondered how to present them. If they were seated around all four sides of the table, singing and watching each other for entrances—so tricky in madrigals—they wouldn't want a bunch of flowers in their line of sight. Anyway, it was a non-Valentine's event, so the flowers should be there as decoration, not a statement.

He gathered up an assortment of small vases and cleaned them, ready to set around in all the rooms, including one small one for the guest room.

He phoned the RCMP depot and left another message regarding last Saturday's incident on the trail, adding that he would keep calling until someone agreed to speak to him.

He checked the wine cupboard. Who was drinking all the wine? No mystery there. Tim knew his daily glass of wine, which he so enjoyed, was often flowing into two or more. Was that a problem? Should he curtail his consumption? Should he treat wine the way Dr Muhammed had said to treat coffee, to dial it back if he got the jitters?

Alcohol wasn't caffeine. Maybe alcohol jitters was not as bad as too much coffee? He didn't have jitters from the wine, but he would pay attention to that, some day.

He knew he was spending a lot of money to keep the wine cupboard stocked, not only with a quantity of week-day plonk, but with some very tasty choices for Sundays. Money, whether spent on cleaning services or on fine vintages, all came out of the same pocket eventually. Maybe he'd bring it up with his accountant at tax time.

Regardless, he had to visit the liquor store now. He soon regained his buoyant attitude of the morning with a cart-load of weekday standbys and vintages.

To ensure that he stayed out of the way of Elaine and the painting contractors as they worked this evening, he rented a bagful of movies, though he wasn't curious about any of them. He considered picking up some greasy, salty take-out for supper, but virtuously decided to save that money. And there was the matter of his too-tight jeans.

A lean chicken breast and a baked potato were his supper. Surely he needn't deny himself a glass or two of *Vendredi Blanc* to go with that.

When he woke, he turned off the hissing movie screen, the electric fireplace, and all the lights, and went to bed, eager for the morrow.

February 13: On the trail

Saturday

What did Tim expect to happen today?

This was not so much a question about the unknown outcomes of various errands, as about what he should wear while discovering those outcomes. Since shopping for books and a door were on the list, he certainly wouldn't go around wearing the plaid woodsman's jacket with the quilted lining. It wasn't cold enough for that and, anyway, that was for night-time emergencies only. If ever. Same for the hat with the pull-down ear-lugs, and the knee-high logger boots. All of these were in the trunk of his car, not to have them at the ready but because it was the best place to store them.

The backpack was there, too. It still contained the four-battery silver flashlight, the binoculars, and the new compass-and-whistle trinket.

It was a decent day. February could deliver anything, weather-wise, from deep cold to unexpected warmth. It had been doing all of that. Today was sub-freezing cold, but no precipitation was falling nor forecast. Tim felt he could handle a short, innocent, stroll along the Old Train Line Trail. He was curious about something and wanted to check it out—prudently. No need to drop himself in any hidden pond to prove that water was wet.

But first, he'd give the day a chance to warm up a bit while he did a little shopping. He went to Mahone Bay, hoping to find the bookstore open. It was such a pretty town; every time he drove down Main Street and saw the picturesque churches on the waterfront he wondered if he would enjoy living here. South River's main charm was not its scenic beauty—it had precious little of that, despite being cleft by a river estuary below the bridge and a tumbling falls above it. Mahone Bay had scenery, South River had stores and related commerce. It wasn't a solid argument, but coupled with inertia, it was enough to keep Tim in the larger town.

There was a notice on the door of the bookstore, but not the same notice he had seen the last time he was there. This one didn't say they would be open on weekends. It said SORRY WE'VE CLOSED, and recommended a bookstore in Lunenburg. Drat! A small enterprise, especially one selling books, needed more than four months of tourists to pay twelve months of rent and inventory. Score one for the commercial cluster.

Back to Blockhouse and the building supplies store. They were open and busy. Yes, they did sell aluminum doors, not the same one Robert had chosen, but a similar model, one that should not dent if a newspaper was tossed at it. They'd need measurements. No, not all doors were the same size. Yes, they could provide an installer. The clerk gave Tim a pre-printed door sketch with arrows indicating what measurements they needed to order the right door for him.

This wasn't a step forward nor backward. It was another reminder of how much work went on in the background before things could be started or finished. He wasn't all that curious about the process of aluminum door replacement. It was not a delving topic.

~

It was mid-morning. The day was unlikely to warm up much more, given the overcast sky, so he decided to investigate the trail next before driving down to Lunenburg to hunt for books.

Before he stopped at the trail, he drove around Blockhouse to see what was nearby. He remembered he had felt closed in and far from houses as soon as he entered the trail, because the trees were tall and thick on both sides, like a fence, and he hadn't heard any road noises.

He was surprised to find a street nearby, parallel to the trail for a short distance and then turning away from it, curving back to the paved road just before it met the highway overpass. On that street were several homes, and little lanes running off left and right. A tiny village was hidden there. He had assumed it was only woods and then the highway.

He drove slowly around those streets and lanes several times, trying to peer into yards of houses that might back on to the trail. He saw nothing of interest, nothing suspicious. What had he expected to see? He didn't know. He hadn't expected to see the very well-to-do homes there amongst some that had seen better days, but that was not a clue to a mystery.

What was he curious about, anyway? He knew that people had fallen into hidden water, reportedly, and both had survived. But why would they have gone into the brush?

He parked back at the trail entrance, slung the backpack over his shoulder, put on the ordinary tuque, and carefully walked to the site of last Saturday's excitement. It didn't take him long to get there. It had seemed far when he was portaging that unfortunate woman out.

At least, he assumed he was where he had come upon her. There had been snow flurries off and on, plus a little rain, in the past week. There weren't any discernible boot-prints. There were depressions at the edge of the trail that might have been made by people, but as he looked he could see them all around, just contours made by the boulders and hummocks in the area.

Tim began to step into the undergrowth, then stopped. To be a third victim was not on his *To Do* list. But how could he see any clues if he didn't go exploring? How far in there might they have gone? He peered into the undergrowth but all he could see was undergrowth. He leaned against a boulder to think, and removed his backpack. He tried the binoculars, but it was hard to focus on anything without knowing what to look for.

He replaced the binoculars in the backpack, and saw the compass gadget. He took it out and held it level. Had he ever used a compass? Eons ago perhaps, in school, maybe. He held it until the needle stopped swinging. The red-tipped side of the needle was supposed to point North, he knew. Either the compass was a useless toy, or he had misjudged where he was, because north wasn't where he'd expected. That slight curve in the trail was more pronounced than he had guessed, maybe.

But it wasn't north he was looking for, it was a water-hole in the woods. He could only make a wild guess, because he hadn't seen where the woman was dragged from. Or had he?

He moved to the middle of the trail and stood where the scene had taken place. What had he seen and heard? A few weeks ago he thought he was The Great Observer. He had even tried to practice observing the little details that had made Sherlock Holmes so famous. Well, that had flown out the window here. Give him one life-or-death crisis and all he'd observed were trees and rocks and snow.

Easy now. That wasn't fair. Sherlock often sat in quiet thought, his fingers steepled, tolerating no interruptions; was he snoozing, or was he reviewing details in his great mind, to observe in retrospect? Everything involving Tim had happened right here, or a yard or two in either direction. What had he observed?

He looked up and down the trail to make sure nobody was coming to disturb him. He closed his eyes. He saw people bending over the woman who was lying on the trail. There was urgent chatter. What were they saying?

She fell in. She's cold. Might not make it.

Tim had asked *Where'd she fall in?* It seemed like a stupid question at the time, but not so stupid now. The man had pointed into the bushes, which wasn't helpful, but they had not wasted precious time to explore that detail.

Keeping his eyes closed, he mentally reviewed the scene. Where had the man pointed? He had raised his arm...and pointed into the brush...past the extra-wide trunk of a big maple tree.

Tim opened his eyes and looked for the tree. Nearby trees were slim aspens and birch. He looked around. Two or three yards beyond was a very large tree. He walked over next to it. Yes, this was the place. He looked into the woods again, and again saw no pond.

He brought out the binoculars again, and focused straight in, where the man had pointed. He couldn't make out any details other than gray and brown trunks and branches, but—there— might be something that was not a tree. He couldn't tell if it was something painted, or maybe a piece of clothing.

Setting the binoculars down, he carefully noted the direction of the piece of colour. He held the compass and waited for the needle to steady. When it pointed toward the swatch of colour he raised the binoculars again, found it again with some difficulty, and checked the compass. Close enough. Then he looked at the opposite side of the compass and noted that direction. If he could get on the other side of this wood, he'd know what direction to look in. Maybe. If it worked like that. He wrote the directions in his notebook.

He wanted to mark the tree so he could find it again, but he had no tool for that job. He must add a small knife to the backpack. Or string. He broke a few nearby twigs and hoped he would recognize the spot again if he needed to return.

As he started walking back to his car, he had a brilliant idea. He returned to the big tree, aimed himself toward the trail entrance, and walked steadily, counting each step until he arrived at the edge of the paved road. He wrote down the number of paces.

It was only a short distance back to the street leading into the little hamlet, but it was uphill and snow covered the roadside, so he drove and parked again. He consulted the notebook for the number of steps and began to walk in, carefully keeping his stride the same length as much as possible. No traffic interrupted him. It was a quiet Saturday morning, like all Saturday mornings here, he supposed.

He knew the street curved to the right, toward Highway 103, and the trail curved to the left, but he didn't know how to allow for whatever difference that might make, so when he reached the number of steps, he stopped. He had the compass in his hand, and got it to settle so he could find south-west instead of north-east, where he had spied the bit of colour in the woods.

The bit of colour was revealed as a wide swath of every colour. A fully-loaded clothesline stretched across the yard behind a mobile home that backed on to the wooded area between it and the trail. Sheets, jeans, t-shirts, socks, colourful onesies, and a dozen cloths, possibly diapers, were crowded on the line, all frozen stiff.

This domestic display served as a curtain for the forest behind, and Tim was not about to tip-toe into the back yard of this busy family home to see if he could find a pond to fall into. He turned around and counted his steps back to the car to confirm his findings. In the car, he made note of his observations. He had no idea what any of this meant, if anything. He didn't know how to use the compass, had no map, and wasn't sure what relation two roads curving in different directions might have, if any.

But he had stayed dry himself, and had not hurt his back, so he was ahead by what had not gone wrong, at least.

~

He was hungry and still wanted to see about books, so he drove to Lunenburg along the straight road that undulated over picturesque drumlins. He thought of the Robert Frost poem about two roads diverging in a yellow wood and wanted to sing it, but couldn't recall if there was a tune. The drumlins led him to "Unto the Hills", so he sang what he could recall of it during the fifteen-minute drive.

> Unto the hills around do I lift up my longing eyes.
> Oh, whence for me shall my salvation come,
>   from whence arise?

His salvation would not come from that bookstore today. *Closed for inventory*, the sign said. *Sorry for any inconvenience. Phone us for special orders.*

Tim copied the phone number from the sign. He peered in the window. Someone was in there, a hopeful sign. He would place his order right away, in hopes that his little piece of business would help them survive the rest of the winter.

He found a restaurant open nearby and ordered a bowl of chowder. He wondered how he could find out about a simple pond to satisfy his growing curiosity. Who would leave a hiking trail to thrash through very thick brush—not at all easy to get through—and plunge into water? And why? And how? Not wearing skis, that's for sure, not in that tangle.

The domestic scene of the humble trailer and clothesline hadn't appeared at all sinister. The woods beyond their back yard—what he could see of it—didn't lead to a body of water. Nothing made sense, nothing led him from one possibility to another. Last month, when he was chasing his Aunt Stella's suspicions, everything was a possible clue, and he found that hugely difficult. Now he had zero clues, and that was harder.

He needed a clue, some direction. Aside from his own stressed recall of the man pointing vaguely into the brush, he had nothing.

What had he written in the list of delving topics about evidence? *First, the evidence. Period.* He was trying to work with nothing but his own curiosity, a good start, possibly, but not the first thing needed. As he had learned with other projects this past week, things had to line up *before* one could begin. He needed to measure the door before he could get a new one. He needed to know what possessed people to leave the trail before he could find out why they found water under ice.

He checked his watch. Just enough time for one more thing before he went home to make pizza for supper. He drove along the scenic bank of the river to South River and parked near the office. The contractor's vehicles were parked nearby, a good sign. Inside, the painters were at work on the walls. They had finished the ceiling and some of the walls.

Elaine was in her office, smiling broadly. "I'm surprised you stayed away this long," she said. "They're making great progress."

"One coat or two?"

"One in some places, like behind the banks of storage cabinets and Mr Barss' filing cabinet empire. Two in others. They'll finish tonight. They worked all last night. We'll leave the heat turned up to help dry everything, and the place should be quite habitable by Monday morning."

Tim went upstairs. It was beautiful. Soft white walls, bright white trim, a nice wooden Venetian blind at the window. And his old office chair was at the table, waiting for him to comfortably lean back in it.

He could do a lot of delving in here.

Back downstairs, he stopped at Elaine's office again. "Nice chair?"

"Very nice," she said, and tapped her feet on the floor. "My feet actually reach the floor in this one, so my legs won't go to sleep."

"You must've rushed right out to get it."

"I did. It was on sale."

"I like the sound of that. See you tomorrow at four."

~

When Robert arrived, he quickly checked the grocery items Tim had picked up. The menu was to be mostly tapas, trays of small bites that each could select as much or as little of as they desired.

While Tim assembled their supper pizza and put it in the oven, Robert sliced and diced items to prep for tomorrow's menu. They shared the cooking space amicably, a first, Tim thought, but Robert wasn't wound up with pre-concert jitters when nerves made him touchy. Tim quite enjoyed this middle ground.

"Can I see the music you brought for tomorrow?" Tim ventured. "Maybe have a quick run-through?"

"Nope. Not fair. Everyone will be on the same footing, more or less, except for *moi*, of course. Don't fret, I've chosen pieces you can sing, or will have fun trying to, anyway. I must say, I'm looking forward to this. I rarely get to make music for music's sake."

Tim's pizza was cheesy and saucy, crust done just right. They put an old Western in the DVD player, but when the gunfights didn't grip their attention they lowered the volume so they could talk a bit. They each had a little bit of paperwork to work on as well. Neither was concentrating very hard on anything, and both were enjoying that freedom.

At one point, Tim asked, "Do you think I'm gaining weight? My jeans are tight."

Robert didn't even look up to respond. "I hope you are. You were getting too thin. You wouldn't even make good soup. Put some meat back on those bones."

Tim put down his notebook. He couldn't think of anything useful to write about what he had seen—or not seen—on the trail or around it. He couldn't find the water the people had fallen into. Why? Because he was a prudent man and wasn't foolish enough to rush in where his better angels told him not to go. But was that the right thing to be seeking? Was that the reason he couldn't find it? If he did find a pond, what would he know? He still wouldn't know why anyone would be drawn to it.

He thought of the fresh white room that had been restored out of the dusty shadows downtown. He was sure that the good thoughts were in there, maybe even answers. He'd go get them Monday morning.

February 14: Valentine's Day

Sunday

Hosting dinner guests who don't know each other can be stressful, especially when the event coincides with a celebration of romance. But today's dinner didn't elicit any stress in the hosts. On the contrary, both were eager for it to start.

But first, church. To his credit, the minister didn't try to link Cupid or Valentine's Day to scripture. Instead, he delivered an interesting talk on The Four Loves: *Storge* (community), *Philia* (friends), *Eros* (romantic), and *Agape* (love of God). It was inclusive without being patronizing. It could have gone awry in so many ways, but he handled it with a light touch, and kept it short.

The choir approved of the final hymn, "Love Divine, All Loves Excelling", so they sang it earnestly. Tim's fellow tenor, Spencer, made it all the way through the service without making lame jokes. Tim thought he might even feel a little *storge* for Spencer if he continued behaving like a grownup.

Home again, Tim prepared sandwiches and tea for their lunch while Robert created the tapas plates. It seemed like a lot of work for a simple dinner, but Robert was not one to under-do.

Tim set the table, put the gerberas in vases on multiple surfaces throughout the parlour and dining room, and took one upstairs to the guest room for Helen. He laid the wood in the real fireplace, noting that he must make a trip inland to see Buck, the supplier of excellent kindling.

Just before two o'clock the doorbell rang. Robert went to greet Helen.

"My god, girl, you must have flown!" She was the minister at a church in Dartmouth, a ninety-minute drive if all went well over the Halifax bridge and along the highway.

"I didn't dare drive over the limit but I made the sermon pretty short."

Listening from the dining room, Tim liked her already. He went to the foyer for introductions, and then asked Helen to follow him as he carried her bag up to the guest room. He apologized for the shared bathroom upstairs, but it was a very old house and—

"Goodness, don't worry about that," Helen said. "I'm a minister, remember, which means I have the privilege of living in whatever shelter my parishioners can afford to provide. A shared washroom is fine, especially since it's indoors and has hot running water!" Her laugh seemed to come easily. "Now, where's this beast I'm here to tame?"

Tim led her back downstairs to the parlour and Helen immediately sat at the piano and played scales. "Professor Kirk," she called. "Have you lost your hearing?"

"Hmm." Robert replied. "Sometimes I wish."

"Don't worry. I can fix."

Tim placed a tray bearing a sandwich and tea on a side table next to her tools. He closed the parlour door so she could tune the worst of the jangling strings without worrying that she was disturbing anything. An out-of-tune piano is an aural assault for those who can discern such things, but hearing a piano being brought into tune is an odd kind of pleasure, at a distance.

An hour later, Helen called Robert to come in, and they discussed her results. Tim couldn't hear the details, but he was very happy that the consultation was going on about his piano, in that parlour, in this house, with those fine people. His mother came to mind frequently, usually due to tension-filled memories, but at this moment he wished she were here to experience this: smart, skilled, caring people in the house, having fun, with music. His people.

Robert came back into the kitchen and propped the door open. "She did it." He saw the pensive expression on Tim's face and said, "What's wrong?"

"Not a thing. I was just enjoying this." Tim waved his hand to indicate kitchen and parlour. "How'd she do?"

"She did her best, such as that is," Helen responded as she brought the lunch tray to the counter. "It's passable, so my teacher says. In the middle octaves, anyway."

"She did well," said Robert. "We can use it now if we want to."

"That's not a usual preacher skill, Helen," Tim said. "How did that come about?"

"Purely through self-preservation. I mentioned having summer placements where the loo was outdoors? This was on the prairies in my student days, but still, the traumatic memories linger on. Anyway, most of these churches were kept un-heated and damp year-round, until Sunday, when they were like the fiery furnace, so their poor old pianos were always in desperate shape. Since I was also expected to play them, I acquired the tools and got some instruction on how to tune them. The ones that were salvageable, at least."

"So my piano...?"

"Not like those, ha-ha. It's old but still a good instrument. Tuning's not quite at A440, but your technician will have less work to do in the middle bits when he comes."

"Good to hear. I feel I should pay you for your work."

"And you will. You'll have to listen to me singing, Robert tells me."

"Oh well, I'm sure I'm the lightweight in this crowd. But I'm really looking forward to tackling whatever Robert thinks we can do. I think I'll get the fire going now. Elaine will be here shortly."

~

Introductions went swimmingly. Elaine and Helen were both easy conversationalists. Their career paths were quite different, but they shared rural roots, and that made them cousins. Robert evidently enjoyed them both, and Tim was loving these new energies in the house. The food and drink were all self-serve, so the wines and waters were on trays with glasses and everyone was encouraged to partake as they wished.

Tim excused himself to answer the phone. "Oh, hi, Aunt Stella, Happy Valentine's Day. How are you?"

"Valentine's Day, indeed. I'm calling to thank you for the lovely bouquet, Timothy. You shouldn't have."

"Why not? You deserve flowers. Though you likely have lots more from your admirers. Or admirer singular?"

"No, I don't."

"What? Your mystery man didn't—"

"He's gone."

"What? That was fast. My goodness, what happened?"

"I won't bore you with the details. Let's say we didn't have much in common. Nothing, as it turns out."

"I'm so sorry, Aunt Stella."

Laughter erupted from the parlour.

"You have visitors. I didn't mean to interrupt. Thank you again for the thoughtful flowers—and the card, if you are indeed 'The Delver and the Pied Piper'."

"I confess. Yes, we're having, uh, some choir members in for a bit of a sing-song."

Tim tried to make it sound like this was a duty, not a fabulous dinner-party that didn't include Stella. They wouldn't have included her in this group anyway—he had never heard her sing a note—but given her news, he didn't want to let on that he was having fun when she obviously was not. Darn Valentine's Day anyway. It was hard on the lovelorn.

"Are you around this week, Aunt Stella? Can we get together?"

"There's no need, Timothy. I'm fine. Carry on. Hello to Robert." And she hung up.

Back in the parlour, Tim said, "Her majesty says hello. Mister Diamond Earrings is history." The man with whom Stella had parted ways—Tim was not certain he'd ever been privileged with his name—had given her a gorgeous pair of earrings last month.

"Oh, boy," Robert said. "He must've made a mistake. I'm sure she allows only one. Good for her."

Robert was distributing packets of music. The other three

quickly shuffled through them with cries of delight at what they would be singing, as well as laughter when they saw challenging pieces he alone believed they could sing.

He asked them to put down the music. He struck Helen's tuning fork, hummed a note, said, *"Dona Nobis Pacem,"* and pointed to Helen.

She began to sing the familiar piece, followed in turn by Tim, then Elaine. What a glorious sound they made! When they finished singing the canon they erupted in laughter at their enjoyment of singing, and at the misses and near-misses each had made, dredging the lines from memory.

"Aren't you going to sing with us?" Elaine asked Robert.

"Sure am. I just wanted to hear you all first, director's prerogative. Now we know you can sing. Let's see if you can read."

"Oh, Robert, before we do, can we do one more, a round?"

"Sure, Helen, what do you have in mind?"

"White coral bells, upon a tender stalk," she began, and each singer entered in turn and carried on.

> Lilies of the valley deck my garden walk.
> Oh, don't you wish that you could hear them ring?
> That will happen only when the fairies sing!

With each piece they sang, their voices blended better and better. Eventually, they moved to the dining room. Tim had inserted a leaf in the table so each person had room for food and music and beverages. The food was fabulous, of course, a surprise for the women and a source of pride for the men.

By times they sat to eat, stood to sing, sometimes strolling around the room, or wandering across the hall to the piano when they needed support. Each piece ended in laughter, or murmurings of enjoyment, and occasionally, shared silence. Sometimes, someone would mention when they had first or last sung a piece, or confess they never had.

Robert encouraged them to sing gently, and Tim's little gelato balls soothed their throats. When they finished the food and music they returned to the parlour for final wine or coffees, and some nibbled at the plate of chocolate-dipped strawberries. Tim stoked the fire and they chatted amiably.

Helen went to the piano. "Here's one for you, teacher," she said to Robert, who was surprised and impressed by the short piece she played.

"When did you learn that?" he said. "I didn't think you had any spare time?"

"Since your inspiring recital last month, I've made more time for my music. My congregation took too much of my time, and my well was always low. Working on music fills me up again. I'm filled tonight, filled with joy and good food, and wine, too, a rare pleasure."

Elaine soon took her leave. "This was such fun," she said. "Thank you all so much. It was lovely to meet you, Helen. I have a busy day tomorrow, as I'm sure everyone else does, but these wonderful songs will be in my head for some time. I expect we'll see you dark and early, Tim?"

"You know you will. Gotta see all that fresh paint!"

Then it was Helen's turn. "Thank you both so much. If you'll excuse me, it's time for some sweet repose. Please wake me half an hour after you get up in the morning, or whenever the bathroom is free."

Tim and Robert cleared the table, put the scarce leftovers in the fridge, rinsed the dishes, and sat in the glow of the fire with a little wine.

"I'd love to do that again sometime, Rob."

"I'm ahead of you there. How about we sing a quartet in church?"

"What? Gosh, I don't know about that. I was just thinking to relax with food, wine, and song, like this. Can we have wine if we sing in church? We'd sing really well. Anyway, Helen can't come; she's got her own church. Don't you go getting big ideas, now."

"Hmm," Robert replied. "D'you think Stella will be okay? Tough to break up at Valentine's. That guy's a bum, whoever he is."

"She'll recover. Maybe we should be feeling sorry for the guy: she won't have let him get away without at least a couple flesh wounds. But still, I only just discovered that my aunt has feelings, and I'm sorry they were hurt. I'll check in on her."

February 15: Vibes

Monday

Helen had the ability to blend into her surroundings, so her presence in the house on Monday morning was not intrusive. Robert was on his way out the door as she came downstairs.

"Good morning, Helen. Gloria here is prepared to make you an infusion of your choice: espresso, cappuccino, latte?"

"Gosh, Tim, that's very kind of you, but any of those might be too exciting, so early in the day. May I have a mug of hot water, instead?"

She repeated her thanks, and was soon following Robert to the city. The morning was very cold but nothing new had fallen from the sky to make the driving risky, so Tim bade her take care and turned to his own day.

First, he loaded the dishes in the old dishwasher, but decided not to turn it on because he was going to leave the house. The last couple of loads had stayed on one cycle or another for a very long time, and he feared that there was a good chance of a flood or fire from the thing. What good he could do about either if he were home, he didn't know, but at least neither would be a surprise and he could call the fire department before the house burned down.

He knew that was just magical thinking. The dishwasher needed to be serviced, maybe repaired, maybe replaced. He could arrange for a service call, but he knew he'd pay a lot of money for someone to come only to tell him that parts weren't available. He might as well spring for a new unit and have the peace of mind.

That's what Elaine would do, he thought. He admired her dither-free decision-making. Of course, it wasn't her money she'd been making decisions with, but he felt she was managing his business responsibly.

He wrote his *To Do* list for the day, or for some of it, anyway. Not everything got done in a day, but that was all right, as leftover tasks propelled the following days along. He didn't like having nothing planned. Doubts crept in then, and he didn't need to encourage them.

On Friday, he had felt like his boat was underway, moving ahead with a good breeze.

On Saturday, he hadn't been so sure. With the confidence of someone completely lacking in knowledge about a compass, he had taken sightings and checked out reciprocal directions with no clue as to whether any of that indicated anything. Good thing he wasn't the navigator on a real boat. Of course, boats had charts that showed where the shoals and harbours were.

"Come on now, Tim," he said aloud. "Stay positive. Let's give the new-old room a chance to inspire us."

~

He hastened to see the freshly-painted offices of *The Times*. There was a hubbub as the staff arrived and admired the new brightness of their workspace. The front reception area looked inviting, professional. This had been a good decision, he saw, an outgrowth of his simple wish to have a private room to work in.

So that wish had been the actual beginning, putting all the necessary steps in motion to lead to today. For the staff, today marked the end of drab walls. For Tim, it marked the beginning of deep and satisfying delving.

He marked himself IN, waved at a few employees, and went up the bright white stairway to his new office. If a plain white room could inspire, this one was ready. He raised the Venetian blind so he could see the whorls in the glass.

There was a small envelope on the table containing a handwritten thank-you note from Elaine. That was classy.

The oak table and black chair looked good together. He turned them to face the window to facilitate day-dreaming, maybe even thinking. He moved the plain oak chair to the wall near the door; he wasn't planning to entertain visitors. He closed the door.

He was ready to begin, or to resume beginning. He had the room and his thoughts and his notes, and no distractions.

He took out the notebook where he had recorded his observations at the trail and little streets in Blockhouse. Observations. What had he observed?

He gazed out the window. He liked how the bubbles in the glass made the distant trees and hilltops undulate when he moved his head.

He thought back to the previous Saturday when he had come upon the woman and her rescuers. She was suffering from hypothermia. Why? Because the man—who was he?— said she had fallen in water. Where was the water? *There*, he'd said, and pointed into the brush. How did *he* know?

The woman wasn't wearing shoes or socks. Tim supposed she had lost those in the water. She was wearing only tights and a top and a light shirt, such as you would expect to see on the trail in mid-summer, not in mid-February. Had she lost her jacket in the woods?

All that made no sense at all, but the Big Question that had been forming in Tim's mind ever since the event unfolded was simply *Why*? What would motivate a person to leave the trail and thrash into that thicket, fall through ice into a hidden pool of water, and crawl out again? What about the report in his own newspaper?

Maybe you can't believe everything you read in the papers.

Tim brought his focus back to the notebook and jotted these observations and questions. Then he took out his phone and hit the first speed-dial number.

"Good morning, *The Times*. This is Rachael speaking. How may I help you?"

"Good morning, Rachael, It's Tim. Is James Olsen in?"

"Good morning, Mister Brown. Oh my goodness, you should see the office, is it ever beautiful! Miss Fong has certainly done a great job getting it painted so quickly. I hope you like it!"

"I'm sure I will, Rachael. Is James in yet?"

"He should be, let me check, one moment, please. Yes, he is, shall I connect you?"

"No, thanks, Rachael, that's all I need to know." Tim had repeated Rachael's name just to let her know that he did know it, and to remind himself what it was.

"Oh, well, all right then. You have a good day now. Be sure to drop in."

He left his quiet room and went downstairs to James Olsen's desk. "Good morning, James. Got a minute? I have a question for you about the people who fell in water off the Old Train Line Trail. Did you ever speak with either one of them?"

"Gee, Mister Brown, you surprised me. We're not used to seeing you here. What people, now?"

Tim reached for a copy of last week's paper and opened it to the Community Notes article. "These people."

"Oh yeah. Sure."

"You spoke to the woman on the skis?"

"Yes, why?"

"Where was she when she went through the ice?"

"Um, on a trail, I think."

"You think?"

Tim was speaking quietly, but he could see it was dawning on James that he was being interrogated.

"Yeah, on a trail."

"Where? I thought you told me first that it was in the woods."

"Well, yeah, trails go through woods. What—?"

"So, what does this sentence mean? 'We reported last week that one person skied cross-country from a trail and sank into a hidden pond that had not frozen solid.' When did the skis materialize? I didn't find any mention of skis in the previous issue."

"Oh, well, it must have got edited out. Sorry about that."

"What's that person's name, James?"

"I—I can't divulge that information, sorry."

"Why not?" Tim was leaning on James' desk with both hands.

"Uh, because the, um, the incident took place on, um, private property."

"Trespassing?"

"You could say that."

"I'm not saying anything, James, you are. So, you're saying that someone was trespassing on private property and fell in a pond there? On skis? And got out again?"

"Yep."

"And they reported this to you directly?"

"Affirmative."

"Interesting. Can I see your notes?"

"I don't have them with me."

"James, something doesn't add up. What if I said to you"—Tim stood up to stretch his back and leaned over again—"what if I said to you that your little story didn't happen the way you told it? What if I said to you that *you* were the person on the skis?"

Tim had still not raised his voice above a low conversational tone. The person in the next cubicle would never know that James was being grilled unless they could see his beet-red face.

"Now, whether you went through the ice, or where, is not of interest to me at the moment. Maybe you made it all up so you'd have a story to file, small as it was. I'll ignore that for now. But let's move on. I assume you also wrote this sentence: 'This past weekend another hiker reportedly broke through ice into deep water...' Am I correct in that assumption?"

James nodded.

"You didn't actually speak to anyone about this incident, did you? Your only clue about it was my phone message about it, am I right?"

"It was your tip, sure, but I did check with my, uh, sources."

"Thank you, James, you've been a big help." James looked very glum. "Really, you have. Also, you've committed a number of serious errors which could jeopardize your job and did confuse my own investigations. I now know I can overlook the careless skier—who was likely joyriding on the golf course and found himself in one of the water hazards."

James' look of astonishment was worth the risk of Tim's wild guess.

"You're not the first to do that. But I know that little red herring is not at all related to the incident on the Blockhouse trail because I was there for that. Now here's what's going to happen: you and I are not going to say anything more about this, for now, to anyone. Whatever you're working on right now—I assume you're working on something good, a keen reporter like yourself—you will exercise due diligence and keep accurate notes, and report only facts. Am I clear?"

James nodded again.

"Good. Now. I may need some assistance in the process of my own investigations, and I will expect your full cooperation if so. Also clear?"

"I thought you were taking the year off."

"What I'm doing is no concern of yours, unless I make it your concern. Got it?"

Another nod.

"Okay. Now, James, you've just received a valuable lesson in ethical investigative journalism, which you told me you were very interested in, at least the investigative part. I'm not going to fire you over this, because I think you're a whole lot smarter now than when you came in this morning. So hang in there, straighten up, and fly right."

Tim put his hand on James' drooping shoulder, gave it a shake, and went back upstairs.

What brought that on? How did I know James' story was bogus?

To be honest, that idea wasn't fully formed in his mind even as he was going down the stairs to speak with James. But James was giving off shirky vibes. *Score one for observation. Or hunches.*

He recorded this encounter in the notebook. As he was writing, he remembered last month's understanding of the importance of hunches. He wished he had last month's notebooks handy so he could read what he'd learned. That would seem more efficient than having to learn the same things over again. Tomorrow, he could pack up all his January papers and bring them here. The locksmith would bring keys so he could leave everything out within easy reach.

He went down the dusty hallway and looked in the other rooms. They hadn't looked great before, but they were positively dowdy now, compared to his bright Thinking Room. However, there was an old wooden cabinet in one, like the bottom half of a kitchen counter, and it had a shelf inside the doors. It wasn't attached to anything, so Tim gripped one end and slowly began to drag it down the hall to his room, being careful of his still-tender back.

A moment later, the caretaker appeared at the top of the stairs. "Need some help?"

"Oh, is it noisy?"

"Most of the staff are hiding under their desks. It sounds like a cement truck is running up here."

"Oops, sorry. Yes, if you don't mind, can we move this into my office here?"

"Sure. Wait a sec, will you? I'll be right back."

Tim scouted around for anything else that was loose and looked useful. The place was bare, except for the file cabinet at the end of the hall, the star of a recent nightmare.

His helper soon returned with a square of old carpet with a wooden strip attached at one edge and a rope handle looped through the wood. They manoeuvred the carpet under the counter and then quietly push-pulled it down the hall and into place in the new room.

"Anything else?"

"Sure, how about this filing cabinet? Is it too heavy? It looks like it's made of cast iron."

"Or maybe a navy destroyer, but I think the two of us can do it."

They tipped the cabinet to one side and slid the magic carpet underneath. It was slower going, but it moved.

Tim was excited. Tomorrow he would bring some rags to clear the dust of the ages from these new treasures, and then he could place his papers on or in them.

What time was it? Nearing noon. He wanted to retrace his Saturday tracks. If James' light-hearted article about silly hikers was falsely presented, what else was false?

On the road to Blockhouse, he mused about how easy it is to build on any idea presented as fact, whether it is or not. *If a truth is based on a falsehood, is the truth still true?* This was a good question, and he hoped he would remember it long enough to write it down.

His memory wasn't bad, not in a clinical sense, but there were so many thoughts and distractions. Also, he didn't always trust what he learned, let alone what he wondered about. As Robert had said, he had no experience in starting, and things seemed to involve a lot of starting.

He thought about that bobbly compass needle: it pointed all around the circle, eventually settling on *N*, but what if you didn't want *N*? What if you wanted *SSW* or *ENE* or any of the three hundred and sixty points around the circle? If your *N* was wrong because you had a magnetic flashlight distracting the needle, wouldn't all the other points be wrong, too?

And did a metaphor contain any useful instruction for a real-life situation?

These thoughts didn't lead to any revelations, but they did entertain him until he reached the little street parallel to the trail in Blockhouse. He turned in and drove slowly to the mobile home again, where he had counted the paces roughly equal to the distance to the scene of action on the trail. He shifted the car to Park, but before he got out of the car he made a promise to the man in the rear-view mirror: "Do *not* go off the beaten track. Do *not* trespass. Be *sensible.*"

He felt he needed this extra safeguard against impulses because of what he noticed in the back yard: the clothesline still held laundry. Sure, a family with a baby in diapers likely did laundry every day—what did he know about such things?—but this was the same laundry he'd seen on Saturday, he was certain. He had looked closely at the clothesline then, admiring the care with which the items had been sorted and hung, arranged by size and colour, right down to the tiny socks and the row of cloth squares which he hoped were diapers, not tea towels, due to the smudges on them.

Everything was still there, just as before, except some of the clothespins had failed on the sheets and their corners were hanging down.

He got out of the car and walked along the lane. He didn't see any other dwellings, but maybe this lane also turned right and joined up with other streets. He walked slowly past the home, not wanting to stare, but eager to observe.

There was no vehicle in the driveway, and no tracks or footprints discernible in the snow. He walked on until he determined that the lane ended at the trees a short distance farther on, so he turned around. From here, he could see the back yard and side entrance of the mobile home. No sign of activity.

He stood there for a few minutes, just listening. If there was a baby in that mobile home, shouldn't it be crying? They don't cry all the time, he supposed. The drapes were closed across the picture window, so he couldn't see inside. No sound of radio or television.

Tim's feet were demanding that he walk in, maybe knock on the door, but his head had promised he wouldn't. What would his story be if someone did answer the door? He could pretend he was a Jehovah's Witness, just coming to share blessings, but he didn't have any of their leaflets with him—or anywhere—so that wouldn't fool anyone.

No, his head said, *you just stay out here in the lane and think about this.*

He didn't know what that clothesline meant to him or the woman on the trail, if anything at all. Sure, he was curious, but he could think about what things meant without plunging into deep snow on private property. The place gave him the creeps, anyway.

Before he drove away, he checked the signal bars on his mobile phone: one was showing steady, flickering to two. It was laughable how these phones were meant to serve you when you were mobile, but they worked only if you stayed in one place. He'd like to delve into that topic, but it was already in the news constantly, even in his own paper. The largest provider paid for advertisements in *The Times* featuring a map of the province with blue blobs indicating where you should be able to get a signal. Perhaps that would improve in time.

He considered walking along the trail to re-visit the emergency scene, but he had already done that on Saturday. He didn't have a new hunch to investigate and, again, he wanted to keep himself away from the temptation of exploring the treacherous woods.

Another thought was gnawing at him, and it needed prompt action. That old dishwasher was fully-loaded and in jeopardy of not living through all the cycles. He left Blockhouse and drove to the appliance store where the laziest clerk in the world had hidden from him a few weeks ago, and marched up to the counter.

"Hey, good morning! How can I help you today?" Not the same clerk, he was relieved to see.

"A dishwasher, please. Mine is loaded and ready to go, but each time I start it up, it sounds like it's eating the dishes. I think it's time to send it to the landfill."

"You've come to the right place, then," said the helpful clerk, whose name tag said *Manager*. "Let's have a look."

They looked. This was another area of life about which Tim thought he was not very curious. The manager mentioned the exciting features and benefits of each model, and the related prices. Plus tax. Plus installation. This one was your basic model, not meant for daily use. Was there a large family in the home? This one was a good workhorse, but the interior was limited in size. This one was the Cadillac of all. You could put your glassware and fine china up here, and all but the largest of roasting pans down here, and it would scrub, rinse, dry, and shine every piece, with no breakage. Quietest, most energy-efficient washer on the market. "Wisper" quiet. Five-year guarantee. On sale until Friday.

Then he asked the dreaded question: "What size is your opening?"

"I have no idea," Tim said.

"No problem. Let's do this. We'll write it up, and I'll check the installer's schedule. Meanwhile, when you go home, measure the height of your counter top and the width of the existing machine and phone it in. In some of our older homes, the counters are too low for these machines, in which case we'll place a special order. Here's my card: you just call and ask for me."

Tim carefully returned his credit card to his wallet, and did his best not to do mental arithmetic, adding this new purchase to all the other expenses at his home and office. *Different pockets*, he told himself, *and none of it is unnecessary*. Well, the whole office paint job was optional, although Elaine hadn't treated it as such, and the staff seemed really happy with it, which was worth something.

Speaking of staff, he wondered if he'd been a bit harsh with James Olsen. Perhaps Tim had misled him about the trail event, but James should have checked, darn it all.

His tummy told him it was past lunchtime, and he knew where there were some tasty bites. He went home and warmed up the leftover tapas. He found a tape measure in the kitchen drawer jumble, measured the dimensions of the old dishwasher, and called the store manager. The old appliance was oversized for its age, but the new one would fit the space perfectly. Tim's mother likely went for the top of the line when it was new, however long ago that had been.

"How about Thursday for installation? Will the lady of the house be there to let the installer in?"

"The lady of the house? There's no—oh, I mean yes, yes she will. Anytime after seven-thirty."

He chuckled as he envisioned Mrs Aquino scowling at any mess the installer would make, but he thought himself clever to get the job done on a day when Mrs A could clean up after it.

But first, he had to deal with the incumbent appliance, which was loaded for action. He decided to remove the roasting pans and baking sheets and just go with dishes, in case he had to unload mid-way. He closed the door, pushed Start, and the old thing began sloshing and grinding its way through the cycles.

Tim went to the study to work, far enough from the kitchen that the noise wouldn't give him a headache, but close enough that he would hear if trouble erupted.

He sat back in the chair and steepled his fingers. That posture seemed somehow to be an aid to thinking. The window in his new office was, too.

He turned to look out the window in the study, but it had aluminum storm windows, likely installed a century after the windows downtown were. The screen had etched the glass so the view was permanently foggy. He wondered how much it would cost to replace the window—just one—but pulled his attention back to the matter at hand.

The matter at hand was...well, what was it, exactly? The identity of the woman, also known as "the victim"? What did he want to know that for? Because he had helped rescue her? Yes, but from what? Hypothermia? What, precisely, had happened to her before he came on the scene?

Tim broke his steepled reverie to write these thoughts down.

> Victim > young woman > hypothermia > how? > water? > lightly dressed, no shoes–

Then he shifted his mind's eye to the home on the other side of the treed area.

> Mobile > laundry > baby > unoccupied > relevant?

"Congratulations, Timothy," he said aloud. "You always manage to come up with a list of what you don't know."

But of course. That was part of delving into things about which one was curious, surely, the very essence of it. One would have to make a list of all the things one knew, or didn't know, or needed to know, and then address them all until one of them came out on top. What was it he had done last month—looked for one of the options to start blinking? Nothing was blinking yet, but he hadn't started listing things. Perhaps he'd make a grid of all the factors; what would the rows and columns be?

Here were other things to consider:

> RCMP > no call back
> Other guy on trail > where did he go?

Tim really wanted to check out the woodsy space between the trail and that next lane, to see if there was a water-hole in there, and if the old trailer was more or less in line with the trail, though its relevance to this story still was far from established. Safest way would be to go with someone. He knew immediately who he would take, but he didn't want to do that until he had formed his hunches better.

He phoned Stella: no answer. He left a message he hoped was cheery-but-supportive, just calling to say hi. If she'd listen before erasing it.

He took the front door sketch and a tape measure and did his best to record the correct measurements of the damaged door. He'd take that back to the store this week.

Chores taken care of, he returned to the desk and began doodling a Delving Grid about The Situation on the Trail. This did not go smoothly, but he knew that good questions don't always pose themselves. He needed to write down all the elements having to do with the situation, and hope they'd eventually sort themselves into categories, and the questions would come from there. Then, and only then, could he expect answers.

This was like everything else he wanted to do lately: he couldn't begin and expect to be at the end in one simple step. He had to cover all the steps that came first: the seed, the fertile soil, the sun, the rain...on this cold mid-February day these were pleasant thoughts, though more metaphor than method.

The floor around his desk was soon covered in balled-up notebook pages. The pages were too small for this; he couldn't read his own writing squeezed in the tiny grid spaces.

He retrieved some sheets of manila flip-chart paper which he had put to pretty good use last month. He taped them to the dining-room door and began to mark the clues down the left side of the sheet. By 'clues' he meant everything he had observed about the rescue on the trail. Across the top, he wrote Who | What | When | Where | Why, and drew lines down and across. He stood back to examine his handiwork. He knew that this exercise didn't always lead anywhere, but even if everything was a dead end— well, he didn't know what came after that. Surely not everything would be a dead end, everything except one thing. There were empty boxes on the sheet, and each one was begging for a word.

He wanted to write a title at the top of the sheet, but he hesitated. What was he after, anyhow? Did he want to know if there was a hidden pond in the woods? Was that his big question? Was he hoping to reveal a risk to public safety? He would if there was one, but he had a hunch that wasn't the real question.

What about that unfortunate woman? He wondered how she was doing. Many accident victims were whisked to the hospital by ambulance and then discharged, and he didn't agonize over how they made out. He did have a short but intense connection with this one.

Was it about how she came to be on the trail? Did that teenage boy go in and drag her out, or how did she get out? Where was her coat? If you went for a hike and somehow got off the well-marked trail and into deep water, you might lose your boots and socks, but would you lose your jacket?

Was it about why that guy at the scene just disappeared? He didn't look like a hiker to Tim, not that you had to go to the sports outlets to get an outfit before you could walk on a public trail. But still—Tim closed his eyes to try to recall this man's appearance— he looked like he'd be more at home in a tavern than on a trail. *I'd better keep my judgments to myself.* Judgments could get judgy, and it wasn't his intent to criticize. The guy didn't look "suspicious", but it did seem odd that he didn't follow them out to the ambulance or offer any help. Maybe he simply assumed there wasn't any further need for his presence, which had turned out to be true.

Speaking of odd appearances, Tim recalled how he must have looked to the bystanders attracted there by the sirens, first wearing nothing but underpants, then an old blanket as a skirt. But he'd stayed to see the matter through to a conclusion of some sort. His motivation was entirely on the welfare of the victim. Now his motive was curiosity, because nothing added up.

As he reviewed the large chart, he saw several hunches, a few suppositions, and a thing or two that might be red herrings. These were good. These were the bits that were needed before he could begin. These were the measurements, left to right, top to bottom, inside and outside. These were the cleaners and the crack-fillers. This was his tool-box. He knew that installers or repairmen didn't bring only a tape measure or a screwdriver to a job. They'd lug a whole toolbox full of gadgets and gizmos they weren't expecting to use, but they'd come to the job site prepared for anything. Well, so would Timothy Brown.

He'd take this sheet of possibilities to his prepared thinking-room, along with assorted paper, erasers, pencils, markers and tape, and he would get to the bottom of whatever this was. He en-titled the grid *CURIOUS* and then laid the assembled tools beside the door to take tomorrow.

He unloaded the dishwasher. Everything was clean and dry. "No need to show off now," he told it. "You're being laid off this Thursday."

He spent the rest of the evening in the company of Sherlock Holmes and Doctor Watson.

February 16: Doors

Tuesday

"It is a capital mistake to theorize before one has data," Sherlock instructed Tim. "Insensibly, one begins to twist facts to suit theories, instead of theories to suit facts."

Actually, Sherlock had imparted this wisdom to Dr Watson, but Tim took it to heart. It wasn't exactly a new thought. He had discovered this principle during his adventures in January, but it was gratifying to see it stated so clearly by so respected an observer as Holmes. Sure, Holmes was the creation of a fine writer of fiction, but that didn't diminish the wisdom.

Once Tim got set up in his private room down at *The Times* building, he would write Holmes' wisdom on one of the large sheets and put it up on the wall as a reminder. Or get his staff designer, Ed Garamond, to "posterize" it for him.

He was fairly confident that he hadn't yet twisted facts to suit theories. He had un-twisted what facts he had so he could lay them out for dispassionate consideration. That was the magic of the grid he had constructed last evening. Facts and theories could lie side by side there so he could scrutinize them.

He was less confident that he had all the facts required, but the grid would expose that, too. Titling the grid *CURIOUS* was another sign that he hadn't drawn conclusions.

One difference between the project he'd been cajoled into working on last month and this one was the pace. Last month, he felt like Stella was on the phone daily, hectoring him about her puzzle and why he hadn't solved it. For this matter of The Woman on the Trail, Tim could take all winter if he wanted to. He saw no urgency, no one had asked him anything about it, and the RCMP seemed to have closed the file, or the part in which he was concerned.

His interest in the case was purely for exercise. And because he was curious. Things didn't add up, but he hoped the grid would eventually spell out the story.

He had been on sabbatical for a month and a half now, and he still woke at the same time as before. The alarm rang because it was set to do so, but he was almost always awake before the bell.

He didn't mind. It wasn't sleep he was seeking, but less stress when he was awake. With a few exceptions, he felt he was gaining on this quest, and his 'whenever' approach to the current project was a hopeful sign. He didn't want to slip into letting everything slide; he hoped to be able to point to some accomplishment at the end of the year, though the shape of that was still very much unknown.

He wondered if and how creature comforts might inspire good thoughts. He liked the empty-room feeling of his empty room, and didn't want to clutter it up with the usual office debris. But as he made his breakfast toast and coffee, he decided it might be nice to have some coffee in it. This would eliminate trips to the drive-thru for coffee he didn't particularly like, and donuts ditto.

He rummaged in a bottom cupboard and produced a thermos, a long-ago gift from someone. He rinsed the inside with hot water and filled it with his own brewed coffee. He wrapped the toast in waxed paper, put those items and a mug in a paper bag, and took it all downtown to search for theories.

~

The locksmith worked quickly. Tim placed the keys to the new locks on his key ring. He closed the door, sat at the table, poured himself a steaming mug of black coffee, and unwrapped the toast and jam. The coffee aroma filled the room. This was nice. Quiet. Peaceful. The preliminaries were over. The elements had all been assembled. Now he could Begin.

He had a good start on beginning. He unrolled the *CURIOUS* grid and taped it to the wall behind the door, opposite the window. Should someone come to the door—and he didn't plan for visitors here—this chart wouldn't be the first thing they'd see.

He took care to put a blank sheet of paper behind the one he was working on, to protect the wall. A few dots of marker ink had leaked through at home when he'd been engrossed in underlining and crossing out and circling on the page, and he'd had to scrub very hard to remove the most obvious spots. He wouldn't sully these fresh walls like that.

The grid looked like business there on the wall. He would enjoy contemplating the categories and questions and filling in the empty boxes. But first, he had a few errands. Now that he saw errands as necessary elements to achieve desired outcomes, rather than nuisance interruptions, he was more willing to do them.

The first errand took him back to Blockhouse to order the front door replacement. He looked for the man who had given him the drawing. He wasn't in sight, but several other men were behind the service counter.

One came over, said, "May I help?" and then grinned and said, "Hey, how're you? Aren't you the fella that brought that woman out of the trail that day?"

"Uh, yes, I guess so, unless it happened more than once. How'd you know it was me?"

"I'm a volunteer firefighter, and we were called over." He leaned over the counter to look at Tim's legs. "I hardly ever forget a fella walking on the trail in February without his pants on!" This was said at hardware-store volume, and the other men behind the counter looked at Tim and grinned. They had obviously heard the story. Tim hoped he wasn't blushing.

"Well, thanks for answering the call. I did start out fully dressed, but I thought that woman needed my trousers more than I did right then. Say, do you know what ever happened to her? Do you know who she was?"

"No, I don't, but you could check with the hospital."

"I did. She was discharged, that's all they would tell me. But I was wondering how she ended up in that state. Someone said she fell in a pond in the woods, but there's no pond in there, is there?"

"I don't know, sorry. I live over in Big Lots. There's lots of swampy places in the woods, though. Whatcha got there?"

Tim handed him the sketch of the screen door with his measurements written in, which apparently made sense. He showed the man the style of door he wanted, the one Robert liked. It would have to be ordered in, of course, but should arrive in about ten days. Once it came, they'd call him and set up a time to install it.

"What do you want done with the old door?"

"I certainly don't want it. Can your people take it away?"

"Sure. Some people like to put them on their hunting camps."

"Oh, well, I don't have one of those. Do you?"

"Yeah, back off the Aylesford Road."

"Does it have a screen door?"

"No, it's just a camp. Pretty rough."

"Maybe you'd like my dented door, then? I can tell the installer to bring it to you."

"How much would you want for it?"

"Goodness, nothing! If the installer charges you something for bringing it over, you can discuss that with him, but I'll be happy just to dispose of it. Let me have your name so I can make sure it gets to you."

"Donnie. Donnie Isnor."

"Okay, Donnie, I'll send the door to you, and let's hope the installer doesn't bend it taking it off the house. Oh, one more thing about that trail call: the Mounties that came, where would they have come from? I can't seem to get a peep from the detachment outside South River."

"Might'a been from Lunenburg."

"Of course. Thanks a lot, Donnie."

~

The forecast promised snow, and strong winds starting late in the afternoon. Not a blizzard by the meteorological definition, but nasty enough while it lasted, and power outages were expected.

Tim's next errand must be to get more kindling from Buck who supplied his Christmas tree and firewood.

Buck's place was "upriver" on the opposite side of South River and about half an hour from Blockhouse. Given that it was mid-morning, and his thermos of home-brewed coffee was in the office, he permitted himself a detour into Mahone Bay, for the scenery, for the drive-thru, and maybe for the two Dutchies that got added to the order.

He had to return to Blockhouse to get back to the highway. He detoured to the lane behind the trail, and glanced in toward the mobile home. Most of the same washing was still on the line. That's all he wanted to see. He would not permit himself any out-of-vehicle excursion.

On the highway with coffee and treat, Tim hummed a hymn, and sang a bit when the first donut was gone:

> In the bleak mid-winter, frosty wind made moan,
> earth stood hard as iron, water like a stone;
> snow had fallen, snow on snow, snow on snow,
> in the bleak mid-winter, long ago.

The washing on that clothesline would be down under snow on snow by the time tonight's bleak mid-winter storm was finished with it. Too bad. The whole place looked sad, abandoned.

He bought three large bundles of kindling from Buck, and then wondered where he should go from there. The newspaper office was busy constructing this week's paper. He was very curious to see what Elaine and Stella had done with "In The Ring", but if that blew up he wanted to be able to say truthfully that he didn't know, hadn't seen, wasn't even there.

"You're a chicken," he told the man in the rear-view mirror, who replied, "No, I'm prudent. A prudent chicken."

He decided a prudent chicken should go home and check the supply of batteries for flashlights, and food to eat without cooking if it came to that. And wine. He had forgotten to return the old Western movies he had rented last week, but he expected there'd already been a pre-storm run on new releases, so he decided to re-watch whatever he had in the bag until the power went off or he fell asleep.

~

"Oh good, you're home. Just calling to see how you're doing, Aunt Stella."

"Why, am I ill? I hadn't heard."

"No-no, neither have I. I was just checking—"

"Timothy, I appreciate your interest, but surely you must know there isn't a man yet born that will get the better of me. But your flowers are still lovely."

"You're tough, Aunt Stella."

"That's not news. How's the editorial going?"

"What editorial is that?" inquired Prudent Chicken.

"Don't play dumb, Timothy."

"Not playing. I'm on sabbatical, remember? I have nothing to do with editorials, have not seen whatever you're asking about. The paper will be out tomorrow, if the snow doesn't slow delivery, and we are quite proud of our record in snowstorms. Me personally, I'm delving into an interesting event that happened recently on a hiking trail—"

"I must go."

He was prepared for her to hang up suddenly. She said she would before she did, though, an improvement there. While Stella was not an enemy, she was often an adversary; even seemed to like the role, or was comfortable in it anyway. Tim preferred not to do anything adversarial with anyone, but occasionally prepared his defence in advance, as he had just done. He gave himself a small thumbs-up.

He looked up the number of the Lunenburg RCMP and called it. He explained the nature of his inquiry as simply as he could—woman on Old Train Line Trail in distress, taken to South River Memorial by ambulance, Blockhouse Fire Dept and Mounties also attended, she had been discharged from hospital, but he wished to speak with the constable who attended the scene on the trail. He was told that no one was in who could help him but someone would get back to him. He left his name and number—remembering to give his mobile phone number as well as his home number —and hung up.

A few big snowflakes whirled past the window in a gust of wind. He pulled on his jacket and carried the kindling bundles in from the car. He placed one bundle next to the electric fireplace to lend it a little authenticity, and stacked the others beside the real fireplace. He brought firewood in from the sun-porch but didn't light it yet. He'd save the wood. If the power went off later he'd need it then.

To his regret, the big chart of curious topics was now at the office and he was here. He had worked profitably all through the last big storm, with charts taped up all over the house. Now that he had achieved his dream of a "room somewhere", it wasn't where he was.

Neither, he realized to his annoyance, were his notes. That wasn't progress. How long was this storm supposed to last? Maybe he should run downtown right now to fetch his notebooks.

He was surprised at how reluctant he was to make the five-minute drive downtown for this important errand, but he did go. He parked in the No Parking zone out front, unlocked the new lock on the door at the bottom of the stairs, took the stairs two by two, and unlocked the door to his room. He retrieved the notebooks and thermos from the table, rolled up the chart from the wall, and left the building. Nobody paid any attention to him.

During the few minutes he was in the building, the snow had already laid down a white carpet of big, wet flakes on the streets, making both stopping and starting slippery.

At home, he searched amongst his stash of briefcases and portfolios for one that matched his sabbatical persona. There was a stylish, slim leather one with disappearing handles, but shouldn't he use something large enough to carry a thermos? If he'd had the thermos with him in Blockhouse today he wouldn't have been tempted to get those donuts. There'd likely be many times when he wouldn't know if he'd circle back at day's end or not. So a big briefcase was the better choice, though it didn't look as nifty as the other.

He was reluctant to fold the flip-chart page to make it fit in the briefcase. What if he copied it over on a sheet of foolscap and carried that around? Yes, he'd try that.

Elaine's suggestion that he get himself a lap-top computer came to mind, but he wasn't sure he knew how to work with the grid program in a computer and he didn't want to get bogged down in technology. Flip chart paper and markers were his preferred technology, and foolscap came a close second.

He opened a double sheet of foolscap and copied the grid, altering a few items as he went. It was a good grid. He carried the briefcase, the notebooks, and the foolscap into the den and turned on the electric fire. He looked outside to assure himself that he was helplessly storm-stayed, then relaxed in the big recliner chair.

He'd been raring to go first thing this morning, but the prematurely darkening afternoon and the wind whistling at the window soon lulled him into an afternoon nap. When the telephone rang, he was disoriented, but managed to answer before it went to the answering service. It was the Lunenburg RCMP.

"Oh, thanks for calling me back. Are you the constable who came to the trail in Blockhouse where the woman was suffering from hypothermia?"

"Yes. What is your connection with the incident?"

"I'm the guy who carried her out, along with a woman who found her first, I guess. It was her son, I think, who ran for help, right? You went back along the trail with them to see where she had fallen in—or whatever happened to her, I'm not sure."

"I'm sure she appreciates your help. What can I do for you now?"

"Well, I—I wonder how that all happened. You went in there. Did you see any pond for her to fall into? The other guy who was there said she fell in, but I couldn't see any water, could you?"

"Well, no, we didn't investigate that. Nobody mentioned water. I didn't see any danger to trail users, who are expected to stay on the trail, and there's no criminal investigation, so there's really nothing more for us to do. We consider the file closed."

"What about the other guy that was there? He seemed to know her, but he made himself scarce before we got her out to the road."

"I suppose he doesn't seem like a Good Samaritan, but that's not an offence. We do appreciate your quick thinking and help getting her out, Mister Brown, but there's nothing more to do."

"So—so you won't be taking my statement?"

"There's no need. I've taken notes as we've been talking here, and I'll add them to the file, but as I say, the case is closed. It's slippery out there now, you stay home and stay safe."

"Thank you, Constable, you too."

Was he being stonewalled? Was there a cover-up? Or was there really nothing more to the story?

This official wet blanket hadn't dampened his curiosity in the least. He wondered if James Olsen would've said okay to the Constable and left it at that. An investigative journalist should make up his own mind, shouldn't he? One should respect authority while questioning authority, shouldn't one?

Tim had snoozed for over an hour. It was dark now, and when he turned on the front porch light, he could see snow stuck to the windward side of his car. How lucky was he not to be out in this mess.

It was time for supper and a glass of *Tempête de Neige*. He enjoyed them in front of the fake fire while watching two spaghetti westerns in a row.

February 17: Tempête de neige

Wednesday

The heavy snow and strong winds had pulled down some power lines in the town and county. The local radio station most likely reported that schools were closed, some businesses were closed, some were open—the usual confusing array of attempts to ignore the storm while dealing with the effects of it. The wind was subsiding, so power crews would be out making repairs as soon as they could safely do so.

However, because the power was off in Tim's house, he heard none of this. But he was familiar with snowstorms and their aftereffects. His drafty old house lost heat quickly without the furnace blowing every few minutes. Town water still had pressure, and the water in his tank was still hot, so he chanced a quick shower, dressed in sweatpants and sweaters, and went downstairs. No electricity meant no coffee; that was the real deprivation.

He peered through the frosty front door windows to see if there were any newspapers. *The Daily* was on the porch, delivered from Halifax. Amazing that someone had driven a truck down the highway, through a snowstorm, in the dark, to get the newspaper to his doorstep, dry in its plastic wrapper. After all that effort, he felt obliged to bring it in and read it.

He lifted the lid on the special box for *The Times*, his own publication, printed in the industrial park not five miles away, due today. It was empty. The daily paper replaced itself every day. If a weekly paper missed its due date, it was late for a week.

He lit the fire and closed the parlour doors to try to keep in the room what heat didn't go up the chimney. He wrapped himself in a blanket, but it was difficult to keep it on his shoulders while read-ing the newspaper. And it was difficult to ignore the fact that he didn't have a coffee.

He went to the front door again and looked out at the street. A plow had gone past. The snow it pushed into his driveway looked wet and sloppy but not impenetrable. Across the corner at the strip mall he could see lights on in some of the stores. Were they just emergency lights? Unlikely that they would power their bright street signs on batteries. They must have electricity on that side of the street. If so, somebody must be selling coffee. Was it worth the risk to go hunting for a hot cup of java?

Yes, it was. He closed the glass doors on the fireplace, stepped into his boots, pulled on his tuque, and blasted the car through the driveway barricade. Sure enough, a nearby burger joint was open. Sure enough, their drive-thru lineup was long and slow. Everyone was likely ordering full breakfasts for their whole families shiver-ing at home, with no thought for a thirsty man who just wanted one blessed hot coffee. He pulled into the parking lot, parked, walked into the restaurant and right up to the counter, and ordered a large coffee, double-cupped to keep it hot, please.

The clerk told him the coffee was free if he bought breakfast, so he ordered a breakfast sandwich, pancakes, and home fries. If that was what the people in the car lineup were waiting for, he felt he had won this round, simply by getting out of the car.

Spinning back into the driveway, he saw that *The Times* had ar-rived. He was very curious about this week's editorial, "In the Ring". He sat very close to the revived fire, laid out his repast, in-haled the hot coffee, and began to read.

"In the Ring" was very good. Excellent, in fact. Elaine had briefly recapped her points of last week, then introduced "several thoughtful responses," leading with one from the MLA for South River and the Harbours, Stella Johnson. Stella kept her arguments concise, to the point, and sharp enough to keep the reader inter-ested.

Tim was proud of both Elaine and Stella. This was very good stuff. Amazing how a non-relative editor could get a good argument from Stella. He might invite them both to dinner sometime. Or maybe not: that much power at the table might cause indigestion.

He called Elaine's direct number.

"Good morning, Tim. Got your copy, I guess?"

"Elaine, you are a pro! 'In the Ring' is brilliant! You managed to convince the MLA to debate rather than attack. I'm impressed."

"Thanks, Tim. It wasn't that difficult, once she listened to my rules of engagement."

"Hmm, I'm not sure that's what she listened to. I think she heard the voice of a strong woman, the only species of human she respects. Good for you, anyway."

Tim's mobile phone began to ring. "Oh, I bet that's herself on my mobile phone now. Must go. Bye."

He fumbled his phone out of his pocket. "Good morning, this is Tim Brown."

"You're sounding lighthearted for so early in the morning."

"It's not only early, it's friggin' cold here on the hill. I just got in with a coffee and breakfast made on the other side of the street, but here in the high-tax ghetto, we're in the dark ages. How's it with you, Aunt Stella?"

"I have power. I'm fine. I called to tell you that you have a very fine editor sitting in for you this year. She knows how to manage debate on important topics."

"Well, well! I'm delighted that you think so. Is there any special reason that you would call me at seven-thirty in the morning to tell me what I already know?"

"No special reason. Just wanted you to know. I must go now."

"Wait! Wait a sec, please, Aunt Stella. I wanted to speak with you about something else. I need to see a detailed map of an area around Blockhouse. Can you get that for me or tell me where I can find it? And I also need to know who lives in a home there that doesn't have a street name or number."

"I'm not a mapping service."

"I know that. But you know who does everything."

"You should, too. That's the jurisdiction of the municipal tax office, I should think."

"But I don't have any connection with the people who live there —it's an old mobile home—so I might not get cooperation if I go through regular channels asking questions. Any clues? You know where all your voters live."

"No street name?"

"No. No sign, anyway. It's just a lane, really, the first left turn up the hill past the Old Train Line Trail."

"Leave it with me."

"Yes, I will, gladly, and thank you very much," Tim said, but Stella had already gone.

He savoured the coffee and ate the breakfast sandwich, but pushed the greasy potato patty and pancake aside after one bite of each. Was the free coffee really free if the parts of the 'meal-deal' he paid for were unpalatable?

He wondered where he should work today. He had neglected to ask Elaine if the heat was on there, but he guessed it was or she would have said. Stella had power. Maybe it was only his side of the street that was out of luck.

His waking thought came to mind, the one that came right after noticing how cold it was in the house. It was that he didn't want to use the briefcase he had selected last evening. It reminded him of his regular job, and he didn't want that reminder. Last month he was feeling disoriented without his regular work trappings, but now he was pretty well disconnected from all that.

He dashed out to the car, popped the trunk, and ran back with the backpack. That was more like it. It looked casual, maybe even sporty, definitely un-businesslike. He brought the briefcase into the parlour and transferred its contents to the backpack.

While he was putting the briefcase back in the closet, the fridge began to hum, the microwave beeped, and the furnace rumbled into action. The electric world had returned. He didn't want to dodge snowplows this morning, nor did he feel like changing out of his sloppy clothes, so he settled in to work at home.

~

Tim taped the large sheet of manila paper to the pantry door and examined the grid of questions. He decided to proceed methodically, top to bottom, left to right, in hopes of filling each box.

First on the list was The Victim.

"Who am I?" he asked aloud, in her voice. "Well, I'm a woman, I'm about—what—thirty? Twenty-five? I could be a mother, but don't you go pinning a baby on me just because you saw diapers on a clothesline somewhere."

Fair enough. No twisting facts to suit theories. He added *Baby* to the list of questions.

"What else about me? I'm outdoors in freezing temperatures without shoes or stockings or a jacket. I would not have left home like that, would I? So when or where did I lose my shoes? Or why? And where was my coat? Was I even planning to go outdoors?"

This girl had some good questions, and Tim was jotting them down as quickly as he could on the foolscap. He'd transcribe them to the big chart later, after she'd finished talking about herself.

He closed his eyes to review the scene on the trail. What had he seen? Sherlock Holmes had told Watson, "You see, but you do not observe."

Sure, Sherlock, but it's challenging to calmly observe once you discover a dying woman on the icy ground and then run toward help with her in your arms. In my arms.

Eyes still closed, Tim focused on the woman he had held so tightly against his chest to give her some warmth, her head right under his chin...

"I have a bracelet on my left wrist," Tim-as-Miss said quietly. "It's light blue, one of those stretchy bands. It has something printed on it in white. A name, maybe?"

This was good stuff.

"I have dark brown hair, parted in the middle, tied in a pony tail. I smell...nice. Clean."

Was that relevant? Wouldn't anyone smell fresh if they'd taken a dunk in an icy pond?

"Hello, Miss," Tim said, in his own voice. "About that pond. If there is one, and if you broke through ice on it—you couldn't weigh much more than one-thirty or I couldn't have carried you." He noted her weight; she didn't argue. "So, if you did manage to break through ice that was hidden by snow, that ice couldn't have been on a lake or a pond, because there's no darn lake or pond in there, I bet you there isn't. There might be a swampy patch in there, maybe up to your knees. If so, if you fell in swamp water, you'd be covered in swamp muck, wouldn't you?"

That was a good point. She didn't respond. Perhaps her silence was agreement. Her cotton shirt, tank top, and stretchy pants were wet, or damp anyway, but her feet didn't look like they had been in the peaty black water one might expect in a swampy area. Tim hadn't observed any trace of debris or sulphurous odour from decaying bog matter on her clothes or his after he'd held her tightly to his chest while carrying her down the trail.

"Okay, Miss, we are going to set aside the fell-in-a-pond story. That was a big red herring."

With a confident stroke of a red marker, he eliminated that false clue. If he were ever invited to go fishing, he'd say he preferred to catch red herrings. Sure, they were confusing and misleading initially, but so was everything else. Once a fish was marked "red", you could set it aside, making the list of clues just that much shorter and the conclusion that much closer.

"Now, Miss, how did you get to the trail? Did you start out walking on it and just happen to lose your shoes and jacket? No, I didn't think so. Did you decide to take a life-threatening shortcut through the woods to or from somewhere? I ask this because the brush is very thick there and it's hard to get through and there are boulders under the snow. Please don't make me have to go in there. Just tell me what happened."

He stood up to wander around the house in case the answer was in a different room. He wished he was staring into the middle distance from the office window, letting the old glass distract him enough that he would stop thinking and just be open to—

"I didn't *plan* to go outdoors without my shoes and jacket." Tim could almost hear her speaking. "I'm not nuts. It was a—a surprise."

Tim looked at the box on the grid named *Other Guy*. "Were you chasing her?" he demanded. "Is that why you were there? Was she running away from you? And if so, why?"

Calm down, now, he said to himself. *Let's be methodical about this, and let's not pick sides, at least not yet.*

He noted these questions in Other Guy's box and returned to The Victim. He crossed out that name and wrote *Miss*, which seemed more sympathetic.

"Miss, did you know that teenager or his mother before...before they found you lying on the trail? I'm going to say no on your behalf. I didn't get that vibe. They would have said something, like, 'She's my sister neighbour baby-sitter friend.' Right? We were busy and working fast, but there was plenty of opportunity for one of them to say they hoped Cassandra or whatever your name is was okay. Right?"

He decided he was right about that, and noted it.

He had now jotted suppositions in the boxes below Who, What, When, or Where. Nothing under Why yet. That was the magic box. When he began writing in Why, he was certain that something would start flickering.

~

He took a break from communing with the absent, and negotiated with Gloria for a latté. What he wanted wasn't in her power to withhold now: they had reached an understanding about the making of infusions last month. What he was working on now was the charming decorations he had seen in the froth in the city cafés. His attempt this morning was better, still not award-winning, but it tasted good. That was one amenity his downtown office couldn't offer.

Back to the grid, he focused on the Other Guy. Why was he on the trail that morning? Was he chasing the young Miss? What was the order of players appearing on that stage, anyway: the young woman, the other woman and her son, then this guy? Was Miss already lying there on the trail when the others came by? Was she in the woods in an invisible water trap of some kind, when the others came along?

How would they know she was in trouble, if so? She hadn't appeared to be in any shape to call for help when Tim got there. The woman and her son did seem to be legitimate hikers—walkers, anyway—when they came upon Miss and Guy.

"Darn it," Tim said to the grid. "The Mountie knows that. Mother and son would've told him the story when they walked back to the site."

He closed his eyes and envisioned them going back to the scene. They wouldn't have walked in there in companionable silence: they weren't out for a stroll with the Mountie. The Constable would have asked them to tell him what happened, and they would have told the story as they saw it.

This discussion needed a separate box.

On a new sheet of foolscap he listed all the players, and drew vertical lines on the right for their order of appearance. He made several columns, as he expected this would change before he was through.

"Okay, everybody: places, please. Who comes to centre stage first?"

Not Mom and Son. They were just a-strolling along. Nice to see them doing this together. He marked Three and Four beside their names. The space beside Miss and Guy was blank for now.

Back to the Guy. He had seemed out of place on the trail, to Tim. *Give the man a chance. Don't twist facts to suit theories.*

"Who am I?" he said as the Guy. "I don't have to tell you. I heard all those sirens and decided to scram because..."

Tim couldn't supply the answer to this.

"Why, Guy? Because you are 'known to authorities', as they say?"

"I live nearby. I cut across the trail sometimes. It's a free country. I was on my way to the store."

Why not? There must be shortcuts between those cute little streets and the convenience store out on the main road. Maybe the store was too close to justify driving the car but too far to walk for a lottery ticket or a pack of smokes. As the crow flies, a shortcut would be just right.

That day had been Tim's first time on that trail, and he had gone only as far as it took to get embroiled in a rescue. He hadn't known what was just around the bend. Once into the situation, he'd been preoccupied with the hazards in proximity to where the Miss had been lying, namely the woods and the mysterious Invisible Pond that lurked out of sight.

Who said anything about a pond, anyway? Tim closed his eyes and tried to observe what he had seen and heard.

She musta fell in there, the Guy had said, and he'd pointed into the woods. Tim had asked if he meant she fell in water, but he hadn't waited for the answer as there was a very cold Miss on the ground. But wait: he said something else: *I just found her.*

"You *found* her? Let's see what that does to this scene-play."

Next to Guy he marked *Two*.

"Well, Missy, that makes you Numero Uno. Did you make your way onto the stage alone? In your condition? How long were you there before the rest of the cast showed up, first your Guy in tarnished armour, followed by Mom and Son, and last but by no means least, The Dashing Delver, who carried you out while you wore his pants!"

Tim paced around the house with this scenario playing. He placed a sheet of paper on the dining table, and drew a long arc from side to side, representing the trail. A vertical line on the right represented the paved road going to Highway 103. Another arc above the first, curving toward the village and back. A straight line at the bottom representing the secondary road between Blockhouse and South River. He marked where he thought the old mobile home might be, only because it was the only other landmark he could recall. And he marked an X where he thought everyone had met on the trail.

This exercise revealed exactly nothing except that he needed more information about the surrounding area. He checked the weather. *No, no, no*, he told himself. *The snow, the wind, the roads.* The trail wouldn't be cleared anyway. It wasn't a public road. Probably a local association maintained it and they'd clear it when they felt like it, most likely not before Saturday.

Back to the Guy. Did he have anything more to say?

"I just found her there. I took the shortcut from my place. It comes out on the trail and then there's another path that comes out behind the store. I didn't know what she was at first when I saw her. I thought it was a deer or something, and I went over to check so I could tell somebody. Then that woman and her kid came and then you. Why did I disappear? It's...it's personal. Was I afraid of being caught? No, 'cause I didn't do nothing wrong. But the way things work around here, if I'm found with an unconscious woman on a trail, and there's a lot of sirens coming, they'll take me somewhere to answer a lot of questions. All I wanted was a pack of gum."

Fair enough, Guy.

"Do I know her?" Tim-as-Guy was exploring all options, though not all questions had a chance of answers yet. "Probably not socially. Maybe."

"And besides, she knows what happened to her. Why not ask her?"

Not that easy, Guy.

Tim finished recording this "interview" and was going to move on to the next when he had another thought. He put Guy on the stand again. Apparently this was both a trial and a play: whatever it took. Did he say she fell in, or fell *in there*? There was a difference. Tim had jumped to one conclusion. Sherlock would be annoyed.

"Did I say she musta fell in water, or fell in *there*, in the woods? What difference? Does it matter? She was on the ground, so I figgered she musta fell down comin' out of the woods, maybe stumbled over the boulders, maybe hit her head. I don't know. I didn't see nothin'. She was just lyin' there, moanin' and shiverin'. She wasn't wearin' enough clothes to keep her warm, that's for sure. Like I say, I use the shortcuts, and the kids have them wore down good."

Tim thanked the Guy for his testimony, and apologized for giving him bad grammar. That was judgy.

He reviewed the grid, and the cast of characters at the bottom. One, two, three and four were still in the same order. He realized he had left out a fifth actor, one he was certain knew least about the scene, but who had definitely been there: TB.

"Do I need to interview you, Mister Brown?"

"Nope," replied Tim-as-Tim. "The purpose of this quest, the reason for our curiosity, is to learn what happened leading up to my arrival, not after. There is no mystery about what I did, since I did it."

He stood up and stretched. This had been a productive morning. He knew a lot more about what he didn't know and what he needed to know. His toolbox was collecting tools. After lunch he'd see if any of them had handles or were sharp enough to use.

While the kettle was boiling for tea, Tim returned to the grid and added a question mark after Guy's #2. He'd imagined a good story about taking the shortcut to the store for gum, but he had not unhooked him from the possibility that he had more to do with Miss's condition than he let on. Was she running from him? Was he chasing her? They'd still be first and second, but the speed of the scene could be quite different. And the reason for it.

~

Sometimes things happen precisely the way you want them to, when you need them to. This was Tim's reaction when the doorbell rang and Spencer was standing there with a cardboard tube in his hand.

"Hi, Spencer, what's that you have there?"

"Hello, Mister Brown. Miss Johnson asked me to give this to you." He handed the tube to Tim. "She said to tell you not to thank her for it. I don't know what that means."

Tim laughed. "Oh, I think I do, Spencer. I can thank you for delivering it, though. How's the driving?"

"No problem at all, not in that vehicle, not with me behind the wheel."

"I bet you're even enjoying being out, then. Better you than me.

Thanks, Spence. See you tomorrow at choir?"

"Yessir. I try not to miss it."

Spencer touched the brim of his cap and returned to the vehicle to which he had referred.

Tim laid the cardboard tube on the desk and returned to the kitchen to browse the rest of *The Times* with lunch. It seemed like six days had passed since he had brought it in the house, not six hours. That was the grid-effect, he thought. Closing his eyes and re-visiting the scene of the crime-not-crime was like Einstein's time travel. When he was trying to re-see what he had seen but not noticed, time moved differently.

Time was passing at an ordinary pace now, and Tim was eager to see what was in that tube, so he couldn't concentrate on the articles in the paper. He quickly finished the peanut butter and banana sandwich, and took the remainder of the mug of tea to the desk and opened the tube.

"Oh, Aunt Stella, this is beautiful!"

It was a map of Blockhouse and environs, showing every street and every building, with pertinent information about each printed in neat, tiny handwriting. It was Stella's campaign map. Undoubtedly she had this detail for every square inch of her constituency of South River and The Harbours. No wonder she won successive elections. The electorate wasn't a mob of unknowns to her: it was people, and she knew each individual one of them.

From a lifetime of conversations with Stella, Tim knew that "don't thank me" meant "don't ever speak to anyone about this, or else". Whatever "or else" meant could make you wish for a stab wound. Stabs could heal.

He unrolled the map on the dining table and anchored the corners with salt and pepper shakers, a tape dispenser, and a small vase with one of Sunday's gerbera daisies, still looking good. He found the Old Train Line Trail, and traced his path. Not far along the curve, but farther than he had walked that day, a lane came in from the paved secondary road and cut across the trail, but it didn't lead to any houses, and seemed to dwindle out in a wooded area. Perhaps that was where Mom and Son had parked to walk on the trail that day.

He moved his finger along from there to where he had entered the trail, and back again to a spot which could be out of sight of either place. He placed a Royal Doulton basket of pansies on that spot, the possible scene where the event began.

Next, he began to widen his search. At the top of the map someone had printed *Highway 103* with an arrow pointing to the top. Below that were the curving streets and lanes of Inner Block-house.

Tim was impressed to see the amount of personal information next to each house and outbuilding—not only names and telephone numbers, but children, pets, jobs, cars. Stella left nothing to chance. She knew that people like to be remembered, and here was her memory bank, in remarkable detail.

Where he had entered the trail was very near the four-way-stop that was one of Outer Blockhouse's distinguishing features. Given that there were very few traffic signs in the whole county, and next to no traffic lights other than a rare flashing orange, an actual four-way stop was a significant landmark, and often used as such.

From the four-way stop, he noted where the trail crossed the paved road leading to the highway, and then his finger took the first left turn, and stayed left.

It was the lane he had measured his paces on, and he was right: it didn't connect with any other street. There was the old mobile home. Tim felt like an eagle hovering high above the ground he had trudged over, and he was pleased to find things where he expected them to be.

But he was surprised at what was written beside the mobile: "Unocc."

That can't be right. That busy clothesline was clear evidence of occupation, and by more than one occupant, since a baby in diapers couldn't keep house for itself.

This was disappointing. He hadn't expected Stella's detailed census of everyone, but once he had seen it, he hoped it would give him information on Miss—if indeed she had come from the trailer, through the Impenetrable Woods, onto the trail, in bad shape. On the other hand, if she belonged to one of the other homes, he had no way of knowing which one.

He switched on the chandelier over the dining table and turned it up to full brightness so he could read the topographical markings on the map. He wasn't sure how a pond or swamp would be indicated, so he looked around until he found a small stream marked at the left edge of the map, outside his area of interest. Nothing like that was in the space between the trail and the old mobile. No squiggly outline of a pond, no name in a cartographer's neat hand identifying "Slough of Despond" or "Tarpit" or anything else an ordinary person might fall into. Anyway, no sensible person would have tried to cross that narrow piece of real estate because it appeared impossible to do without a chainsaw, with or without shoes on.

He examined the south side of the trail, between it and the secondary road to South River. There was even less real estate there in which to hide a pond, and none was indicated.

The eagle's eye view had failed to reveal an obvious clue, but it did raise some new questions. He added *Trailer/Mobile* to the list of questions.

Was there a good reason why an unoccupied trailer would have a full clothesline? Was it unoccupied now? Information about people in a neighbourhood could go out of date between elections, of course. People came and went, changed jobs, had babies, and the impressive notations on this map would be updated only when Stella or one of her minions picked up the information, or when there was a campaign.

But still, he had no reason to link the trailer with the events on the trail. The Guy had vaguely gestured in its direction. What would Sherlock Holmes say about that? *Just because something takes your fancy,* Mister Brown, *doesn't mean it has any significance to the case.*

This was inarguable, and not helpful. Not only was it difficult to observe the right clues, it was challenging to discard any without knowing for certain why they didn't apply.

Thinking about the Guy's alibi, Tim looked closely to see if a shortcut was indicated on the map, but of course none was. Unofficial paths made by the frequent passage of children and smokers wouldn't be marked on topographical maps—if there even was such a path. He examined the details marked beside each dwelling, in case any of it rang a bell, but none of the names meant anything to him, none called "Other Guy" or "Miss".

He'd like to take another look in person.

When was he going to do this? He looked outside. The snow wasn't falling, hadn't been when Spencer arrived with the tube. The temperature had risen above freezing, so the combination of that and salt on the roads likely made them safe to drive on. He checked the calendar. Tomorrow was full enough, being Thursday: Mrs A's day to clean, the dishwasher installer (who he hoped was also the taker-awayer), breakfast at the Daisy Café, Robert's arrival for supper and choir practice. There'd be time in the middle of the day to go have a look-see—as long as he stayed in the car and didn't go charging off into the bushes, where things could go wrong.

After some dithering, he decided to stay put and continue with the grid for the rest of the day. Perhaps he'd come up with more questions that he'd seek answers to tomorrow. He'd prepare Thursday's supper today so he wouldn't have that pressure if something delayed his return.

What could go wrong?

February 18: The scene

Thursday

A February gloom was establishing itself outdoors: a system of warmer air crept in over the snow banks and fields of snow and lakes of ice, which gave back a thick, damp fog. Visibility was poor, but if you needed to slam on the brakes, you'd likely have good traction. Winter driving in South River was often a trade-off: this, but at least not that.

Gloria cooperated to make a fine latté, and Tim practised his foam-drawing skill, better today. The good thing about this quest was that you could drink your mistakes.

Not like his mother would have done. She had indulged herself by writing a cheery food column in her latter years. To her credit, she did make every dish she featured, but if it didn't suit her, the whole thing went in the garbage, even if its only failing was that it didn't look good enough in the photos.

Tim knew that was a trait of a perfectionist, and he knew perfectionism was a heavy burden for those who suffered from it. He'd had to endure her burden as well, and that left many memories of his mother unresolved.

He shook his head to disperse those heavy thoughts. Today was not about Brownie Brown. It was full of purpose, potential, promise, and would end with some moments of choral delight and a clean house.

He wrote out the cheque for Mrs Aquino and laid it on the kitchen island. While he waited eagerly for her to arrive, he rolled up all the big manila sheets on which he had worked until quite late last evening, and put them in the cardboard tube Stella had sent the map in. Once he had made certain that all notebooks were in the backpack and nothing was left lying around for Mrs A to treat as clutter, he paced around until she arrived at precisely seven twenty-five.

"Good morning, Mrs A. How're you today? Driving okay?"

"Winter no good," she replied.

"Ah, well, spring's coming."

They rarely engaged in small talk, but some occasions invited it. "Your cheque is there. Oh, by the way, we're getting a new dishwasher today. The installer will be here this morning to take the old one out and put the new one in. They say it won't take long."

Tim laid the store's business card on the island next to the cheque. "He's from this company. If you would please let him in, that will be much appreciated. I have appointments, so I can't stay."

Mrs A acknowledged this information with a baleful look. She did such a good job cleaning, but would it have interfered with that in any way if she would lighten up a bit? Would she even hear the doorbell once she started thumping around upstairs? He wasn't interested in watching the exciting process of re-dishwashering himself, and was eager to get going.

With a black marker he wrote RING AND KNOCK LOUDLY on a sheet of paper, taped it to the inside of the front door glass, and left.

He was looking forward to breakfast at the Daisy Café. Since he had assigned that visit to a day—Thursdays—the anticipation of a greasy platter made the other days' less festive breakfasts seem more noble, less like a sacrifice.

But on the way to that happy destination this morning, he decided to change the order of things. He'd run over to Blockhouse right now to survey the neighbourhood, referring to the map which was here in the car, if need be. Then, by the time he was back at The Daisy, the regulars would have dispersed and maybe he'd get that table in the front window again.

He didn't stop at the drive-thru for a coffee to take along, either. He stayed on the secondary road to avoid the murky fog on the highway, and was soon in Greater Blockhouse. He drove in and out of every street, lane, and dead-end truck-turn he could find. He looked in on the trail: he could see tracks of skis, boots, snowmobiles, and four-wheelers at the entrance, but he couldn't tell how old they were.

He drove into the lane to the "Unocc" mobile home: some laundry was still on the line—the smaller pieces—but most was gone, presumably on the ground under the latest snow. He peered through the fog to see if he could see any shortcuts through the woods leading to the trail and the convenience store beyond. The dull sky and fog had erased all colour and shadows from the landscape. Nothing stood out.

When he had perused the map yesterday, none of the names or other details about the residents of these houses had rung any bells. Further, since he was trying to place the Guy in the neighbourhood, none of the occupations listed seemed to match this fellow, neither teacher, nor business manager, nor the several retireds.

Had Guy moved in with his retired mother since these notations were made? If so, there were several options, modest homes in which he could be sitting right now, watching some vacuous morning television show, smoking in spite of his mother's lung conditions, waiting for her pension cheque to arrive.

"My goodness, Tim, get your head out of that rabbit-hole," he said to the rear-view mirror. "You've created a villain all on your own. Take a deep breath and mind your manners."

After making another slow circuit through all the streets, he drove to the convenience store where he'd imagined Guy bought his cigarettes, and went in. He picked out a package of gum, as one does when one really only wants information.

He said to the clerk, "I have an odd question for you. Do you know if there is a shortcut that kids in the village use to come across the trail to get to here?"

"Kids in the village? You mean from Mahone Bay?"

"Uh, no, I mean back there—" Tim pointed in the direction of the woods behind the store.

"Dunno. There's some kind of school back there, I guess, but they don't come here. They're all organic and that. We don't sell carrots or whatever they eat."

"I saw the school. But I mean, is there a shortcut behind here that leads to houses up there, that people take to get here?" Tim felt he was losing his ability to communicate. Should it be this hard?

"Well, nothing's far. You go to the four-way stop and turn left, and then—"

"Got it," Tim said. "Thanks for your help."

Maybe it was the weather that gave Tim the creepy feeling he was in a horror movie where people denied things existed that he could see with his very own eyes, *right there*. But he couldn't see them either, since he'd made everything up, so what was he fussed about?

He was frustrated and hungry, and he knew the Daisy could re-solve at least one of those.

Evelyn's loud faux-flirting often got on Tim's nerves, but as everyone said, she meant well, God love 'er, and she did have a way of re-setting the crankies. Tim didn't order the big greasy breakfast as he had dreamed of doing, for fear it wouldn't settle well in his current frame of mind. He didn't take the table in the window either, since it was occupied by some shoppers. He sat in his usual booth and tried to re-direct his mood.

He had brought a notebook, in case he had a brilliant idea. None came. He doodled random words: *hunch, red herring, dead end*. He sketched a stick figure, with a hump on its back, holding a fishing rod from which dangled a magnifying glass. He entitled it *The Hunch-brain of South River Fishes for Red Herrings.*

"Hey, you're good!"

He looked up to see the source of this friendly voice. It was the ambulance driver from the trail. *What are the odds?* Likely pretty high in a small community like South River and environs.

"Um, yeah, thanks. I'm good, but totally undiscovered. Say, listen, have you got a sec? I've been wanting to talk to you. Do you re-member meeting me?"

"I sure do." Her voice was as cheery as Evelyn's, but lacking innuendo. She didn't even mention his missing pants. "But I can't stay, sorry. Busy day. Off duty."

"Of course. Just one minute, though? I've been looking into that event where we met, and something doesn't add up. I have one question for you, if you'd be so kind. Please?" He extended his hand. "My name's Tim Brown. I don't believe I learned yours?"

"I'm Sally. Okay, but make it quick." She squeezed into the booth.

"You likely can't answer my question, Sally, but I'll ask it anyway. That young woman we rescued in Blockhouse, she wasn't hypothermic, was she? I mean, she sure was cold, but she hadn't fallen into water, had she? Because I can't find any water anywhere around there for her to fall into."

Sally looked directly at Tim, not reacting.

"You could say you don't recall," Tim offered, "but I think you do. I think she was in some kind of trouble, medical or otherwise, but not due to exposure. Am I right?"

Still nothing from Sally.

"I've been puzzling over this ever since that day. The RCMP won't tell me anything. They say the file is closed, but I think something happened that should be investigated. I wonder if she said anything in the ambulance? I know you were driving, but you might have overheard."

"That's all confidential," Sally said.

She knows something, Tim thought. *Otherwise she'd simply say that the girl didn't say anything.*

"Can you tell me anything about her, like her name, or where she lives?"

"Sorry. Too many calls for me to keep that info in my head."

"Of course. Thanks, by the way, for letting me know that she recovered and was discharged. That eased my mind a lot."

"What's your concern?"

"Well, there was another person on the trail with us, I don't think you would've seen him. He was there with the woman and her son and the, uh, our victim, when I came along. But when the woman and I picked her up to carry her out, he disappeared. Like *poof*. That seems odd to me. I wondered if she was in some sort of difficulty, and if he might've had something to do with it. My concern? Something's fishy. I'm not inquiring because I personally want to know the private dirt about anybody, it's not that. But I do want justice to be done, if there's an injustice at all."

Sally nodded thoughtfully, and then shifted out of the booth. "Give me your phone number. No promises."

Tim quickly wrote both numbers on the page next to the Hunch sketch, added his name, and handed it to her. "To my first art critic," he said, "with appreciation."

~

Upstairs in his white office, Tim was pleased to unroll and hang the map and the several pages of grids recording Topics and Clues. He remembered to put a blotter-sheet behind the grid-sheets to protect the fresh paint from over-zealous markering. He did the reverse for the map; he wasn't going to mark on it, but he hung a blank sheet over it to keep inquiring eyes away, should any such eyes penetrate the defences of two locked doors.

This precaution was timely: there was a knock on the upper door: he had neglected to lock the door at the bottom of the stairs, so James Olsen had come right up, the sound of his footsteps on the stairs covered by the noisy rustling paper sheets inside.

"Hi, Mister Brown, got a minute?"

"Sure, James." He stepped out of the office to the hallway outside, closing the office door behind him. "What can I do for you?"

"Uh, I wanted to talk to you about something. Can we—what, here?"

"Yup, right here's good. What's on your mind?"

"I—I just—do you have any leads I might follow up for you? Any story ideas? I'm a little dry this week."

"Are you, now? A snowstorm in February isn't news? Well now, you never know. I might. Wait here."

Tim left him standing in the hallway and went back into his office for a notebook. Then he led James to the room across the hall and sketched the location on a page from his notebook.

"You know the four-way stop in Blockhouse, right? Okay, heading toward the highway from there, you cross over a trail. Immediately past the trail is a lane on your left, and on your left in there is an old mobile home. It's supposedly unoccupied, but, until this last storm, there was laundry on the clothesline, including baby clothes. I'm curious: whose laundry is that, and is the place occupied or not, and if so, by whom? Can you scare up those details?"

"Most likely. Can you give me any clues about why you want to know? I mean, was there a crime?"

"Can't say, yet. That's what we're trying to discover. An ambulance came to rescue a woman who was found injured—well, no, but almost unconscious—on the aforementioned trail. My hunch is that she was a victim of something, I just don't know of what, yet. I can't help thinking that this trailer figures into it somehow. So, dig, okay? Here's my mobile number: call me when you have answers. Or questions. Both are useful."

"Is this connected to the, um, issue you were talking to me about on Monday?"

"This is Round Two of that topic, yes. We won't speak of this to anyone, James. If things work out, nobody will be able to connect what was in those "Community Notes" with what you will write. But we have work to do. *Tempus fugit*, James."

"Uh, *danke schoen* to you, too, Mister Brown."

"And keep my name out of it for now, okay, James? You make your own investigations in your own way. Call me with whatever you learn, or don't learn."

Tim went back across the hall and closed the door, happy that he had managed to keep James and his brain-waves outside the room.

A moment later he went downstairs to visit with Ed Garamond, the newspaper's typesetter.

"Hey, Ed, I'm here for a couple favours."

"I'm always happy to do something a little out of the ordinary, Boss."

"Just plain vanilla this time, Ed, sorry. Can you make me a sign for the stairway door back there that says 'Please call Tim Brown for permission to enter' and then put my mobile number on it? I don't expect any visitors, but I don't want unexpected ones, either."

"Sure. I can do that. I'll put it on nice card stock. I'll stick it up for you if you're gone."

"Thanks, Ed, that'll be great. The other thing is, can you arrange for some calling cards for me? I have boxes of business cards that proclaim that I'm the head cheese of this enterprise, and I'm sure they'll last me a lifetime. But this year, while I'm off, I'd just like to be Timothy Brown with these two phone numbers. No title, no address. Can you do that for me?"

"Sure. How many?"

"Oh, I dunno, fifty?"

"That's easy. Can I choose the font? Please? Serif or sans? What's the impression you want to give? Solid and mysterious? Relaxed and playful? Hard to get? I know a font that is really hard to read, especially the numbers, 'specially good if you don't want people to call you but want to pretend you do."

"Don't strain yourself, Ed. These are not for making an impression at all, but simply to save myself the onerous task of writing down my name and phone number. Other than that, go for it. Oh, and don't print them on glossy card stock: I might need to write on them."

It was well past lunchtime and Tim was hungry. He hadn't packed the thermos nor a lunch today because he had been eager to vacate the house before the installer came. He couldn't go home yet because Mrs. A would still be there with all engines roaring. The poor installer was probably freezing in the fresh breeze. How long would it take to replace a dishwasher, anyway? That was another thing he didn't know and wasn't curious about.

He was hungry, though. From Ed's cubicle, he wandered over to the water cooler in the lunchroom. Sometimes staff brought muffins or other goodies to share. Technically he wasn't staff this year, so it would be cheating for him to take anything, but he knew they wouldn't mind.

Sadly, there was nothing to take today. There was some tarry sludge in the bottom of the coffee-pot, but he knew that was not fit for human consumption.

He poured a glass of water and took it upstairs. Two sticks of gum would have to serve as lunch this time. He made a note to get some granola bars to leave in his room for situations like these.

Staying with the task at hand, he transcribed notes to big sheets, mumbling comments, waiting for inspiration to strike, until it was past three-thirty and safe to go home without crossing paths with Mrs Aquino. He had a casserole bubbling in the oven when there was a heavy hammering at the front door, accompanied by multiple doorbell chimes.

He quickly opened the door and was surprised to see Robert standing there. "What's all the ruckus for?"

"I'm just following instructions," Robert said, and pointed to the sign Tim had taped to the door in the morning. "I knocked loudly and rang. What's my prize?"

"I let you in, you goof, that's your prize. I put that note there this morning so the dishwasher installer would be sure to get Mrs A's attention. The thing's installed, so it must've worked."

~

Choir practice was the usual array of enjoyments: a new piece to sing through; a favourite anthem to practice for Sunday, which Robert expected them to be in better voice for than they were; and a short discussion of the Easter concert in April, which was to include the "Hallelujah Chorus".

"Just because it's familiar, don't think for a minute that you know it well enough to perform it," Robert reminded them. "It's dramatic, but it's not a foghorn, so we'll touch on the highlights in the weeks to come. Oh—here's news—I think we'll have a trumpeter to add some drama."

The choir was excited about the extra musical dimension the instrument would provide, and those concerned with fundraising knew at least an extra twenty tickets would sell because of it.

At home, Tim and Robert nibbled on smoked gouda and crackers with their post-practice port. They sat in the cosy den with the lights off and recounted their days by the warm, rotating light of the electric fireplace until their yawns overtook the stories.

It's a curious fact that one can be very sleepy until that sleepy head hits the pillow, when it comes wide awake with some unresolved thought. Tim had been feeling a little guilty about recent conversations with Robert. He did his best to keep the focus on Robert and his pursuits—worth every minute—but it wasn't only because he cared about Robert and his interesting career. He also wanted to avoid having to tell Robert about his own pursuits of late.

Developments at the office building, Elaine's gentle nudging and amazing connections to get the place cleaned and painted—especially his new hidey-hole private workspace—all of that was available for discussion, and it made good storytelling. Even the dishwasher and the new front door got air time, not so much for the mundane items themselves, but for what Tim was learning about what goes on behind the scenes, before things start, about how what appears as the start—the arrival of a new appliance, say—was actually the end of a whole process about which he had been privileged to be mostly ignorant, until now.

But the Incident on the Trail was not a tale about which he chose to share details. Sure, he'd strained his back there and had to skip church the next day because of it, but Robert always followed his lead on things like that. When Tim was in pain, Robert stepped up. When Tim appeared to be healed, Robert moved on unless there was a reason to bring it up again.

Robert lived his life at least one beat in the future. That was his training as a music conductor: if he wanted his choristers to arrive at the same measure at the same time, he had to give the downbeat ahead of them. As a performer, if he wanted anything to happen in the future, he had to be working on it now, so his thoughts were most often on tomorrow. When a major recital was imminent, as one had been last month, he became disoriented and stressed. That's when he would make plans for an elaborate dinner with a menu challenging enough to keep him in the present, chop-chop-chopping in the kitchen, concentrating on keeping his talented fingers out of the way of sharp knives and hot pans.

Conversely, Tim's attention was more on the past in this Year of Delving. He was challenging himself to uncover what had already happened, or reveal some meaning in past events. This was almost as frustrating to Tim as Robert's work was challenging to him. Robert knew what he wanted to do, and practised and focused and obsessed to give his intentions the best chance. Tim couldn't alter the events of the past, no matter how hard he tried—and he did try sometimes, filling in suppositions and fictions as placeholders in a story.

His challenge was, simply put, to keep guessing. Discussing wild guesses with someone who knew less of the sketchy circumstances than he did himself seemed pointless, and would frustrate them both. Robert didn't ask for help figuring out fingerings to use in a complex organ opus played on three manuals plus pedals.

So perhaps they were even. They'd both enjoy sharing and hearing the story after the successful conclusion. If there was one.

Having rationalized this issue, Tim slept well.

February 19: Proving

Friday

While Robert was in the shower, Tim took out a cast-iron fry pan, buttered slices of bread on both sides, cut out the centres with one of his mother's many cookie-cutters, placed the slices in the pan and dropped an egg in each hole. While that was cooking, he whispered to Gloria that it was show-time. He set place mats and a few hardy daisy survivors from last Sunday.

"Hey, nice table," Robert said. "Special occasion?"

"Hmm?" said Tim. Then he proudly served the latté, with a perfect *R* painted in the foam.

"Bravo! Congratulations! You *have* been busy, and on a worthy skill, too!"

Robert leaned over to inspect Tim's cup, which also boasted a floating *R*.

"Hey, that's not a T. Did you forget your own initial?"

"No, smarty. I didn't practice the T yet. Gloria suggested I do *R* on both so I'd have two chances to get it right this morning. Gloria's a good teacher."

"*In excelsis*," agreed Robert.

After Robert departed for the city, Tim put their dishes in the gleaming new dishwasher, along with those from yesterday's supper. The machine seemed larger inside than the old one, and he wondered how many days of dishes would accumulate before it would be economically sensible to run the thing? A new problem, but it would solve itself.

He supposed it would be prudent to read the instruction manual first. He put it in the den for this evening's reading. The installer had left a bag of goodies on the counter, including a sample of detergent recommended for this model, and a round magnet with *Clean* on one half and *Dirty* on the other.

Tim knew he would never use that; he would forget to turn the magnet like he forgot to mark himself IN or OUT at the office. Neither really mattered.

He made a thermos of coffee, and a peanut butter and raisin sandwich which he sealed tightly in plastic. It would last a long time if he didn't eat it, should he get a better offer. He placed these, plus an apple, plus the remainder of the pack of gum, in the backpack. Now he was ready for the day, wherever it might lead.

~

At the beginning of the month—a mere two weeks ago—he had decided to spend time in the upper office, for privacy, and to wander around amongst people, for random inspiration. He had achieved the private office in jig-time. About random inspiration, though, he was uncertain about from where it might come, or from whom. That's the thing about random.

For certain it wouldn't just walk in the door to his office, not now. He laughed to see the sign that Ed had made for the door at the bottom of the stairs:

DO *NOT* KNOCK.
> ENTRANCE FORBIDDEN<
without
SECRET PASSCODE
Code may be obtained *only* by calling this number:
902-123-4567
IF NO ANSWER, GO AWAY QUIETLY.
HAVE A NICE DAY!

Tim was hoping to hear from two potential sources of inspiration: Sally, the paramedic, and James Olsen, the dubious reporter. Either one of them could confirm some of his suspicions, possibly leading to a hunch.

He doubted that he'd hear from Sally, because of her job and his lack of one. She might think he was some fellow who'd been out for a walk when he was called upon to rescue a maiden in distress. She wouldn't be wrong. Never mind. He wasn't going to get down on himself because he didn't have a grand job title. He had one before, and might take it up again, but right now he was Citizen Brown. But he was also curious.

James was more likely to bring something like a report, however ragged it might be, because Tim was his ultimate boss, even while on sabbatical. Inside this building, Tim had status.

He was inhaling the steam from his coffee when the phone rang.

"Timothy Brown," he announced. He thought that sounded better than "Hello?"

"Mister Brown? Are you here? I mean, up there?"

"Good morning, James. I'm in my office, yes. What's up?"

"Can I come up? Do I need a code?"

"You don't need a—I mean, yes, a code. It's secret, but I have assigned one to you. Yes, come on up, and bring a spare chair with you."

Tim took the straight-backed chair from his office to the dusty room across the hall. James came up the stairs with a chair of similar vintage and style.

"In here?" he said. "Don't you have a nice room over there?"

"I do. Sit down. What's on your mind this morning, James?"

"Well, I went over to Blockhouse like you said. I found the old trailer, where you said."

"Any sign of activity? Tracks in the snow, that sort of thing?"

Jimmy consulted a small notebook. "No tracks. She's abandoned, Mister Brown. I looked inside—"

"You did *what*? That's trespassing, James!"

"Maybe, maybe not. I went up the steps and knocked on the door, which isn't trespassing. Nobody answered, so I opened the storm door and knocked on the inside door. But it wasn't locked, y'know? It kinda pushed open when I knocked on it. That's not trespassing. It was accidental, right?"

"Don't tell me you went inside."

"Nope, I sure didn't. The place stinks to high heaven, Mister Brown. I'll never go in there. I was going to say I thought I heard someone call for me to come in—that's my ready excuse about trespassing, in case you want to know."

"Please don't tell me that. I don't want to know, and I don't want you trespassing, okay?"

"Okay."

"Okay. What else? The place stank, so then what?"

"So I looked inside. It was the kitchen door. There was a garbage can near the door, full to overflowing, and maggots everywhere, makes me retch just thinking about it. That's likely where the stink was mostly coming from. No lights on, no heat on, nobody moving around. I called, nobody answered. So then I closed the door. I couldn't go in, the stink was putrid."

"I got that. What next?"

"I looked around outside. I noted the clothesline. All I saw on the line was some baby things, at the end where I was standing. I couldn't say if there were other items on the ground, under snow, and I didn't walk over there, but I can go back and check if you want me to."

"Not right now. I had thought that if the laundry wasn't on the line, and wasn't on the ground, maybe somebody had come to get it. Like maybe nobody lived there but someone was using the clothesline. Any thoughts about that?"

"Gosh, I didn't think of that. But I didn't see any tracks in the back yard, if that's anything."

"Right. Good. What else?"

"I went off the doorstep and looked toward the back yard, where it meets the woods there. I thought I saw something but I didn't know what I might be walking over, so I was careful—"

Tim's phone rang.

"Hold that thought please, James. Timothy Brown."

"Hello, this is Sally."

Tim's heart skipped a beat. "Sally! Nice to hear from you."

"Thanks. Here's what I can tell you, but please, *please*, do not tell anyone you got this from me. I'm trusting you with confidential information because I think you might, uh, do some good with it. Okay?"

"Scout's honour."

"Thank you. So, you asked me if that patient was suffering from hypothermia, and the answer is yes, definitely. You did nothing to make her condition worse, and I would say you did a lot to save her life. She was in grave danger. You also inquired if there was some other condition. All I can tell you is that she had bruising on her upper body. I can't comment on the cause."

"Can't, or...?"

"Can't. Don't know."

"Fair enough. Can you share a name?"

"Nope."

"Okay. Anything else?"

"No. Just...just keep asking questions. Follow your instincts. They seem to be good."

"I will. Thanks so much for this. Do you want me to follow up with you?"

"No, please. I see a lot of people in distress every day, and it's not healthy for me to follow their cases. Pick up and deliver safely, that's where I try to keep it and that's hard enough. Gotta go now."

"You're the best. Take care of yourself."

Tim pressed *End*. His head was spinning. Hypothermia was back on the grid. And bruises added. What did this mean?

"James, I need a pee break before we continue. Would you like a coffee?"

"No thanks, Mister Brown, but I'll wait here if you don't mind. It's kinda neat up here. Dusty, though."

Tim locked his door before going down stairs. People were going to get the impression that he was hiding something in there. When he was Editor and Publisher his office door was always open; now he had locks everywhere and was issuing codes, courtesy of Ed Garamond's sense of humour.

Well, that's the way it had to be. He was solving puzzles here, and he absolutely needed the sanctuary of his office to help with the solving or whatever it was. It was apparent that his best thoughts did not come to him in the washroom, anyway.

"Sorry about that, James. Had to take that call and answer the call, ha-ha. Now, let's continue. You had stepped off the doorstep and were heading somewhere?"

"Yeah, the back yard. I noticed something back there, and it looked odd. Everything was white, right? Covered in snow. But there was this one very black thing, like tar paper, but not covered in snow. There was junk in the yard, bits of boards and a kid's trike or something, stuff like that, so I was walking carefully. Figured you wouldn't want me to get hurt on the job."

"Not on or off the job, James. It's always good to be careful, especially when trespassing on private property. So…"

"So I got closer, and I could see it wasn't tar-paper. Guess what it was?"

"Please don't tease me, James."

"It was a well!"

"A well?"

"A well. A hole in the ground, filled with water. That's why it looked black, and wasn't covered in snow. Now, as you may know," James was evidently enjoying his revelation, "open wells are illegal in Lunenburg County, for reasons which may be obvious. They are very dangerous, for one thing, and the water in them wouldn't be drinkable, anyway, 'cause critters would likely fall in."

"An open well." Tim was trying to place this unexpected development on his mental grid along with what he had surmised, and what Sally had just told him.

"Yeah, well, here's the kicker. It looks like this wasn't always an open well. There were boards around it, laid across the top, see? Some were broken, and some were scattered."

"James, how far from the home was this well? And how far—a guess is good for now—how far from the public trail do you think the well is?"

"My guess? Maybe halfway between the trail and the trailer."

"I was on the trail. I looked and looked and couldn't see anything through that thick brush. Are you sure?"

"Yeah, pretty sure. You wouldn't see the well anyway. Nothing sticks up, no well cover or anything like that. There's a path to the trail but it doesn't cut straight through, maybe that's why you couldn't see it. When you're at the well, you can see the trail if you look on an angle, like. I can show you."

"Did you take pictures, by any chance?"

"I sure did, Mister Brown. I can get them printed—"

"Do that. Right away. Now! Quickly!"

As James ran down the narrow stairs, Tim called after him, "Great work, James!"

Tim followed James down the stairs at a more leisurely pace, and searched for the building's caretaker, John. He always had to be sought; whatever he was working on seemed never to be in plain sight.

Tim found him in the low-ceilinged basement, where plumbing delivered hot water from the ancient oil-fired boiler to the radiators above, and where John maintained an array of sump pumps so that runoff from the hill behind or a rare flood from the river in front would not get into the boiler.

"Hey, uh, John. Can you do a quick job for me?"

"Good morning, Mister Brown. Depends, as always. Gotta keep a close eye on this baby this time of year."

Tim noted the old recliner chair set up next to the boiler. It looked well-used. He was tempted to put his hand on it to see if it was warm, but he didn't. "I need one of the rooms on the second floor vacuumed and dusted. Just a quick once-over. The first on the left at the top of the stairs. And can you find two spare chairs to bring up, please?"

That room was twice the size of his front-of-building office but it was empty, so the requested removal of spiders and their webs wouldn't take more than ten minutes.

"I guess I can fit it in. When do you want this done?"

"Right now, please. See you up there."

Tim left, ducking his head under the beams.

On the main floor, he searched in corners and closets for a small table that might be considered excess. He spied a narrow lamp stand next to the stationery supply cabinet, likely a relic from before his mother's reign. If it wasn't exactly excess it didn't appear to be essential. It held a box of envelopes. He placed the box on the floor and quickly made off with his find.

Uncharacteristically, John was already at work upstairs. Tim had left the bottom door open when he came down, so John wouldn't have seen the notice to call for a code. Just as well. He might have taken that as a reason to delay. Tim was pleased to see he had brought two chairs.

"This place needs a good going-over," John shouted over the noise of the vacuum. "I never come up here."

"I know," Tim shouted back. "Can you fit it in? One room at a time, maybe?"

"Okay, but not regularly, right? If we're talking adding a whole floor—"

Tim shook his head. "No, not regularly. Do one at a time until the cobwebs and top ten layers of dust are gone."

"What about your room there?"

"Nope, thanks, I'll take care of that myself. This'll do for now, though. Thanks very much."

After the caretaker left, Tim closed the bottom door and returned to his sanctuary. He thought his effort to maintain privacy in this room might seem a bit obsessive, but so be it. He was happy to have it, had invested some thought and money into carving it out for himself, and he wasn't going to expose it to the staff of *The Times*.

Now he had added an ante-room, creating a suite. How cool was that? It reminded him of Sherlock Holmes' "quarters" on Baker Street.

Indeed, there was some similarity, though he was lacking a Watson to listen to his theories, and also a Mrs Hudson, their landlady, to announce his visitors and bring up his tea. Never mind, he'd manage.

His goal for the year was to delve into matters of interest in the town and area. If he could only resolve this thing about that woman on the trail, he could get on with that.

He felt that a resolution was close, maybe even imminent. That call from Sally from the ambulance was disturbing. He had eliminated hypothermia as a factor. Why? No water. He lifted the cover sheet on the map and looked closely at the area behind the mobile home: no pond, no swamp. Was there a well? The topographical map contained various symbols, most of which meant little to him. There was a tiny circle behind the mobile at the edge of the wooded area. Could be a well. One shouldn't have to guess about that.

Sally asserted that Miss was suffering from hypothermia as a fact. A fact! Facts had been very hard to come by. He could plant a flag in this one. If this was a fact, then everything else would have to lead to it or follow from it, perhaps not directly; perhaps there would be more than one step, but nothing he considered from here on could be contrary to this fact: she was suffering from hypothermia.

He started a new sheet, entitled *HYPOTHERMIA*, and wrote *WELL* at the top of the left-hand column. Was this how it should go? Maybe not. If she got hypothermia and the source was unknown, that's how it should go; the well could be one source, but should he keep looking for others? On the other hand, if he *knew* she had fallen in the well—jumping to that conclusion just for a moment—then the well would be the prime topic, and he should look for contributing factors, such as why she'd been there and did she know the well was there and why did she get in the well and how did she get from the well to the darn trail, anyway?

He decided to make a sheet titled *WELL*, and work both angles until the boxes on one contained more good answers than the other. He taped both to the wall, careful to add a blotter sheet behind them.

James phoned. "I've got your prints, Mister Brown. I think you'll like them. Would you like me to pick up a coffee for you? I'm at the drive-thru now."

Tim glanced at his watch: noon already. Time really did fly when your curiosity was being teased. He shook the thermos: empty.

"Sure, James, that'd be great. Large steeped tea, please, black, no sugar. I have a sandwich here, but pick up something for your lunch if you like. I'll reimburse you."

"It's my turn to pay. Be there in a jif."

"Good. Come right up. Your code's still valid."

James was shaping up. Had he been too hard on him about shoddy reporting? Or had that scolding helped him focus on his work? Asking Tim for leads had been a smart move. Gutsy. It seemed like it would be good for Tim, anyway.

~

"Gee, that was quick!"

"Yes, well, I don't really enjoy sitting in a place decorated with cobwebs like a Hallowe'en display, and I imagine you don't, either, so I got John to give it a lick and a promise, and bring some chairs. I found this table for our coffees."

"Uh-oh. Miss Fong will be after you for that."

"She will? Why?"

"It's hers. She brought it in so we wouldn't be leaving stuff on the floor when we're taking stuff out of the stationery cabinet. That's where you found it, isn't it?"

"Guilty as charged! Good eye, James. I'll bring something in from home, then. Thanks for the coffee. Let's get to work. What've you got?"

James handed the photographs to Tim one by one, and pointed out what he'd noticed at each.

The interior of the trailer, shot from the door, looked like raccoons lived there, and perhaps they did; but raccoons didn't hang the wash on a clothesline. The back yard, shot from the lane, was a nondescript area of lumpy snow. But under the trees, as seen from the doorstep and then from the back yard, there did seem to be a black hole. Successive photos, each taken a few steps closer to the mystery object, revealed more detail, until the photographer seemed dangerously close. It definitely was an old well; the prints revealed the rock lining where the covering boards had been pushed aside. It was very dark inside. Several boards, apparently rotten, were broken.

Tim lifted his head and blinked. "These are fantastic, James. I'm not comfortable with you getting so close to that hole, though."

"I used the zoom. Don't worry, I wasn't interested in falling in cold water—not a second time." He glanced at Tim. "I let my camera do the risky stuff."

"Good. What's in the rest?"

"These are that path I was telling you about. See, it's open there between the trees. Could be a path."

"Were there any—did you see any tracks in there? Footprints?"

"Lemme see." James took back the photo. "I guess I was looking at the trees, looking for an opening. I can't remember if it was used or not. Sorry."

"No problem. When were you there, James?"

"Yesterday. I went over right after you mentioned it."

"Are you free right now to go again?"

"Sure. What do you want me to do?"

"Not sure. I'm going with you. We'll see when we get there. Bring that camera. I'll be down in ten minutes. Oh, take back this chair you brought up. These are all I need up here. Mum's the word about Miss Fong's table."

Tim was particularly intrigued by the photo of the path through the trees. He tried to place it on the map. Of course, a path wouldn't be marked unless it was an official right-of-way of some kind, but a local shortcut such as The Guy had mentioned was entirely possible.

Correction: Guy hadn't mentioned anything. Every word he'd 'said' was a figment of Tim's own fertile imagination. "Give yourself the credit," Tim said aloud. "The shortcut was a hunch. Now, it seems, there really is a path. Congratulations, me."

It wasn't where he'd expected, though. As he scrutinized the map, he saw that the mobile was not parallel to the lane it was on, as most houses were, but angled slightly, with the doorstep closer to the lane than the other end. So, if one stood with the trailer at one's back and followed the path, one might come out a few steps farther along the trail than Tim had been. If he could find that end of the path, he should be able to walk back through to the mobile home—avoiding the dangerous open well which was in desperate need of a solid cover.

He put the thermos in his backpack, locked the office door and the door at the bottom of the stairs. James was waiting for him in the reception area—and so was Elaine Fong. She was grinning widely and holding out her hand.

"My table, please," she said.

"Busted! James, did you squeal?"

"No, he didn't. I knew it had to be you. No one else would dare. It's very useful where it was." She shook her hand at Tim as though she was demanding that he hand over a candy bar.

"I'll put it back tomorrow, I promise. I'm sure I have something similar at home. We're on our way to—we have to go now. Gotta run. C'mon, James!" The two men laughed as they escaped.

James offered his sporty four-wheel drive, and Tim was happy to accept. It was rare that he was a passenger in any vehicle and this one looked like fun.

James took them to the highway, where the stiff suspension and rag roof made it a rough, noisy ride. *More fun to look at than to ride in*, Tim decided.

They took the Blockhouse exit, and he directed James to park near the trail entrance. There had been enough traffic on the trail since the snow on Wednesday that it was relatively easy to walk along if they watched where they stepped. Frozen footprints were as treacherous underfoot as stones.

Tim stopped at the spot where he had encountered the people. He asked James to take a photo of that place with the big tree trunk in the shot. Then they walked slowly on, past that place, looking into the brush for an opening that could be a shortcut back to the old trailer on the next lane.

"Here it is, Mister Brown! Look!"

He looked. There was a path through the trees, a path in the air, anyway. It was difficult to know what it was like on the ground, as it was elevated above the trail just enough that they couldn't see.

"Much as I don't want to do this, James, let's go have a look for footprints."

"No problem!" James leapt up on a boulder and promptly slipped off.

"Careful! We don't need another injury. Are you okay?"

"Ouch. Yeah, ow. I'll live. You be careful, now. Here, let me give you a hand." James reached his hand out to Tim.

"Maybe there's another way," Tim said. "Hang on."

He walked another couple steps beyond the boulder and found a place where the cut through the trees was obscured but there was a lower path leading to it. He stepped off the trail and easily walked through to the cut, farther in than where James was sitting on the boulder, rubbing his ankle.

"Can you take a couple photos here, James? One looking that way, and one this way, and then one from the trail looking in. I want to do that before we put our own footprints in the snow."

James did as he was asked. Tim was quite enjoying having a sidekick who had a nifty camera. He tried not to enjoy watching his young sidekick knock himself about as he had done. Going outdoors wasn't supposed to be injurious every time, was it? At least, if either of them was injured this afternoon, the other could go for help.

"Now, James, it is my theory that this path is a shortcut leading somewhere, though I cannot think where or why. Who would want to get to an abandoned and stinky mobile home in a hurry?"

James turned around and looked from the path toward the trail. "Maybe not to go that way, Mister Brown. Maybe to go this way." He pointed across the trail, and Tim turned to look. Not far away was the secondary road from Blockhouse to South River, visible beyond the corner of the building that housed the convenience store.

"Oh, for heaven's sake," Tim said. "I am certainly a townie, James. I think I expected all streets, roads, trails, and paths to intersect each other at right angles. It is a well-known fact that the shortest distance between two objects is a straight line, but that straight line doesn't have to be parallel to the earth's lines of latitude and longitude—and nobody would clamber over a huge boulder if they could go around it—no insult intended."

"Whatever you said, Mister Brown. I'm not insulted. This is one of the most interesting days I've had since I joined the newspaper. Which way d'you want to go now?"

Tim smiled. He felt the same as James, and his own date of hire went a lot further back.

"Let's stick to this side of the trail, and go see about that well you mentioned. But listen—" Tim reached out to grab James' shoulder. "Do not, under any circumstances, fall in that well. Got me?"

"Don't you worry. I have no intention of falling down a well." James limped ahead. "I've already got my war wound for the day."

"Good. I mean, good that you're careful. Wait up, now, James. What do you see on this path? Are there footprints? Is anyone using it?"

Both men bent over to examine the path. It *was* a path, seemingly made by the passing of feet over time. It zigged and zagged around rocks and stumps, but they could see that occasional branches had been sawn or chopped from trees to clear the way, and a few saplings had been cut down and pushed aside, otherwise the woods would have been as impenetrable there as they were everywhere.

"Talk to me, James. It looks like people created this path, only people, not a lands and forest crew or it would be fifteen metres wide with ditches, right? Do you see any fresh cuts, or has it been like this for a while?"

"Hmm. No fresh cuts. This is fun. I haven't ever done this kind of investigating before. There's some tracks here. Deer, I'd say. This'd be a perfect place to hang out in hunting season."

"Yeah, until you fired your gun. Then it would be a perfect place to get arrested. You might bag yourself some hikers, though, or someone taking a shortcut to the store."

"Ha-ha, yeah, serve 'em right for wanting a bag of chips."

"Another thing to look for, James: let me know if you see any piece of clothing in here, like shoes or a jacket."

"Nothing like that so far. No footprints since Wednesday, either." James stopped. "Actually, since yesterday, right? It was still snowing some in the morning, right? Maybe not as much in here, under all these trees, but still, only one day ago. Maybe nobody was out of whatever that store sells in the last twenty-four hours. Or they drove. It's slippery in here now, icy, right? I'd drive around if it was me, of course, but not everyone has a hot rod. You know, I always wondered: if the snow doesn't fall as heavy under the trees, where does it go? Does it say, 'Can't fall down there, gotta keep driftin' along?'"

Tim thought James was a little over-curious, but he was engaged, so he didn't criticize.

They proceeded slowly through the narrow path, James chattering, but both with their eyes on the trail, looking for clues to they knew not what. They emerged from the trees behind the trailer, the open well gaping not more than two giant steps from where they stood.

"Holy!" James said. "I didn't expect to see it this close. Careful, Mister Brown!"

"*You* be careful." They grabbed each other's arms like Hansel and Gretel in the forest, then quickly separated and stepped a giant step away from the well.

"That is one dangerous thing right there," Tim said.

"Yup."

Then James re-traced his giant step toward it.

"James!"

"Don't worry. I'm not going any closer."

He lifted the camera strap from around his neck, and lowered its cover. He fiddled with the buttons—Tim could hear its tiny electric motor whining as the lens moved in and out. Then James held it high above his head, pointed it down into the well, and pressed the shutter button. He lowered his arms, pressed more buttons, and showed Tim the pictures on the screen on the back of the camera.

They couldn't see how deep the well was, how far to the bottom, but the water level was close to the surface, with only a few rows of icy stones showing above the water. It was an old well, judging by the stone construction and the boards that had covered it, now rotted and scattered. It was dark down there, and the dark water reflected the puffy clouds in the sky.

Tim looked up. The sky was uniformly overcast. No puffy clouds visible.

"James, is there a flash on that fancy camera? Can you take that shot again, with the flash?"

"Sure can." James pushed more buttons, raised his arms, aimed, and pressed the shutter. The camera flashed, the shutter clicked, and he presented the screen again.

"What the heck's that?"

Tim sighed. "Pretty sure it's a woman's jacket, James. But it's just her jacket and not her, thank God. Caught on a nail, most likely, or a piece of broken board. She must have been terrified. Save those pictures, James. We'll put them to good use."

"Can you fill me in on what this is all about?"

"Soon. But first, we need to prevent actual drownings. This hellhole has to be covered, but not by us. I bet it is super icy right over there, and another person could slip on the ice and slide right in through those old boards. That would hurt. Anybody going by could slide in, or a dog. Do you see anything we might use to close it off? The municipality will have to fix it, but we can't leave it. It's been open—what—almost two weeks already. Some dogs are possibly already down there."

"Maybe we could push these boards—"

"No way. They're rotten, and those stones don't look too stable either. The ground around it is frozen, but it still might collapse. I bet the whole thing was covered in leaves, rotting away for years, and nobody knew it was there. Gosh, what to do?"

Tim looked up at the mobile home and the sagging clothesline. "Come on, James. Let's take in the washing."

They carefully skirted the well and trudged up the driveway to the doorstep. They removed the remaining items from the clothesline and knotted them together to make a line. The knots took up quite a bit of length, so they looked around for something to add. Tim walked cautiously into the yard below the line and kicked the snow. The clothing items he had seen two weeks ago were all there. The frozen legs of pants and sleeves of shirts that had fallen provided enough length now to tie one end to the last slim tree at the edge of the woods where the trail came out—but how to anchor the other end?

James wrestled the little red and yellow plastic trike out of the snow. They tied the line to it and pulled it tight to serve as a warning for anyone coming by.

"Okay, let's go. We have some calls to make. What time is it?"

It was mid-afternoon already. Much had been discovered, and much had to be reported.

They hurried through the path back to James' adventure-wagon, a little more quickly than they had come, though James was still favouring his ankle.

In the vehicle, Tim said, "Let's go over to the building supplies store first. I have an idea."

They went in and Tim led the way to the order counter. He asked for Donnie Isnor, the volunteer fireman he had dealt with about his door order. Donnie was busy, could someone else help him?

"Well, I need to speak to a volunteer fireman. There's no fire, it's not an emergency, but there's a very great danger."

Four heads turned, and two of them came over to see what Tim was talking about. An open well, you say? Did someone fall in? Someone fell in two weeks ago? We answered a call about it? Is it on private property or municipal property?

Tim didn't know the answer to this question, but he knew jurisdiction might have something to do with whether the fire department could do anything about the danger, so he replied that he didn't know, thought it was maybe both, right on the line.

The men said they'd report it, but Tim wasn't convinced. If he called it in as an emergency, a crew might be dispatched, but not if nobody was actively splashing around in the well. It was after three o'clock Friday afternoon. Few work crews would turn out on a new project at this hour.

"James, would you mind if I drive while you make some calls? The county must cover that well. I'm nothing to nobody, but you're a reporter for *The Times*, so use your title."

"Sure, Mister Brown, but it's stick shift. Can you—"

"Oh, right. Nope. Just keep your attention on the road while talking, then."

James gave an impressive performance on his mobile phone. He reached the Public Works Department for the county (phone number stored in his phone's memory) and told them he had already called the local fire department, but they'd said they needed the county to take remedial action before they dared visit the site. He was passed on to the manager, and informed that gentleman that one person had nearly died there already, and there was "some evidence" that another person or animal may have gone through the well cover and he would keep calling until the well was covered, and if it wasn't, and since they now knew about it, there might be charges of negligence, which would make for interesting reading in the newspapers.

Tim enjoyed listening in, even though James skated on factual thin ice a few times. They pulled up in front of *The Times* building, and Tim was happy to get out to let James drive right back to Blockhouse, to meet the Public Works crew, who had promised to bring a heavy steel plate to cover the well temporarily. The Manager said he would contact the Fire Department after he had seen the site.

~

Back in his private office, Tim was happier than he'd been since he didn't know when. This was a different kind of happy from the usual. He had supposed and guessed and surmised a lot of things, and he had discovered that some of them were true! He had taken James Olsen along, and he turned out to be a bloodhound on the scent of a story, well-suited to chase a worthy quarry, as he had said about himself.

What was that about being judgy? One should not.

Speaking of judgy, he knew he didn't have a good resolution to the nature and purpose of the character known as Guy, but he wasn't ready yet to dismiss him as a simple passer-by. Sally had told Tim to keep looking. Was there a sinister element involving

Guy?

He checked the time: after four. Should he go home and come back tomorrow? The big sheets of paper were downtown now, taking up an impressive amount of wall space. He felt he could think better, maybe see patterns better if he worked with them rather than a little notebook.

He was hungry, but addressing that would take too much time, so he got a glass of water from downstairs, and served himself two sticks of gum. Granola bars would come in handy for times like this.

He lost himself in a happy hour of adding, deleting, and moving items on the grids until his phone rang.

"We got 'er done, Mister Brown." James sounded exultant. "They came right over with their truck and a piece of that metal they lay down when they're missing a manhole cover. It was getting dark, but they drove in where I showed them, and they could see it in their headlights. Good thing there was crusty snow down to slide it on or we'd never have got it there."

"We? Don't tell me you were helping?"

"Sure. I had to. Those two old guys couldn't lift much."

"James, that's far beyond the duty of a reporter. You don't make the news, remember? You report it."

"Well, you said yourself it had to be covered, and everybody said it was dangerous. Oh, and the Fire Chief came over while we were there. They're gonna pump the well out tomorrow, in case anything or anybody might've fallen in. They wanted to know how I came to discover it, and I said I couldn't reveal my sources at this time. Pretty cool, eh?"

"Very cool, James. What time will they be there with the pumper?"

"Nine, I think. I'll be there to report. Will you?"

"Most likely. Come to think of it, absolutely!"

"Oh, and you'll like this: I told them about the stink in the trailer. I'm not sure who does what about that yet, probably county, but I'm pretty sure that thing'll be hauled away. I hope nobody's walking on the road when it goes by."

"Why's that?"

"There'll be a lot of wiggling stuff falling out of it. I doubt the floor is even solid. It'll have to go on a flatbed. But some poor schmuck'll have to check it out first, in case there's—you know—a body. Sure smells like it. One of the county guys woofed his cookies."

"Thank you, James. I get the picture. I could smell it when I was at the clothesline today. So, what now for you? Have you pitched this story to your editor yet?"

"I'm gonna call her now, but I wanted to check with you first. Can I tell her that you're involved in the story?"

"Nope, and thanks for asking. We are collaborating, it's true, but for two different purposes. You are a newspaper reporter looking for a story to tell. I'm just a curious citizen. If you say I'm in on it with you, it'll go to front page because of me and you'll wonder if you really earned the credit. So, make your pitch. She saw us leave the building together anyway, so there's no secret, but don't lead with my name. Use yours. Okay?"

"Sure, but you still have to tell me the back story, right? I really like working with you, Mister Brown. You can teach me a lot."

"I'm no teacher, James. But we did a good job observing and investigating today. How's your ankle?"

"It's okay. I have sports injuries worse than that all the time. So, about the back story?"

"Oh, right. I can fill you in tomorrow morning while we're watching the pumper action at the well. Take that marvellous camera. See you then."

Tim pumped his fist in the air. He felt the urge to sing, to dance a jig, to yell a victory yell. Because of James' desire to get a story, Tim would solve his, he was sure of it. The fire department would bring a pumper to that old well in the morning, and nothing drew a crowd like a fire truck pumping out a well. Oh yes, he was sure there'd be a crowd. And he, the Secret Observer, would observe that crowd. Residents of the tiny hamlet of Inner Blockhouse would be there and he hoped to recognize at least one person.

He stopped at his favourite fish and chips joint, and took home a

Highliner: two pieces of fish, extra fries, extra coleslaw, extra "Our Own" tartar sauce. He sang "Onward, Christian Soldiers" on the drive home, not especially for its words but for its ebullient mood. He danced a jig as he pulled the cork from a bottle of *Anticipation Blanc*. He ate the first half of his feast standing up, he was so happy with the day.

Was it still Friday? The day had started so long ago that he could hardly contain it all. And nothing had gone wrong. Was that setting the bar too low? He didn't think so. When one engages in new activities with new people in new environments, and a great good thing is set in motion, and nobody got hurt (much)—well, that was worth celebrating.

And Robert had been tickled to see his initial in the coffee foam. Life wasn't all big gestures and "marching off to war". One must win the peace, too.

February 20: Face in the crowd

Saturday

Tim sprang out of bed and turned off the alarm before it rang. This was going to be another Very Interesting Day, starting with something very interesting to observe. He was thinking about the day, brushing his teeth, when he pointed the toothbrush at the man in the mirror and said, "No. No, no, no. No."

The crowd in Blockhouse that would be attracted by the fire department's truck had come to mind. Perhaps "crowd" was overstating it a bit, but he did expect some local residents to wander over to see what was going on, especially since the weather was simply dull and wouldn't force anyone to stay inside. Neighbours must wonder about the old trailer; perhaps they even knew the people who had lived there and now apparently didn't. More about that might be revealed this morning.

He was reviewing the scene when the idea came to him that he should dress to blend in with the crowd, and that led him to the quilted plaid jacket still in the trunk of his car, and a selection of things to wear on his head, all comfortable, none attractive. It wasn't attraction he'd be dressing for, but camouflage; and comfort too, of course, because standing around for a couple of hours in winter can give a person a chill.

Didn't he have anything warm but unremarkable? Other than the lightweight jacket he had worn the day he went hiking on the trail, he had a selection of long coats he wore to work or church. He'd stick out for sure in any of those, and he might be recognized in the jacket, though by whom he didn't know.

The man in the mirror suggested that he should take all options along—but not a topcoat—and make his choice once he was there. Tim shook the toothbrush at him again and made him promise that he would not get into any ridiculous situations simply because his identity might be obscured.

He boiled an egg, made toast, and asked Gloria for a cappuccino. He wanted the caffeine, but decided against making a larger volume of coffee. He had learned on a previous outing that downing a lot of liquid prior to an observing adventure could send him looking for a place to relieve the pressure. Since he was hoping for curious onlookers, that would be ill-advised.

The grocery list had grown through the week. He and Robert had not discussed hosting any guests to Sunday dinner, which suited him fine. He'd shop for something they could cook together, or maybe they'd go out for dinner.

He had no task this morning other than to observe, so there was no need for any special tools such as binoculars or a flashlight, but they were in the car anyway.

Before he left the house, Tim looked around for a small occasional table or plant stand to serve as a place to rest coffee cups in the ante-room to his office. Several candidates were in the parlour; they'd been there so long he rarely noticed them. He chose one, a little larger than Elaine's and better suited for his purpose. He moved the vase that had sat on it for years to the mantel, took the table to the car, and set off to Blockhouse to see what he could see.

He was early. He intended to cruise around until the action started. He was glad his car was a nondescript make, made even more so by the dried salt and accumulated road dirt on it. His friend and South River's mayor, Garland Greene, also a car dealer, had been urging him to trade up to a big flashy truck. It was a nice vehicle, no question about that, but it would've stuck out like a sore thumb in this setting. His Aunt Stella always owned vehicles that cost more than some homes in this area, but she knew how to wear an accessory like that. His own not-cheap sedan suited him.

He rolled past the fire department, and was excited to see the big doors were open. He cruised around Mahone Bay's waterfront, then drove back to Blockhouse. The big pumper was out in the yard. He drove to the lane past the not-mobile home, and saw that the rope of diapers that he and James had put around the open well was down, replaced by yellow warning tape. That was good: it would prevent another accidental dunking in the well, and would attract the attention of any locals passing by. It was impossible to see if anyone had used the shortcut path because of yesterday's footprints and tire tracks from the municipality's works department.

He turned and drove to the street leading to the homes in this hidden village. There was no sign of life, but it was not yet nine o'clock on a Saturday morning, so anyone who had been working or at school all week would still be home in their pyjamas if they had a choice.

He heard the rumble of the fire truck's big engine as it arrived at the lane. Volunteer firemen were standing around in their gear, waiting for something.

Tim parked as far from the action as possible, where he might still see any bystanders. He opened the trunk and brought the garment bag into the passenger seat. He selected the tuque, pulled it low on his head, and checked in the rear-view mirror. With forehead and ears covered, he barely recognized himself. He slouched down behind the wheel, and kept watching.

Next to arrive was James Olsen, no hiding in his brightly-coloured sports vehicle. He jumped out, the camera around his neck and a notepad in his hand, and approached the fire crew. A truck from the municipality came next, and then everyone moved toward the well. James hung back and aimed his camera.

Soon, the workers returned to their vehicles, and the noise increased from air brakes, back-up beepings, and diesel engines revving as they manoeuvred the pumper into position. Tim looked up and down the streets. No spectators yet. He caught glimpses of James, who seemed to be looking for someone, every now and then.

Tim couldn't see, but heard, the sound of the pumper engine working. Still no onlookers in sight, but he couldn't wait in the car any longer. He grabbed the lumberjack jacket, put it on as he got out of the car, and slowly approached to get a better look at the action.

Everyone's attention was focused on the well, where water poured from the hose and drained into the ground under the trees. He kept to the far side of the lane, hands in his pockets. Nobody paid any attention to him.

Why were there no spectators? Wouldn't anybody living nearby be curious about what was going on back there at the edge of the woods? Perhaps they weren't nearby enough to bother.

Maybe they already knew, a possibility he hadn't thought of before. Maybe the phones had been ringing since the municipal works crew had come to lay the metal cover over the well and put up the yellow tape. Maybe even his and James' diaper-line had started the talk.

Oh well, not all was lost. The well was being pumped out, and he hoped nothing sinister would be revealed in it when the water level reached bottom.

He saw James put his phone to his ear, and a few seconds later, his own phone vibrated in his pocket. He didn't answer it. James evidently hadn't recognized him, standing not fifty feet away, so that was one small satisfaction, but he was disappointed that nobody for whom he wore his simple disguise had appeared.

Wait. Someone was down there near the well, not wearing fire department gear or works department coveralls. How did he get there? Oh, for heaven's sake—through the path, of course. Tim stepped forward and stopped: he knew the crews wouldn't allow him to get closer because it was too close to the well.

The sun was beginning to break through the clouds, putting whoever was standing in the path in dark shade. Tim thought he— it was a man—could be the Guy! He needed to get closer, to talk with him. But how?

There was one other way. Tim turned and shuffled away, hoping to appear uninterested, until he was out of sight behind the parked trucks. Then he broke into a jog, down the paved road and onto the trail. He pulled his phone from his pocket and hit James' number as he ran.

"Hello? Mister Brown, where are you, I've been calling you. The fire truck's here."

"James." Tim was puffing. Talking on the phone while jogging wasn't easy. "Listen. There's a man in the path near the well. Do you see him?"

"A man where? Oh, there he is. Yeah. Who's that? What's the matter—are you running? D'you want me to—"

"Don't do anything. Don't even—*wheeze*—look at him. I want to talk to him. If he comes toward you—*gasp*—try to keep him there, talk to him, ask him where he lives, anything—*wheeze*—till I get there. Gotta go."

He had reached the path already. It was slightly uphill and running in there was risky, so he slowed his pace and tried to catch his breath. In another minute he could see the man, still standing at the entrance to the path, watching the very interesting goings-on.

The idling diesel engines were quite loud, so he wouldn't hear Tim coming up behind him. That could be a problem. He didn't want to frighten the man and have him run away, so he waited a few paces back in the path.

His phone vibrated again. The man didn't hear the buzz above the roar, so Tim carefully took it out of his pocket, pushed the button and quietly said, "Yup." He could see James up by the lane, phone to his ear, looking at the ground, good fellow.

"Mister Brown," James whispered over the machine noise, "there's someone else behind him there now. Two of 'em. You want me to detain them both if I can?"

"Yup." Tim hung up, now convinced that his disguise was impenetrable.

Finally, the pump shut off, reducing the racket enough that Tim ventured to approach the man. "Excuse me," he said loudly, from some distance behind the fellow. "S'cuse me," from a few steps closer, then again "Hi. Excuse me, sorry, coming through." This time the man heard him and jumped to one side, almost slipping on the ice underfoot.

"Oh, hey there, sorry I didn't mean to startle you—hey, haven't I seen you somewhere before?"

Tim was certain—not absolutely, but quite—that this was The Guy from two Saturdays ago. He was wearing an oversized parka, not the nondescript sweater he had on then, or at least it wasn't visible now. Tim had been quite distracted by the hypothermic woman on the trail, and had scarcely paused to observe the man as Sherlock Holmes might have done, other than to observe that he was not very helpful.

"Weren't you on the trail two weeks ago when that girl fell there?"

The man looked past Tim into the thick brush, but not at Tim.

"I was there, too, remember? I helped carry her out to the ambulance."

The Guy turned away to watch the men at work again. Tim stepped closer. "I'm not accusing you of anything. I wondered if you remember any details about how she came to be lying on the trail. Did you find her first?"

"I like the fire truck but I don't like the sirens," the man replied, and Tim had his answer in a flash.

"Do you? I like the truck too. Would you like to see it?"

The man nodded vigorously.

"Mind if I take your arm? It's slippery here."

"It's slippery here," the man echoed, and allowed Tim to guide him to their left, circling away from men and machinery. As they approached the lane, James came toward them with his hand up, ready to invent a reason why they should stop until Mister Brown should appear. Tim stopped, reached in his pocket and hit Redial on the phone. James' phone rang, and when he answered it he heard himself say hello and recognized Tim's wide grin.

"My friend here would like to see the fire truck, right, uh, sorry, what's your name, please? My name's Tim."

"My name is Walter."

"Hi, Walter, this is James. James, can you ask your pals to let Walter sit in the fire truck for a few minutes?"

James, gaping with surprise at seeing Tim as he presently appeared, meekly escorted Walter to the gleaming fire truck. Tim heard one of the volunteers say "Hey, Wally," and then they boosted Walter up into the cab.

Evidently Wally-Guy *was* known to authorities, just not for the reasons Tim had speculated about. Poor Wally fled from sirens because he didn't like the noise.

James returned to photograph more of the action. The works crew were lifting a heavy cement cover into place. In a watery patch nearby were two muddy shoes and the puffy white jacket that Tim had mistaken yesterday for reflected clouds. Nothing else, no human or other remains, thank goodness.

Tim phoned James again. "Can you get a look in the pockets of that jacket? Is there any money or ID? It belongs to the girl they were called here to rescue two weeks ago."

He watched James negotiate his way through the group. Heads shook, but James managed to convince someone that they should check the pockets. They found something. James aimed his camera at the hand of the man who held whatever it was.

James turned toward Tim, and Tim gave a thumbs-up to signal that all was good, no further action needed. He phoned James to tell him he'd meet him at the office.

At the car, Tim removed the bulky plaid coat and the tuque, and smoothed down his haystack hair. He picked up two large coffees at the drive-thru, and half a dozen assorted donuts. He'd wanted only four, but he was told that if he ordered six he'd save the tax, so he took six. It was curious that a donuts vendor was permitted to promote tax evasion. Or avoidance, likely, but still.

~

The little occasional table was perfect, positioned between the two chairs in the empty room. The grouping in front of the window was a bit austere, but Tim liked the look. It saved him from having meetings in the hallway. He placed the bag of donuts and the coffees on the table. That looked more hospitable.

He returned Elaine Fong's plant stand to the storage room, and was surprised at the pile of stationery supplies that had accumulated on the floor where the stand had been. They didn't only need something to put things on while digging for other things, they needed a bigger cabinet. Or fewer supplies.

What a morning! He hardly knew where to start, so many things had happened—things within things. He knew he'd be writing notes on these few hours for some time to come. He had expected the noise of the fire truck pumper to bring out a crowd, but there was no crowd. The homes in the little village weren't right next door to the dead-end lane, and the highway wasn't far off, so perhaps residents had learned to ignore truck noises.

He had hoped to see at least one familiar face, possibly two: the victim, whom he'd named Miss on the grid, and Guy, the runaway witness. He wasn't surprised, really, that Miss hadn't been drawn to truck noise. He didn't know if she was connected with that odiferous old mobile home or not, but his hunch said not. Just because a path goes past a dwelling doesn't mean that a path-user lives there.

It was clear that nobody was living in it now, though the question still remained whether something or somebody had died, and was still dead, in there. Anyway, he assumed that Miss was okay, since she had been discharged from the hospital. She hadn't been motivated to come and fall in the well a second time. Nobody else had fallen in there either; he was relieved about that.

They did find something in that jacket pocket, perhaps a wallet with some ID. James's photograph of it would be interesting.

How about James and his wonderful camera with unlimited capacity? He could shoot at will, as Tim had seen him doing, and examine each shot for details later. He briefly considered getting himself such a camera, but he'd hold off on that. Previously, he'd hand an occasional roll of film to the newspaper's own photographer, who would develop the photos in their darkroom. They had modernized production some time ago so reporters had their own digital photos now, but he hadn't followed how to get the photos out of the camera. It involved a computer, not a darkroom, and he was somewhat computer-averse, happy to remain ignorant as long as it was someone else's job to run the process.

So James had photographed all the action at the well, including the Guy—now known as Wally—appearing at the edge of the woods, and then a tall Mystery Man coming up the path behind him. Tim thought this was the funniest thing. He was grateful that the garb had disguised him, but he always assumed that his height alone was a giveaway.

People weren't all that observant, he knew, since he struggled to be more observant himself and found it challenging. Perhaps it wasn't observation skills at all. Maybe people saw only the things that made them curious. And maybe curiosity came from interest, unless it was trained to be otherwise.

So Guy-Walter-Wally had behaved exactly as he should be expected to, once you realized that he wasn't capable of adult thought or action. Tim felt a twinge of guilt about having suspected him of malfeasance on the trail, but how could he have known otherwise? Yes, he'd been judgy, but wasn't that everyone's default setting? He supposed it was one of the outer rings of prejudice, but that's how people were wired, wasn't it, to be able to pick out friend from foe without having to learn a person's whole history first, to avoid making fatal errors?

Would Sherlock have deduced that Wally was mentally deficient —whatever his condition was—in the fast action of the life-threatening crisis on the trail, bing-bang-boom? Unlikely. Given the nineteenth-century times in which Sherlock was plying his trade as the "world's only consulting detective," he and his author had done well to be as non-judgmental as they had been.

But Tim could see that a hasty attempt to categorize a person was a kind of conclusion without proof, and Sherlock had ridiculed it. This was a worthy topic for delving and he'd think more about it once this current preoccupation was cleared up, which he sensed would be very soon.

James called to say he was on his way and Tim told him to come right up. He took both coffees downstairs to boost their temperature in the lunchroom microwave, and returned to the ante-room to wait. The sun was still shining, and the slice of sunshine that came in the windows at the back of the building carried considerable warmth. These were nice rooms, too nice to be unused. He vaguely recalled some issue with the building inspector or fire marshal or insurance company about the safety of people using them, maybe due to the steep and narrow stairs and only one exit. That was back in his mother's day, when the value of real estate wasn't what it was now. Perhaps he'd look into some renovations to bring the second floor up to code and get some use out of it. They were already heating it, and heat was definitely not cheap.

James didn't phone a second time, but he did knock on the door at the bottom of the stairs even though Tim had left it ajar.

"Enter!"

"Oh hey, coffee and donuts, great! I'm starved!"

"I bet you are. Help yourself. There's an assortment in there, the tax-cheat special. Anything happen after I left?"

Tim and James amicably compared notes on the morning from their different perspectives. They laughed at James' account of the anonymous "local" hanging around in the lane, and showing up again in the pathway behind Wally. James clicked through the images stored in the camera to show Tim the shots of himself in disguise.

"That hat changes your face completely," he said, "but the jacket —with respect—is so uncharacteristic of you that nobody would ever guess it was you in it. It's a perfect disguise. I'm going to look for something like that for myself."

"Do that, and let's keep mine a secret, okay? It's a good story but you can't tell it. I might want to use it again."

The existence of the path had been pure speculation on Tim's part, based on an imagined story by Guy. Guy was really Wally, who couldn't express himself well enough to describe the path or the old well other than to say, 'There!' and point. Wally most likely became a character in the story because of timing. He simply came upon Miss, who had collapsed on the cold trail, suffering from hypothermia.

Tim gave James the briefest of briefings about his innocent walk on the Old Train Line Trail two weeks ago. He told about portaging Miss, downplaying his heavy-duty carrying. He omitted the part about loaning his pants and getting them back, and about failing to hear from the RCMP, and about getting info from Sally. James didn't need any of that. What good would it do to dredge up all that for a story about a dangerous well?

They discussed what the story angle would be. As reporters, they both knew that few news stories are immutable. This story, on the bones of it, was about an old well, with a wooden cover which may have been legal when it was put there, who knows how long ago. That cover had itself become hidden by leaves that fell every year, and the leaves and rain and snow had rotted it. Perhaps a whole generation had passed; maybe nobody even knew the well was there at all any more. Meanwhile, a path was worn through the thick brush by many feet and a hatchet, to save a few steps to the trail or the convenience store beyond. Then one day, a local passerby (name and gender withheld), was entering this trail, perhaps going too quickly over the snow on ice, and slipped and slid onto the rotted well-cover and broke through into the icy water. If there was a skim of ice on the water it would not have stopped the passerby from plunging to the bottom.

"How deep was it?" Tim asked.

"About six or seven feet, I'd say."

"Over her head, then, but not by much. Enough to drown her. What a desperate struggle she must have had. Was that her jacket, I wonder? What did they take out of the pocket?"

"Not sure. I can show you. Look here." James flicked through the picture files again. He turned the camera's screen toward Tim. It showed the hand of the fireman who had searched the pockets, holding something like a business card.

"Did it have any printing on it?"

"We couldn't make out anything. Just some smudges. Weird."

"Who has it now?"

"Um, that fireman, I guess."

"Nothing else? Money?"

"Nope."

"James, can you call right now about that card or whatever it is? Tell them to lay it out on a paper towel and don't touch it until it dries. Say it might be evidence in a police matter."

"Really? Okay. But there wasn't anything readable on it."

James found a contact in his phone's directory. When he completed that call, Tim said, "What did you do, store the entire phone book in there?"

"Yeah, pretty much, when I had lots of time on my hands. But this is the first time I've had a story to use all these numbers on."

They continued reviewing what they had seen, sharing observations, and discussing what could be told about it as long as the donuts lasted. Because he was writing for a newspaper, James needed to present it as news. But because the newspaper was a weekly, the news didn't need to be new, or urgent. It was similar to covering a burning building: there was interesting action, the story could be compelling depending on how it was told, but fires were usually cold by the time the paper was for sale in the stores.

"What's the latest on the old trailer? Will the works department be taking care of that?"

"I guess. Boy, that's a job I wouldn't want. They have to get an inspector to go in to check it first, and try to find the tenant or owner. Then some other people and equipment come to dismantle it. What a mess."

"I agree. Keep on top of it, James. They won't phone you to let you know what they're doing. Some of them won't want you there, so you should keep your eye on the site a couple times a day, if you don't have a local buddy. This is feeling like a two-part story, dealing with two kinds of danger from abandoned properties. Who in the county is responsible for dangerous properties, un-covered wells, maggoty kitchens? Is it the county, even? Or public health? Was there ever a permit for that well? Does anyone check on dug wells? The thing is, you don't have to get all the answers right away, or ever. You just have to ask good questions, and see who squeaks. Okay? Now, if you're finished with me, I have some errands to do. If I can help, you know how to reach me, and I'd love to see some of those pictures. Can you print a few for me?"

"You sure you don't want to co-write this with me?"

"I just did. The rest is between you and your editor. She's wondering, I have no doubt, what parking-lot snow-pile she's going to have to feature on the front page this week. Go pitch a two-part story to her, with a photo spread inside, and then let her work on it with you. She has great instincts."

Tim whistled a hymn as he locked up. He was a good whistler and it sounded cheerful.

~

Tim popped into a salon for a long overdue haircut, and was in luck: the stylist he preferred was sweeping up from a client and could take him right away, she said, "Unless you want foils or special effects."

Tim assured her he didn't know what foils were but he'd appreciate a tidy head. She removed most of the hair that had been giving him a fright wig whenever he removed his tuque.

"Thanks," he said, "that looks much better."

"You're welcome. You are a handsome dude." She knew how to earn a good tip.

Saturday afternoon was not the most efficient time to get groceries if all you wanted to do was shop, as there was always at least one person or couple ready to lean on their cart and 'catch up', but he mostly enjoyed this impromptu socializing. Someone would wheel into the aisle sooner or later and that would be their signal to break it up and move along.

He couldn't settle on what to have for Sunday dinner. A roast...a chicken...steak... scallops—yes, fresh scallops on a bed of basmati rice. Oh, he could taste them now. The best scallops in the world came ashore locally; they were sweet, tender, and expensive. He picked up a generous portion.

For dessert, apple pie and ice cream were fail-safe and favourites. Finally, he bought vermouth to add to the butter in which the pillow-sized scallops would be sautéed, and a vintage white to drink with this fine feast.

He arrived home and put the groceries away. There was time for him to have a quick shower. He had perspired heavily due to his impromptu jog around Blockhouse this morning. Yes, he had been severely short of breath, but he did it and hadn't injured himself. Perhaps he wasn't a clumsy oaf after all.

His new haircut looked great in the steamy mirror as he towelled dry. *Not oaf-like at all, even without foils.*

While he waited for Robert to arrive, he wrote a few more lines in his notebook. He would return to the office and his grids of targets and topics on Monday, and he knew he would fill in or cross off many, as appropriate. He would check James' article to make sure he omitted what was necessary and included what was interesting.

Meanwhile, he was looking forward to taking the next thirty-six hours off.

February 21: Day of rest

Sunday

This was the First Sunday of Lent. The annual discussion of abstinence and sacrifice had begun earlier in the week. While Tim wasn't a stranger to having light and fluffy pancakes for dinner on Pancake Day as a nod to the ancient Hebrews' unleavened bread, he rarely remembered to do it. Nor had he seriously considered giving up anything for Lent's forty days.

At Saint John's United Church, the message from the pulpit was about abstaining from unkindness and other default behaviours, not from chocolate or wine. On a chilly morning in late February, this light touch was appreciated.

On the drive home after church, Tim mused that Lent seemed to come too soon after the avalanche of indulgences that was Christmas. "In December it was 'Get this and party that' and January was 'Pay up and be grateful' and now it's 'Give it all up'. Seems a bit passive-aggressive, doesn't it?"

"Sure does. The church matched its calendar to popular pagan events, thinking the way to beat them was to join them" Robert said, taking a page from one of his university lectures. "The pagans celebrated quite different things on those dates, so the Christian calendar had to adapt. It is a bit of a jumble, therefore. You don't follow it anyway, so don't fuss."

"You're right, but maybe I'd get credit for obedience if the order of things suited my modern habits better."

"Excellent thought! Call it the Church of Laissez-faire. Maybe I'll join, if it has good music."

When Tim revealed what he was planning for their dinner,

Robert clapped his hands in anticipation, and offered to clarify the butter and chop the parsley.

"Are you sure you're okay not to go out somewhere to eat? Or to go for a drive?"

"I might've said yes to either, but those scallops have given me a different focus. Let's just hang around here and have a normal day, can we? I have a little bit of work to do—not much—and we can talk, too, about whatever we like, you know, like if we lived together."

"Normal day? Lived together? Yes, please."

So they spent a quiet day. It was a rare time for them, abnormal, highly-prized, and delicious, including the re-baked apple pie. They savoured seconds of pie in front of the embers in the fireplace, accompanied by the soothing white-noise whispers from the new dishwasher in the kitchen.

February 22: Story elements

Monday

James had phoned twice on Sunday afternoon. The first time was to tell Tim that Elaine had accepted his story pitch, but that she was reluctant to allocate front page space plus an inside photo spread to it for this week's issue of *The Times*, let alone for two weeks running. Tim knew James wanted him to put in a good word on his behalf, not an unreasonable request, but it was too early in his sabbatical year to return to the job, no matter how briefly. Reporting this story through James was close enough. He knew—or expected—that Elaine would accede if he made a firm request on James' behalf, but he didn't think this story justified a management override. Perhaps it was because of his mother's deployment of that very tactic with him whenever it suited her that he resisted it.

"See it from her perspective," he had counselled James. "Ask yourself—heck, ask her, respectfully—what's blocking your way, and don't argue with her, but work on it. It's in her best interest for you to do well."

James was jubilant in the second call. She agreed to front page plus inside single page photo spread, and a strong 'maybe' for next week, depending on what he produced. He wanted to bring the draft over for Tim to read, and Tim was tempted to allow it, but his head was settled in his normal day with Robert by that time, so he deferred James to Monday morning.

"*Very* early Monday morning, like six-thirty early."

"What? I'm not even up then, Mister Brown. Why then?"

"Because I am up and will have been for some time. Come to my house. And bring your camera, please."

And so it was that soon after Robert departed, having enjoyed another monogrammed latté, James arrived, sleepy but on time. Tim welcomed him into the kitchen, prepared his choice of beverage from Gloria, even venturing an impromptu *J* in the foam, and they sat on the stools at the island while Tim read the article and looked over the excellent photographs.

"Did she agree to colour for the photos at all?"

"Oh, I didn't ask. Should I?"

"You should inquire, and push if she appears iffy, but not hard. I think she'll do it anyway. This one, and that one, they're both great. Composition, colour, focus, award-winning, really. I forget: did you study photography, James?"

"Yeah, a bit. I really like it. That's why I got this camera. Digital's where it's at, baby. I still take workshops whenever I see one."

"It shows. Good work. Keep it up. Now, about your writing."

"Not so good?"

"A little too good, maybe a bit hyper. Show, don't tell, remember. If something is bad or good, happy or sad, try to let your fine camera-work show someone portraying that. If you write that the crowd was excited, but everyone in the photo looks bored and there's only two people in the frame, you've written a lie. Pictures always win. Oh, and there's an unsubstantiated claim in your story. Do you know what it is?"

James scanned the pages. Tim put two slices of bread to toast, and brought them to the island with butter and jam.

"I don't see it."

"The jacket, James. You say it belongs to a victim. You don't know this."

"Yeah, but you said—"

"Uh-uh. What I said was conjecture on my part. Unless the Miss comes along to claim her jacket, it's a guess. Now, what am I to your story? Not *my* story, but the one you're telling here?"

"Um, a person walking by? A bystander in a tuque?"

"Correct. An unidentified bystander. What did I say about the jacket?"

"I think you said you thought it might be hers."

"And what does that mean, James, when somebody says they think something 'might be' something? Does it mean it *is*?"

"Oh, I get it. It means…it's a question?"

"Correct. It's in the same category as 'pretty sure'. You and I didn't spend much time working together before I went on leave, so you likely missed this bit, which I have lectured the staff on, many, many times: if you say you are 'pretty sure', you are not sure at all, so don't even say it. Here's a common sentence: 'I'm pretty sure the money's in my bank.' Work it out until you can say 'I have the money', and don't buy anything until you know. Got it?"

"Yeah, that makes sense, thanks. I learn something every day from you. I hope you'll come back to work soon."

"Please don't wish for that, not yet. Give me another ten months; maybe I'll be ready then. Anyway, the moral of the story before us is that you do not know whose jacket that is—although a *bystander* suggested he was *pretty sure* it belonged to someone *rumoured* to have fallen in that well, hence the broken cover. I know you want to tell a complete story, and you can't yet, but this one contains a mystery, and your readers will like a mystery. And so should you, as it makes a compelling argument for a follow-up if the mystery becomes solved, that is to say, proven. By the way, where is that piece of whatever it was you took out of the pocket?"

"Buddy at the fire department has it. I asked him to lay it out like you said."

"Can you get it from him today? Failing that, I'd be happy to go wherever to have a look."

"I'll get it. He thought I was crazy to ask about it, said he'd tossed it out but he could get it. There was nothing on it."

"Funny she'd be carrying a blank card, don't you think? Odd? Curious? I want to have a good look at the object itself, not just a photo."

"You said 'she', Mister Brown. So, d'you think it 'might have' belonged to the woman you saw?"

"Yes, James, I do. Pretty sure, anyway, ha-ha. I call it a hunch. Hunches hound me all day. I just wouldn't put them in print. It bites if they turn out to be wrong."

"Got it. Well, I better be going, Gotta revise this. Will you be at the office today?"

"Yup, going there very soon."

"Why do you go there when you could stay in your nice big home here?"

"Because here is where I live. There is where I think."

"Is that why you won't let anyone in? Everyone wonders what's in there."

"Really? Well, I'll tell you, and you can tell everyone: nothing."

"Truly?"

"Pretty much," Tim laughed. "Four walls and a window, a table, and a chair. Empty filing cabinet. When I try to think here, I'm surrounded by things that generate their own thoughts, like furniture, chores, memories, food. Downtown, I'm free to think the thoughts I need, about the project I'm working on. No external triggers. Simple."

As James was pulling on his boots, Tim asked, "Did you bring that fabulous camera?"

"Oh, yeah, I left it in the car. Yikes. It's not good for the screen to freeze. What did you want me to shoot?"

Tim stepped into his boots and followed James out to the driveway. "See my screen door with the big dent in it? I'd really appreciate a few good shots of that, if you don't mind. Insurance claim."

~

While the coffee pot dripped coffee for the thermos, Tim sat with his pocket calendar. This had come up in conversation yesterday. Formerly, he looked for what the coming week would demand of him. Robert had commiserated, as he, too, was a slave to his schedule.

But now, Tim could choose what he'd like to accomplish in the week. At the beginning of this year he'd found himself flailing about, with no goal or reward in sight. Recently he'd been inserting bits of both. Now he was leaving the house regularly, passing through places where he might have random human encounters to spark new thoughts, and going to the white room where those new thoughts might spark delving projects. He even knew when he would have breakfast at the Daisy Café. That felt more purposeful than simply taking refuge there, though the day he chose for that was definitely selected so he could take refuge from Mrs Aquino.

Today, he would review the grids and ensure that there was nothing more for him to do regarding the Incident on the Trail. He hoped that James' article would shake mysteries loose, if there were any. The RCMP hadn't bothered to speak with him, had closed the file, and might ignore the article or maybe even not link it to the trail incident.

Tim's lingering concern, and that of Sally the paramedic, he sensed, was that the Miss on the trail was the victim of an assault instead of—or as well as—an accident on a slippery path. That suspicion arose because she had bruises and scrapes, which falling in a well would explain. The Guy had been a suspect, too. That's where being "pretty sure" gets you. Wally wouldn't hurt anyone. He could, he was big enough, but it was unlikely that he would, and Tim didn't think there was any reason to go down that rabbit-hole. He felt that file was closed.

He was curious about the white card, though, simply because it existed. Who carries a blank card? It must have had something printed on it before it spent two weeks soaking in the well. It was unlikely that any legible markings remained, but he'd like to see. He went to the den to get the magnifying glass to take along: it might help.

The card was of interest also because of what wasn't in the pocket with it, namely a purse or even loose change. Who leaves home with only a blank card in her pocket and nothing else? Didn't that seem hasty? Or random? Or was she on her way to call a number on that card? Or to visit the person or place named thereon?

"All good questions, Tim. Don't be too curious, now," he counselled himself. "We'll have a look at it, and if something shows up, we'll follow it. If nothing, then nothing. Case closed. We'll have other topics to delve into."

He flipped back in the calendar to the beginning of the month.

What delving had he been thinking about then? Emergency procedures, for goodness' sake. He'd better come up with something more worthy of his time than safety manuals at the plant. As it turned out, he had spent some brief but poignant moments wondering about CPR, and hidden wells, and toxic garbage left in abandoned homes, but they weren't delving topics. He still hoped to explore something of universal value and interest.

Stella said that the region offered only as much depth as a cookie sheet. He was pretty sure she might be wrong, but not a hundred percent.

~

Tim spent a lovely morning in the thinking room. He decided to review this case from the beginning, asking or answering questions in all the boxes on the grids on the wall, drawing a line through any that were explained or eliminated. He had directed James to be absolutely certain of his statements before committing them to print, because once they were in print, presented as facts, the newspaper would be on the hook for them, and that was a risk Tim preferred to minimize. Here, out of public view, supposition, hunches, guesswork and the like were all welcome, but they had to be resolved at some point. He was pleased to see that the number of boxes with lines through them was growing.

At noon, he was ready for a snack bar with the final bit of coffee. It was so disappointing: dry, tasteless, and high in sugar and calories. How was this a health food, as the label implied? If he was stuck in a snowdrift, he guessed he'd be glad to have one handy, but not here, not in this room, the sanctuary of pure thought. He'd rather have a PB&J, or the stale donuts he remembered were in the room across the hall. Donuts had no food value at all, but nobody claimed they did, and they didn't taste like insulation.

He didn't want the distraction of going out for lunch, not even next door, so he made a cup of tea in the staff lunchroom and gave himself permission to finish the donuts through the afternoon.

The newspaper office was humming its usual Monday hum.

Deadline was tomorrow, so the community was calling in late as usual with important notices, the reporters were out at the eleventh hour hoping to find a good story or photograph, and sales people were chasing down advertising commitments and urging the design staff to get it right and get it quick.

Elaine Fong was the ringmaster of all this activity and Tim knew to give her a wide berth. He saw her, and she saw him, but he wasn't part of her circus, so her eyes didn't even flicker with recognition. She was looking inward at a mental image of the entire newspaper. If someone dashed in with an unexpectedly good story, she'd be mentally adjusting page space even before Layout brought her the changes. Tim had stood in the centre ring where she was now, where he was grateful not to be this year.

He knew, and he knew Elaine knew, that each week's issue was a link in a thin chain. If any one was a dud, the chain was weakened, possibly broken. Some readers might not bother to pick up a copy next week; or if they were going to renew their subscription, they might put it off and never come back. Boring kills newspapers.

Tim was confident that James Olsen would keep the paper from being boring this week. After that—who knew?

A large white envelope was taped to the door at the bottom of the stairs, but nobody had called him for the 'access code'. He wondered if he should get a mailbox for such deliveries.

He took the envelope upstairs: James had printed an eight-by-ten glossy of his dented front door. Good. After the new door was installed on Friday he would send the photo and the bill to *The Daily* in Halifax, demanding recompense.

February 23: White card

Tuesday

"Are you up there? I have the card."

"Are you down there?"

Tim went down to James' cubicle in case they needed to consult someone else, though he didn't know who or for what. Things were a little quieter in the circus today, as most decisions had been made, and anything new coming in would be considered TOO LATE unless it was a real, verifiable, bona fide, urgent, terrible, awful emergency. Such occurrences were rare in South River, as James had complained.

"Where's Exhibit A, eh?" Tim drew the magnifying glass from his pocket. "I'm ready to observe."

"Now I've seen it all." James laughed. "You look like Shylock Jones with that thing."

"Thanks, I think. Where's the card?"

James produced an envelope and tipped it to let the contents slide out on the desk: a business card, plus a piece of paper towel. The card was almost entirely blank, as the ink had all but washed away. What remained on the wrinkly cardboard rectangle was just smears.

Tim held the lens near and far, and examined both sides carefully, but couldn't find a letter or an imprint. Only smudges. What would Sherlock do?

"Nothing, right?"

"Hmm, I'm not sure there's anything of interest here, but let's do the exercise anyway. You take notes, James. Is the card of standard business card dimensions?"

James produced one of his cards.

"Yes, it is. Now look there: the edges are ragged. Yours are crisp."

"Sure, Mister Brown, but it was wet for days. Weeks."

"True, but look through the glass: doesn't it look like a uniformly ragged edge? Like it was perforated?"

James squinted through the glass. "Gee, you're right. You'd think that'd go to mush, but you can see the little wiggles. What's that mean?"

"Meaning can wait. We're still observing. Now, what about that trace of ink remaining? Where is it on the card?"

"Where—oh, I get it. Like was it in the upper left or lower right corner?" James rotated the card. "Hard to say."

"Write these things down, James. Notes, notes, notes. Now, what was the colour of this ink? Was it black? Dark blue? Dark gray?"

"I'd say black."

"Tell you what. Take it over to the window—better yet, take it outdoors and look at it in natural light. The lights in here give off some weird hue, I forget what it is, but it's not daylight. I have a quick visit to make. Meet you back here in a jiffy."

Until now, Tim had completely forgotten about the cards that he had asked Ed Garamond to print for him. He walked over to Ed's cubicle and knocked on the partition. Ed's eyes were on his computer screen.

"Busy," he said, without turning. "The answer's no."

"I know," Tim said. "Take a break."

"Oh, hi, boss. Sorry, I thought it was—"

"I know. Just need a second."

"Oh, no worries. I was wondering where you got to. Did you like the sign I made for you?"

"Loved it, Ed. The 'code' requirement actually works. You're hilarious. Just wondering about my cards?"

"Oh, right, I forgot about them. They're right here: are these okay?"

"Better than. Thanks for doing this, Ed. Say, did you print them here, or send out?"

"I printed them here. Super easy to do more when you need

them."

"Cost?"

"No charge. Company expense, so I guess you pay, eventually."

James was back at his desk. "It might be dark blue," he said. "You're right, it does look different in natural light. Still, hard to tell."

"Okay, write that down anyway. You're not colour-blind, are you? You should know that about yourself. I'm not questioning your assessment, only whether you're qualified to judge colours. Although that jeep of yours sure is a bright colour. What do you call that?"

"Jungle orange. The dealer does, anyway."

"Of course they do. Now, what else can we observe? Nothing that tells us anything useful, I guess. Oh, I have an idea. Come with me."

Tim picked up the blank card and returned to Ed's cubicle, James in tow.

"Ed, sorry to bother you again, but we have a mystery here. This card was found in the pocket of a jacket that had spent at least two weeks in water. What can you tell us about it?"

Ed took the card gently, turned it over, and held it up to the light.

"It was likely printed on an ink jet printer. That ink is water-soluble, no surprise there's nothing left if it was soaking all that time. It's from a sheet of cards, ten per sheet. They are connected with rows of perforations so you can pull the cards off—if you're careful. Some people fold at the perforations first but that delaminates the card stock. Looks like that might've happened here, but water could've done that. They're popular with small businesses that can't afford to print five hundred at a time, or don't know if they'll need that many."

"Did you print mine that way, Ed?"

"Yes and no. I used a sheet of plain, un-coated cards, which you requested because you wanted to be able to write on them. But I used cards meant for our laser printer. Come to think of it, this card might have been meant for laser printers, too; ink jet ink doesn't absorb into it as readily, and often smears. Amateur job, anyway."

"Can you tell where that smear is supposed to be on the card?"

"Most likely left or upper left, if it's a logo. Standard placement. Anything else?"

"What colour is, or was, the ink?"

"Hard to say. Take it outside. The light in here is wonky."

Back at James' desk, Tim said, "So what have we learned, James? It was a DIY job, printed on a home printer, most likely. She—the owner of the jacket—either has a small business herself, or was going to visit one. Not a conclusion, but it may be a clue. We also learned that Ed Garamond knows a lot about a lot of things. Respect his time, but use him when you need to. I'll keep this with me, if that's all right with you."

Tim picked up the paper towel to wrap around the card, and stopped. He smoothed the towel out on the desk.

"Look."

The volunteer firefighter had likely pressed the card in the paper like a blotter, and it had absorbed some ink in the process. The towel revealed an indistinct impression of the printed card. The blurred arrangement of a logo and business card information were there in reverse.

"Oh, too bad," James said, squinting through the magnifying glass. "I still can't read it."

"That'd be too much to hope for. But if I saw one like it I might recognize it, wouldn't you? You must remember, James, not to overlook tiny bits and bobs. They may be nothing, or they may be clues, and clues lead to hunches, and hunches lead, well, to dead ends, sometimes. I think I'll go over to Blockhouse for a walk about, stop in whatever shops are there, see what I can see. I'm hunch-less at the moment, so I'll go look around. I'll call you if I find anything of interest."

He parked near the Blockhouse four-way stop and looked around. Nothing much to drop in on there. He'd been in the convenience store before, but hadn't been on the lookout for business cards then.

Inside the store, he saw nothing of interest on the counter, but as he turned to leave he saw a cork board beside the door, shingled with business cards of all descriptions. Several cards appeared to be of the home-printed variety, offering to "mind children in my own home", to "clean your home", to do "odd jobs" or "snow removal".

"What's the local telephone exchange here?" he asked the clerk behind the counter, who didn't appear at all curious about what Tim was looking for. Perhaps people studied the cork board all the time. It *was* interesting. "The phone number, I mean."

"Six-two-four." He pronounced the third number "foh".

None of the phone numbers on the cards he had picked out had six-two-four.

"Something you're looking for?" the clerk finally offered.

"Yeah, maybe you can help me. I met someone about two weeks ago, who was on her way to a small shop around here. Except she didn't make it."

"She mighta been goin' to the NuYu." The clerk pointed to a poster on the wall beside the cork board. The NuYu was a spa. With a six-two-four phone number.

"Where's this?"

"Go out the door, turn right."

"How far?"

"Don't get in your car. I think you can walk that far." The clerk and a customer both found that funny. Cah. Fah.

Tim didn't buy any gum this time. He said thanks, pushed open the glass door, and turned right. Facing him was a large portable sign stating that the NuYu Spa had "New Hours". It was in the same building as the convenience store, on the lower level, five strides away.

He opened the door and bells jingled. The air inside had a pleasant herbal aroma. A sign on the counter asked him to "Please Wait We'll Be Right With Yu". He looked around for another bulletin board or business cards on display, but saw nothing but an orchid in a planter. A woman emerged from behind a curtain and said in a soft voice, "Welcome to NuYu. How may I make you feel better?"

"Hello! I didn't even know you were here—your business, I mean. Do you have a brochure or, uh, or business cards? So I can see what you offer?"

She handed him a glossy colour brochure listing massages and other treatments Tim had never heard of. "We have an introductory rate for first-timers. Have you had any of these treatments before?"

"Uh, no, I guess I haven't. I think I'd like it, though. I strained my back a couple weeks ago, and still get twinges. Do you treat that?"

"I sure do. You can call for an appointment, or we can make one now."

"Can't right now, but I do have a question for you. I'm looking for a youngish woman who might have been on her way here two weeks ago last Saturday, late morning. But she didn't make it. Does that ring a bell?"

The woman frowned. "Why do you want to know? Are you a relative of hers?"

"Not a relative, no, but I am concerned about her. I know she met with an accident on her way here, I think. I'm not sure how much I should tell you because I don't know what she wants to be told. She was—is—late twenties, I'd guess, slim, dark hair. Does this ring a bell?"

The woman sighed. "It may. I was expecting a new receptionist who matches that description to start on the thirteenth, but she didn't show up. Not the best way to make a good first or last impression, let me tell you. This place is busy on Saturdays so it was chaos. When she finally called—I don't recall exactly when, sometime the next week—she said she'd been 'unavoidably delayed.' I told her to frig off. Too bad, because I thought she'd be good here."

"Did you hire someone else, then?"

"I wish. Not a lot of suitable applicants around here this time of year. They need to have a certain look, you know, and be able to talk. The bar is low. Do you want the job?"

"Ha-ha, no thanks, I'm not suitable either, but I may become a client. So, what's the harm in calling her back now?"

"Hmm. No harm, maybe, except I abhor unreliable staff. They're worse than no staff."

"I hear you. Maybe I can help. I'm pretty sure—if this person is who I think she is—that her seeming unreliability was due to cir-cumstances beyond her control. Including two nights in hospital. You can ask her. But, with respect, I suggest that you give her a second chance. As much as you find it difficult to find good staff, there are likely not a lot of good jobs for people like her right here in Greater Blockhouse, either, right? She's probably still looking for a job, especially if she doesn't have transportation to get to work farther afield."

She laughed. "That's hilarious, 'Greater Blockhouse'. May I use that? Okay, Mister Whoever You Are, I will call her and see if her story matches yours."

"I wish you both good fortune." He handed her the first of the new cards he had picked up from Ed. "My name's Tim. You're wel-come to call me if you need further corroboration of her story. Do you have a card, in case I want to reach you? In addition to this lovely menu of services, that is?"

"Sure. They're not fancy. I blew my budget on that fancy bro-chure, so I just quick-printed a few of these for now."

She reached under the counter and handed Tim the very card he had set out to search for, NuYu logo in the upper left corner, ad-dress in the lower right, and the proprietor's name, Melanie, and her professional designations, in the middle. All in black ink on a white card. He found it hard not to cry "Eureka!"

"One more thing, Melanie. This young lady doesn't know me and will have no recollection of me, so don't expect to jog her memory that way. I was present at the scene of her, um, delay, that's all. I don't even know her name, and I don't need to. Thanks very much for your help. You *have* made me feel better today!"

~

He drove the short distance to the dead-end lane where the well and the old mobile home were located. The mobile was there—im-mobile—and surrounded by yellow caution tape. That was good. The officials were on it. James would be right on their heels, or as close as he could be without having to get the awful odours in his nose again. The telephoto lens, what James called the camera's "zoom" feature, would help him see up close.

There was nothing for Tim to do here, no need to get out of the car and wander around a property that had proven itself dangerous to at least one passer-by, and potentially to a resident of the trailer, whether that resident was human or animal. The sanitary-white office retreat was the most appealing place to go. His job was to wrap up this investigation or whatever it was, not to slip on hidden ice and start another story he wanted no part of.

He had observed a cooler with sandwiches on display in the convenience store. He couldn't face another lunch of cardboard snack bars, so he went back to the store, bought a roast beef sandwich and took it to the office.

He reviewed the morning, especially the latter part at the spa. Finding the duplicate of the business card from the jacket in the well was the very definition of a long shot, found in two stops. That didn't happen in mystery stories; if it did, it wasn't credible even if plausible. Even Sherlock didn't just hail a carriage and ride directly to the clue that solved the mystery, did he, now? No, he didn't. He had to scuff around a little, entertain various characters who knew their guilt and tried to hide it, or who weren't guilty at all but left misleading clues all over the place.

Here was Timothy Brown, with his magnifying glass, deducing the type of card—with confirmation by Ed Garamond—and then practically driving right up to the place where the card's mates were. Not only that, but he had learned the reason Miss was on the trail that Saturday morning. After getting herself out of the well, *sans* jacket—an unimaginable feat—she was determined to carry on to her new job rather than go home, because she desperately wanted this job—or hoped someone there would help her. She continued into the shortcut, was on the trail for the short zig, and collapsed before she could zag onto the lower portion of the path that came out at the corner of the very building where her new employer was waiting impatiently for her. Boom!

It dawned on Tim that he was the only person who knew the entirety of what happened that day. Miss knew where she was heading. It was unlikely that she remembered anything after she managed to get out of the well, certainly nothing of her collapse and rescue, not until she was warmed up again in the hospital. Melanie at the NuYu knew only that she didn't show up for work.

He felt a surge of pride. His random wanderings might have salvaged the job for Miss, and secured a needed employee for Melanie. Would Melanie call Miss and invite her to come for a re-do? He hoped she would, was pretty sure she would. If Miss was still available, it'd be a story-book ending to what had looked like a dark situation ten days ago.

The buildings across the river wobbled through the imperfections in the window. It was restful. But now the sandwich was gone and he had things to do. He wanted to finish reviewing the grids before he took them down and rolled them up to store them in the cupboard, near, but out of sight. The map of Blockhouse would go in there, too.

Thinking of the map reminded him of Stella. He hadn't heard from her since Valentine's day. That wasn't unusual, but he made a mental note to call her soon to say hello. She wouldn't do that herself, as she considered a friendly greeting to be a waste of time. He admired her steely resolve in tackling her work as MLA. When she revealed a little crack in that smooth armour, as she had done when her Man of the Moment had split—or been split, more likely—it concerned Tim. Not that Stella couldn't handle it, but whereas Tim had dealt with setbacks and disappointments all his life, and was on sabbatical this year so that the weight of them wouldn't bury him, Stella never gave defeat any space, and he feared that she may not have the tools to cope if she was knocked down. Of course, he would never, ever, say this to her. But he would find a way to say something that she might like to hear.

He wondered what he should tell James, if anything, about why Miss was on the Old Train Line Trail. "Nothing," was what his inner Sherlock told him. He had no proof that she was the no-show at the NuYu. It was conjecture, a neat story, but still only a story without Miss to corroborate it.

He could share the business card comparison with James. That was a slam-dunk. The value of Sherlock's magnifying glass had been proven in the modern age. But he'd wait until this week's paper had gone to print. He didn't want the card to lead James to the NuYu, where he might press Melanie to talk about Miss, to pad the article for the paper, and inadvertently mess up the chance for Miss to get her job.

That job was important, a nice conclusion to the incident, and not necessary for public consumption.

February 24: Snow day

Wednesday

It snowed again overnight, not a storm by definition, but enough to close some schools for the morning, and to cause a few fender-benders. Power lines seemed to have survived the strain, and the world was grateful, since every essential thing in homes and businesses was hard-wired or had a plug on it. Because it had snowed last Wednesday as well, the radio announcers said that it seemed to snow "every Wednesday" in their usual quest to find patterns and theories to talk about.

Having been up and out early quite a lot lately, Tim was happy to grant himself another "snow day" this morning. Anyway, there should be a fresh copy of *The Times* in the dedicated box on his porch. He couldn't speak for other subscribers, but he was certainly eager to read this week's edition.

He drew out the suspense, making a double cappuccino first. Still in pyjamas and robe, he pulled on boots to take two steps on the snowy porch to get his own paper, and *The Daily* as well, carefully placed on the rubber *WELCOME* mat. The unseen delivery person continued to put some effort into creative delivery. Good for him or her, but it wouldn't absolve them of responsibility for the cost of replacing his door this Friday.

Back at the island, he sat, tasted the cappy, so good, and finally unfolded the weekly. There was the lead article by James Olsen, above the fold, with a great colour picture, and large print inviting readers to "See More Photos Inside!" The photos inside covered two-thirds of one page, with a few little ads along the bottom and a major advert on the opposite page. *More Next Week!*

"Nice work, Elaine," Tim said aloud. "This issue will pay nicely." James must be over the moon. He wouldn't call him yet, though, since he protested early mornings.

He turned to the editorial page and read a bit of "In the Ring". Elaine had poked her clever stick into another anthill, and the debate was on. She was managing these responses, he saw, by talking to the respondents before press time and reporting their conversation, not simply printing written statements which were so often self-serving and hugely boring. She had formidable journalistic skills which, he knew, she would take to bigger arenas once her contract with *The Times* was over, maybe to a *Globe* or a *Star*. He would miss her. He would write a glowing letter of recommendation, of course, but it would hurt.

He called Elaine. "You are so good at this, Elaine. Congratulations!"

"Thank you, Tim. It was James' story—and yours too, I guess. He said you didn't want any credit?"

"Correct. I'm on leave, far away, can't be found. James actually did a lot of spade-work on this, and took the photos, of course. I just pointed him toward the topic."

"Sure you did. Keep on doing it if you like. I was beginning to wonder about his value. He seemed so uninspired. But this opens a new chapter for him, I hope."

"I think you're right. He lacked curiosity, is all, or didn't know how curiosity works. On the face of it, this is a ho-hum story about an abandoned well. But I think he has hinted that there could have been a fatality—something broke the rotten cover, anyway—and that elevates it."

"Do you know what broke it, Tim? Did somebody die?"

"Know? As in know for a fact? No, I don't, but the victim does, ha-ha. James may discover more. If I do, I'll pass it on to him."

"Well, please do. This is shaping up to be award-winning photo-journalism, and I'd love to submit it."

"Yikes! An award—us? Little old us in South River? Wow. Carry on, then. Oh, speaking of awards, your 'In the Ring' is superb, too. Submit that somewhere as well as your resumé, will you?"

"You're funny, Tim. But thanks, I'm enjoying it. It's fun to tangle with people who charge in with opposing views. We don't agree, necessarily, but we can debate with respect. If not, they don't get in the paper, right?"

"Right."

"And if memory serves, that was your idea too, wasn't it? So, how's your so-called year off going? We like having you lurking around the offices."

"You do? I like being there. Strictly staying away felt like a restraining order. Being able to wander around—not lurking, puh-leeze—without responsibility feels good. Think of me as a friendly ghost. I grew up in there, spent more time and happier time there than at home, actually. But upstairs is perfect for me. If—I mean *when*—I come back to work, I might stay up there."

"Hmm. Not if you're coming back as editor. You have to be in the thick of it, you know that. Otherwise we'll be just an advertising flyer with puff-pieces scattered in to imitate a paper."

He sighed. "Yes, I know. But it's your job right now, and you're killing it!"

"Thanks again, Tim. Great to have your support."

That was a nice conversation. He hadn't had a bad one with Elaine Fong, actually. He'd watch that he didn't get more involved in the newspaper operations. That was a slippery slope. The white room still appealed to him more than the main floor, so he knew he still needed to give his frazzled nervous system a chance to repair. Maybe learn something new. And delve.

He asked Gloria for a second infusion of caffeine, and, still in his slippers and dressing-gown, continued browsing both newspapers. A real snow-day was fun. There was Elaine, at work early, in the role. He'd watch her, too. Burnout shouldn't be the only outcome of doing a good job.

Skipping the television listings, he arrived at the back pages of *The Times*. He scanned the Obituaries, the one section of the newspaper of interest to everyone living in a small town. He was surprised to see a photo of Arnie Cogswell, whom he'd known since junior high school, Tim's own age, therefore. Known as Cogs. They hadn't stayed in touch, though they'd see each other around town and nod. *Died suddenly*, the obit said, *No visitation by request.* Heart, maybe? Shocking. *Leaving to mourn a wife and two children.* How awful for them. Tim noted the funeral was this Friday at a funeral home outside Lunenburg. He'd go.

By mid-morning, he was bored with leisure. He showered and dressed and went out to shovel the entrance to the driveway. He wanted to finish with the notes, and they were downtown, so he'd go put in a few hours at that. He spread peanut butter on a slice of bread and wrapped it around a peeled banana for lunch and headed downtown.

James wasn't in his cubicle, not marked IN on the board, so Tim phoned him.

"Good morning, James, hope I'm not disturbing you?"

"No, it's fine." James spoke barely above a whisper.

"Okay, you sound funny. Are you all right?"

"Yeah. Just...just camping out for a bit."

"Camping? Not outdoors camping, I hope?"

"No. Just waiting for...something. Can I call you back later?"

"Of course. Bye."

That was intriguing, but intriguing would have to wait. Wrap-up was the matter at hand. There wasn't much to do before these papers could be put away. He decided to wait a couple more days before calling NuYu for an appointment, to give Melanie time to call the missing Miss and invite her over for another job interview, if that was even a possibility. He expected that James might soon have something to report on the contents of the smelly trailer, which did not, as far as he knew, have any connection to the well and the events on the trail, but you never knew about that.

He would add that to the aphorisms he'd like to post on the wall: *YOU NEVER KNOW.* Or, more precisely, *YOU NEVER KNOW FOR SURE.*

"Until you do," he added aloud. All the pieces were dangling, waiting to be tied up.

He phoned Stella. No answer, but she'd see that he called.

He made a mug of tea to wash down his PB&B sandwich, eating

it in the white room and letting his eyes play with the bumps in the window-glass. The snow made South River almost pretty. The scrubby river-bank and plain bridge were obscured by unattractive buildings, and the strip mall on the other bank would never be featured on a postcard, so a fresh coat of snow was South River's best look.

He felt he should be busy doing something. Call someone? Go somewhere? Why? What was it his mother used to say when she thought he wasn't being productive? "An idle brain is the devil's workshop." The devil didn't get a chance to set up a workshop in young Timothy's brain, not while Brownie Brown was within range of it, and by the time she was gone, his brain was automatically uneasy when an opportunity to rest approached. He was trying to unlearn that now.

He chuckled at a mental image of his mother sitting in this room, moving her head slightly back and forth to make the world outside bounce around. That would never have happened in this world or the next.

Was Sherlock Holmes' brain idle when he sat deep in his chair, fingers steepled, for hours on end? He claimed to be deep in thought. *Thought is under-rated*, Tim mused. Action was what people like his mother looked for, and trusted. Thought was invisible, therefore suspected. He laughed again as he envisioned Brownie Brown sharing space with The Great Detective. Neither would have appreciated the other's skills or methodology. Oil and water, they would have separated quickly.

The phone startled him from this reverie. "Timothy Brown."

"Hi Mister Brown. It's me."

"Hi James, is everything okay? What's up?"

"Yeah, sure is. Sorry I couldn't talk earlier. They told me to stay away, so I got up early and parked and waited."

"Wait, what? They who? Away from what?"

"Sorry. Yeah, the forensics people. I told the RCMP I had reason to believe that there was a dead person in that old trailer—"

"You did? Oh my goodness, James!"

"Sure. You didn't go inside like I did. It was epic. Anyway, the county guys weren't going to touch it. They said if nobody was re-ported missing they didn't see what there was for them to do, and they took their orders from higher up, and so on. I made some calls, but nobody wanted to talk to me, especially once they knew I was a reporter. So I told the Mounties that I had reason to believe there was a cadaver in there, which I did. That got their interest. But they told me to stay well clear."

"James! What a story! So, what then?"

"So, we had a snowstorm, that was bad luck, because I was afraid they'd see my tracks in the snow, so I went over real early and—"

"Excuse me for interrupting, but where are you now? Are you at your desk? Do you want to come up to tell me this?"

"No, sorry, I'm home, trying to warm up. I sat there for hours. I had the engine running a bit, but I didn't want to melt the snow on the rag-top. I wanted it to look like my jeep had been parked there overnight. Glad I did, too, 'cause the Mountie gave it a good look. I was freaking that he might come over, but he didn't."

"You're smart, James, but you need proper gear for a winter stakeout. I could give you some pointers on that."

"That's funny. So, anyway, I watched the Mountie go to the door, and push it open, and start to go inside, and it was like the smell just smacked him, y'know? He jumped back, he really did. He didn't go in again, didn't even close the door, which I thought was care-less of him. He drove away pretty quick. He radioed for the medical examiner and that crew."

"How do you know that, James?"

"Oh, I could tell ya, but then I'd have to kill ya."

"What? Oh, I get it. You have a police scanner or something. Is that legal? Don't tell me, I don't want you to kill me. I don't want you to get in trouble either. Did you stay there?"

"Yeah, all day, until just now. I'm soaking in the tub and I'm still cold. My bones are cold." He sneezed, hard. "'Scuse me."

"Bless you. I bet they are. Did the Medical Examiner come?"

"Sure did. He put on a haz-mat suit and a respirator, smart move. He went inside, but the Mountie stayed well outside, don't blame him. The ME was inside for about ten minutes, and came out empty-handed. He shook his head at the Mountie, so I guess he didn't find any dead human inside. But he did get some red tape and taped a big X across the door. Then he taped up a notice."

"What does it say? Could you get close enough to read it?"

"Close enough to photograph it. It says the building is condemned and will be demolished, and trespassing is forbidden, and all that. I have a picture of it. I have pictures of everything. *Ahchoo!* Sorry."

"Bless you. Do you know when it will be demolished?"

"Not yet, but I will, don't you worry. I'm on this."

"I'm not worried in the least, James, except about you catching pneumonia."

"I'll be all right, Mister Brown. Do you want me to let you know when I hear back?"

"Uh, no, I don't, James. This is your story, it's separate from what I was looking into, as far as I can see, thank goodness for that. If you do find a link, you can pursue it. The reason I called earlier was to congratulate you on the fantastic spread you achieved in today's edition!"

"Gee, really? I haven't even seen it, can you believe that? I went over there real early, like I said, and then I had to come home to get warm."

There was a thundering sound from James' end. "Sorry, just added some hot water in the tub. I think I'll live now. "

"I'm glad to hear it. Hypothermia can be deadly, I hear. Seems to be contagious. Listen, does Miss Fong—have you checked in with her today?"

"No—well, I left her a message about five-thirty this morning to let her know that I was on a story and wouldn't be in until later. Should I go in now?"

"That's between you and her. You'll like today's issue, anyway. It's a big coup for you, James. The first of many, I'm sure. She's very pleased. So am I."

"Thanks for your help on this, Mister Brown. You put me onto this story. It was the push I needed."

"You're welcome. Just stay curious—and keep it legal. Or safe. Sometimes both, ha-ha. Oh, and do come to see me tomorrow if you're around. I have a very interesting exhibit to show you, pursuant to our recent discussions. See you later, James."

The snow had stopped and streets were plowed and salted, but it took Tim a full half hour to make the five-minute drive home. An oil delivery truck had gotten stuck halfway into a customer's driveway. This was rush hour in South River, if you happened to be on one of the few streets that experienced this phenomenon, so there was gridlock. Some drivers actually blew their horns, which struck Tim as very funny. In South River, car horns were mostly for greeting people you knew, maybe for warning someone backing out of a blind spot, never for hurrying traffic along unless the drivers had gotten out of their vehicles to chat in the street.

He was still chuckling at South River's New York minute when he was standing in his slippers, pouring *Mercredi rouge.*

"To the day," he said as he raised the balloon glass. "To everything!"

February 25: Loose ends

Thursday

Tim was putting on his jacket to go out for breakfast when Stella rang.

"You called?"

That was odd. Stella might return a call if he left a specific request, but calling back on the thin evidence of a Caller ID? Unheard of.

"Yes, I did, Aunt Stella. How are you?"

"Fine. Did you—what did you want?"

"I didn't want anything, thanks. Just calling to say hi, to check in on you."

"All right, then."

"Wait! Do you want me to return the, um, thing you gave me?"

"No. Please destroy it. Was it useful?"

"Very. I would venture to say it helped me accomplish good things. The feature in this week's paper is related to it."

"I haven't had time to look. Anything else?"

"Yes." Tim was thinking fast. "I was wondering, um, if you'll be at home in the next few days? I thought I'd come by with coffees and something from the bakery. How's that sound?"

"Here?"

"Yes."

"When?"

"Well, my time is more flexible than yours, so you tell me. How about Saturday morning? Ten-thirty?"

"I'll call you if I won't be here."

Her softening demeanour seemed to have thickened again,

maybe even formed a crust. He would indeed take some treats to warm her up again. Some anonymous man had put a smile in her voice for the short time he had been calling on her. Tim hoped his departure hadn't put her into a lasting funk.

~

The Daisy Café was bustling, post-snowfall. The world was knocked off-kilter whenever it snowed enough that the school kids were home, parents had to beg off work to look after them, stores lost sales, cars got dented. The day-after chatter was predictable. "Much down up your way?" was an ever-repeated greeting.

Tim didn't enjoy the weather-talk but he liked the hubbub. He ordered a modified Log-Jam breakfast to compensate for the noxious health bars he'd bought in good faith. This would restore an essential component of grease and protein. He did wish the Daisy made decent coffee, but that'd be a gateway drug to more visits and more grease, no doubt about that.

Evelyn was her usual breezy self. Bad as the coffee was, she never let anyone's cup sit empty, and served their meals promptly. She earned her generous tips. This was her stage, and she obviously enjoyed her daily performances. It was rumoured that she lived in a nice house and drove a nice car—as though she shouldn't. Whenever she retired, it was common opinion that the Daisy would have to hire two servers to replace her, but they'd never measure up.

Tim didn't wait for change when he paid his bill. He smiled and said hello to folks he knew, and walked next door.

The Times office was quiet. The whole paper, with the exception of the TV listings and some contracted ads, had to be re-created from scratch each week, so staff were out digging. He waved at Elaine through the window of her closed door—her eyes were focused today, and she waved back—and climbed the stairs to his *sanctum sanctorum.*

He didn't have much in mind to do here today, but he needed to hang out until mid-afternoon when Mrs A had finished house-cleaning. He thought about that funeral tomorrow. Tomorrow was also the installation of the new screen door, and he supposed he'd need to be home for that. Doors didn't get nailed on from the outside; he knew that much, but little more about door installation, except that they were challenging to measure.

He called the building supplies store to check, asking for Donnie Isnor.

"I was just going to call you, Tim. I'm afraid your door hasn't arrived yet. Storm delay, maybe. So we can't install it tomorrow."

"Well, darn. When, then?"

"Well, we're not sure. Depends on where it's held up, right? If it's in the city, it should be here next week. If it's still in Montreal, well, I can't say. But it shouldn't be long. I'll call you when we have it, how's that? Then we'll get it put in for you."

Phooey. So many things had gone according to plan or better recently that he expected this simple door project to follow suit. When he was learning about the things you needed before you could begin, he found that there were steps to take, measurements to make. He hadn't factored in poor service, regardless of the cause.

Well, nothing to be done about that. At least tomorrow's funeral wouldn't collide with the door installation. The funeral wasn't a silver lining in a cloud, he wouldn't say that, but it was a different cloud. *Dead at thirty-nine, yikes.*

He had crossed out almost all the boxes on the wall as either irrelevant or resolved. All except the Miss who was at the centre of the episode. If she would please kindly respond to Melanie's call to work at the NuYu, that'd prove that she was the one who failed to show up for work, and his purely made-up story would be proven from the well to the trail to the spa with a major detour in an ambulance. Not bad for an amateur.

He was too full from breakfast to want lunch. He was not in a reflective frame of mind, possibly for the same reason. He knew he wouldn't concentrate on any new topic until he heard from the spa, and he didn't want to frustrate himself trying.

He did want a mailbox for the door leading upstairs, so he went off to the big chain stores and strolled around looking at all the tools and appliances he had no idea how to use, finally selecting a small mailbox. He picked up sausages and sauerkraut to bake for dinner, hoping that the inevitable gas production from sauerkraut wouldn't manifest until after choir practice was over.

He couldn't think of anything else to do, and driving around wasn't much fun in slush and salt spray, so he went home.

Mrs A was bringing in the various things she had put out on the clothesline and railings to air. He noticed an area rug she had put on public display on the front porch. Where had she found that shabby, threadbare thing?

"Hi Mrs A. How are you? Where'd that old rug come from? Is it mine?"

She pointed to the bare floor under the coffee-table in the parlour. "Floor look better. Rug old."

"Indeed it is. What if we don't put it back? Hey, I have an idea. I'll take it to my, um, I'll take it away."

He rolled it up and tossed it in the trunk of his car. A new, modern rug would brighten up the parlour and help it shake its nineteenth-century pall, something new to look for when he next felt like shopping. If it didn't cost too much. Otherwise, the bare floor would do.

The old rug belonged downtown with the plant-stand in the Baker Street-style ante-room.

~

It was a good choir rehearsal. The choir seemed energized. Was it the thought of February coming to an end? It was such a drab month. People eagerly anticipated March, cold and windy as it may be, as the month when spring would arrive, according to the calendar if not actually in nature. Many people allowed themselves to believe that *this* March would be bright and sunny, maybe even warm.

March was also the month when the Music Committee would make its long-anticipated decision on the budget for paid section leads in the choir. Robert's guerrilla introduction of the candidates that Sunday morning in January had not been forgotten, and twenty pairs of fingers were crossed for a positive outcome from the committee. Looking beyond that, Easter was early in April this year, when they planned to present a short concert, for which they would work hard because they loved to sing.

Someone asked Robert if they could sing "All in the April Evening" at the concert; they had the music in their library.

"I know," Robert sighed. "Must we?"

Tim and Robert managed to leave the church without any embarrassing sauerkraut gas betraying their supper. With their usual post-practice refreshments in the den, they discussed salient events of their days since Monday morning, which seemed like five minutes ago to Tim.

He mentioned that he was going to have coffee with Stella on Saturday morning, a rare event, as he sensed that she was feeling low. "I wish you could come with me. She always rises to your energy."

"Do you want to invite her to Sunday dinner?" Robert offered this out of kindness but not with enthusiasm.

"Aw, that's kind of you, Rob, but I don't think so. We'll do that soon, but if she's in a funk I think we'd be better off not enduring that for a whole dinner. I'll have coffee with her and see how that goes."

February 26: Lost and found

Friday

The funeral home was packed, more mourners than the deceased's family had expected, Tim guessed, or they wouldn't have held the funeral in a small facility like this. Perhaps Cogs hadn't been a church-goer.

There was standing room only in the parlour, and Tim was one of the standees. He had a good view of the mourners as they continued to file in, many of them red-eyed and blowing their noses into handkerchiefs. He recognized someone every now and then, and they nodded solemnly to each other.

Speakers in the low ceiling emitted tinny recorded hymns, but the snuffling in the room was louder. Ten minutes after the ill-named "Service of Celebration" was scheduled to begin, the grieving family entered from a side door, and the attendants seated them in the two front rows. Accompanying the widow and the two children under ten were Cogs' parents, her parents, and other relatives of all ages. They were all beyond sad, some weeping hard, bending over in their grief.

An urn sat on a pedestal in front of them all, and an enlarged copy of the photograph of Cogs that Tim had recognized in the paper was on an easel. Cogs looked happy in the picture.

The music in the ceiling stopped abruptly, and a man in a suit welcomed everyone. He wasn't wearing a clerical collar but he was the officiant. He, too, appeared grief-stricken. Tim began to sense he had missed out by not keeping up with Cogs. He tried to think what he knew about him, but couldn't come up with anything. Someone sitting near him held a program, and Tim signalled that he'd like to have a look at it. Nothing there about a career, only his dates, names of his wife and children, and the short order of service. Tim handed it back.

Someone tearfully read the Twenty-Third Psalm. Someone said he represented a shelter where he had met "Arnie," a great fellow who loved his wife and kids and talked about them a lot. He said he wished he'd had more time to get to know "Arnie" better, but that was not to be.

Not even a little bit. He was never Arnie.

The service ended with a hymn, accompanied by the piano in the ceiling turned up loud and played way too fast for this crowd. They leaned into the hymn and dragged it out until there was not a dry eye in the place. Even if you didn't know the deceased or the bereft, the images in the hymn were emotional.

> Aaa-bide with me; fast falls the even-tide;
> The darkness deepens; Lord, with me abide;
> when other helpers fail, and comforts flee,
> help of the helpless, O abide with me.

Tim revised his guess at cause of death from heart attack to drug overdose or suicide. He didn't think those tragedies happened all of a sudden. Many things had to take place before the crisis, not a beginning in this situation, but an end. No going back. Likely with lots of emotional damage done to those loved ones who were now moaning their abject despair, and possibly their fear, if Cogs had been shooting or popping or gambling or drinking his pay cheques prior to this untimely end.

Those who were seated now stood while those in the front rows were escorted out through the side door. Someone with white gloves carried the urn containing what remained of Cogs and another took the photograph and easel. The program invited guests to stay for a reception.

Oh, those poor people, having to endure that. Tim wouldn't stay. He had experienced one suicide funeral, a long time ago now, but his mother had been an absolute rock and kept this gut-wrenching grief out of their house and away from Tim. He wouldn't know how these children felt, would have nothing to say to them or their mother, whom he didn't know. "Sorry" wouldn't cut it.

After waiting to sign the guest book in the lobby, he made his way to the parking lot and was able to leave easily because almost everyone else stayed for the reception.

He had been standing for nearly an hour, and his back was complaining. It needed some expert attention, and that gave him a perfect excuse to take the cross-country road to Blockhouse. During the fifteen-minute drive, he hummed "Abide With Me", and tried to think about Cogs. He didn't know what to think. He felt very sorry for whatever horrors had infected his life and would scar his family. His life had definitely not been celebrated.

~

Tim parked and tugged on the glass door to the spa. The bells jingled. The same sign was on the counter, no receptionist behind it. His heart sank.

"Be right with you," sang a voice from the back.

Then the curtains parted, and out came Miss. When he would recall this moment later, he saw it in slow-motion, a beautiful sight. She was the girl on the trail all right, dark hair parted in the middle and held in a ribbon at the nape of her neck. She was again wearing an open blouse over a tank top, and yoga pants. Tim almost leaned over the counter to see if she was wearing shoes, but he restrained himself. He had an urge to hug this person who was very much alive, but didn't.

She was wearing a smile he'd never seen before, and a blue band on her left wrist. "Sorry to keep you waiting. I just got in and was hanging up my sweater. How can we make you feel good today?" She said it so naturally you'd think it originated with her. "Oh, sorry, my name's Lisa. I'm new here, but perhaps you're not?"

"Lisa. Lovely to meet you, Lisa. My name's Tim, and I'm new here, too. I was in the other day and picked up a brochure, but honestly, I've never been in a spa before so I don't know what I need done. I have a sore back." He realized he was speaking to the very cause of that sore back. "I lifted, uh, something heavier than I was ready for, I guess. I'm a bit stiff. What's good for that?"

"I'd recommend a massage to begin with, Tim. The therapist may find something needing more specific attention, and you can proceed from there. Does that make sense?"

"Yes, sure it does. Sometime next week?"

They compared calendars and settled on a day and time.

"Who will my therapist be, Lisa? Just curious."

"It's only Melanie here at the moment. She's the owner. I think she's looking for another person, as there are two rooms."

"Did you just start working here, Lisa?" He couldn't get enough of saying her name.

"Uh, yes. I was supposed to start a couple weeks ago but I had— I was unavoidably detained. Very happy to be here now, though. Can I do anything else for you, Tim?"

"No, you've done it all, Lisa, thanks. You've made me feel good already. See you next week."

Tim's boots barely touched the slushy ground. *Lisa! Lisa! Lisa! Such a lovely person! Not dead! Not unemployed!* He understood why Melanie had been so disappointed to lose her: she was pleasant, smooth, knowledgeable, evidently happy to be there.

He drove around the corner to have another look at the old trailer. The place was festooned in yellow tape, red tape, and orange signs. He supposed that whatever was inside—discarded poopy diapers was a good guess, maybe rotting food—would dispose of itself eventually with the help of nature's disgusting bugs, faster as the temperature rose. Perhaps they'd let that process take place on site before dragging it away.

People who took care of such refuse deserved the community's thanks. Tim included whoever had dealt with Cogs' body, in whatever state he'd left himself, in his gratitude. It was unthinkable.

But he'd found Lisa, sweet Lisa, the picture of life and happiness! Her colouring was healthy, not the gray pallor of one who had nearly spent her life-force fighting to save herself from drowning in the coldest of wells, trapped in her jacket caught on a nail or old pipe, still so determined to get that job that she ran barefoot through the icy path...also unthinkable.

What conclusion could he draw from these contrasting lives? As far as he could see, there was none, or it was too deep for delving.

So he sang, "In life, in death, O Lord, abide with me."

~

He phoned from Main Street. "Hi James, you in?"

"Yeah, not for long, though."

"It'll just take a second. I'll see you at your desk."

Tim dashed upstairs with the new mailbox, left it there to deal with next week, picked up the exhibits, and came back down to James' cubicle.

"Watch this, James. Here's the dried card, and the paper towel. You recall our deliberations about these artifacts, and what they might mean, right?"

"Yes, I do."

"So, whaddya think of this?" With a magician's flourish, he presented Melanie's home-printed business card. James held it next to the blank one from the jacket pocket.

"Ho-lee, Mister Brown! This is it, isn't it? It sure looks like it. Where'd you get it?"

"Right where it says, James. I'd like to say my ESP told me where to go, but it didn't. Better than ESP, I had good luck. It was only the second place I went into. I will take a wee bit o' credit for having a good hunch. I hunched that Miss was heading to somewhere nearby when she slipped into the well, but not to shop, since she didn't have any money with her. So I started looking where the path would have taken her, and *shazam*!"

"I sure would like to interview her for next week's edition, a fol-low-up, you know. Can I have this?"

Tim snatched the NuYu card from the desk.

"Nope. I don't want to reveal my connection with the story. But there's a way."

"How?"

"Here's how. I bet she hasn't seen our newspaper with your excellent article, even though they sell it in the convenience store next door to where she works, oops. Perhaps she doesn't have any spare money to buy a copy. But if you did what I did with the business card…"

"I get it! I'll take the paper in there and ask if anyone knows anything about that well."

"Sounds plausible to me. Just don't mention anybody named Brown, all right?"

"Deal. Wow, you're a great detective, Mister Brown. You should pursue that line of work!"

"Thanks, James, but I'm trying very hard, not entirely successfully, to avoid *any* line of work, especially that one. So this story is over to you. I'm out, and happy on both counts."

Tim remembered the rug in the trunk. He carried it through the office from front door to back stairs without anyone paying any attention. He had become invisible again, praise be.

He unrolled it in front of the window between the two straight-back hardwood chairs, and placed the plant stand in the centre. It was a nice touch. It was out of date at home, but the whole room was out of date here, so it fit.

That was enough. He had experienced the depths and heights of emotions today and he found it exhausting. He drove home and warmed the leftover sausage and sauerkraut for supper. He raised a glass of *Vendredi La Douleur* to bid farewell to Cogs who had been lost, followed by a glass of *Vendredi La Joie* to greet Lisa who had been found, both from the same bottle.

February 27: The spaces between

Saturday

Stella hadn't called to decline Tim's coffee-visit this morning, so he assumed they were on for ten-thirty. He checked the grocery list, which he'd deal with following the visit.

There was something else he wanted to shop for; it had flitted through his sleepy mind before the alarm rang, but it had escaped before he brushed his teeth. Was that a sign that he was losing it, he wondered? He was pushing forty. In the grand scheme of things, he didn't think forty was old, though nobody ever seemed to embrace that particular birthday, due to the loss of youth and—well— just loss: health, hair, handsomeness, memory, fitness, all due to be lost after forty.

What brought on this gloom? Cogs' funeral had been on his mind through the night. Mostly he remembered the grinding grief of his family. Cogs wouldn't have to worry now about losing his memory after forty. He'd lost everything, all at once. Or maybe in pieces over a long time before, who knew? That didn't seem like a good alternative.

"Stop that maudlin thinking," he said to the man in the mirror, and that ancient word led his thoughts to Sherlock Holmes, and then he remembered that what he wanted to do today was find a darn bookstore that was open and order a copy of that darn Sherlock book. There. He wasn't senile after all, just experiencing a delay in thinking.

He snorted at that. That'd be a good excuse: "Sorry, I have delayed thoughts. They'll come to me later."

He decided to have a single espresso since he was going to have more coffee soon, but he must have missed some essential incantation, as Gloria dribbled a weak brown solution into the demitasse, an old habit he thought she had forgotten. "Is it you or is it me?" he asked the Miracle of Plumbing, but she barely hissed in reply.

He drove past Stella's modern mansion on the river to the bakery, an institution located in an old chandlery warehouse, supplying life-sustaining breads to the local world, as well as many sweet treats. Tim picked out two butter tarts, two chocolate squares, two muffins, several loaves of bread, and a jar of jam. He had brought the thermos, and the clerk agreed to put two large coffees in it.

He drove back to Stella's and turned in at her driveway. He set aside two loaves of bread to take home, brought the treats to the door, and rang the bell. The chimes sounded somewhere inside.

Nobody answered. He wanted to ring again, but hesitated. It wasn't good to rush Stella. Finally, he heard her coming, heels clicking on the tile in the foyer. She opened the door and turned quickly toward the kitchen. "Come in," she said over her shoulder.

Tim awkwardly closed the door with his arms full. He slipped his boots off and padded to the kitchen, which was as bare as a real estate developer's demo model. The expensive pendant lights over the polished granite island were not turned on.

Stella was sharply dressed, of course; she wouldn't be caught dead otherwise. Tim was certain she'd specified in her will how she was to be laid out when she was dead, even if she was on her way to the crematorium. She looked good but not good. Her clothes and hair were great, but Stella herself seemed—what?—diminished, somehow?

"Good morning, Aunt Stella," Tim began, at a quieter level of energy than he would have used normally. "How are you this morning?"

"Oh, fine, thanks. What'd you bring?"

Tim went to the cupboards and searched for a plate. He admired the cabinet doors that opened and closed silently, leisurely, at the touch of a finger. He found two mugs, pre-heated them from the instant hot water dispenser, and laid out a selection of the bakery items.

"There you go. Help yourself. Would you like me to make some toast? I brought jam, assuming there was none here."

"Sure, maybe some toast would be nice."

While Tim sliced the bread and located the toaster, hidden in an appliance garage at the end of the long counter, Stella sat motionless.

"Here you go. Now, what's up? You are not yourself this morning, Aunt Stella." He leaned close. "Look at me. What's wrong?"

"I'm fine. I've been working very hard, and…this damn winter's going on too long." Stella slid down off her stool and went to the living room to get a throw, which she wrapped around her shoulders. Tim had found it very warm in the kitchen. She nibbled at the toast. This was not the rogue star that Stella usually was, roaring through galaxies, causing planets to crash out of orbit.

"May I turn on the lights, please?" Tim didn't wait for permission. When Stella shaded her eyes he dimmed the lights.

"Okay, what's wrong? This is not you. I thought you might be feeling low because that Whoosis had disappointed you—"

Poorly as she might be feeling, Stella was able to give a sharp *Pfft* at the mention of the erstwhile boyfriend.

"Okay, whatever, but now I see you're not sad. You're ill. May I please ask again what's the matter, and can you please answer?"

Stella held her cup in both hands and stared into it. When she finally looked at Tim, her eyes were brimming with tears. "They're testing. They don't know yet."

"Oh my God, Stella, testing? For what?"

"Lots of things. Anything. I've had blood tests up the wazoo, and have a bunch of scans and x-rays booked."

"Since when? How long since you've been feeling like this?"

"Hard to say, isn't it? You feel crappy, you get up and power through anyway, don't you? Then, one day, you realize your batteries are very low and not recharging at all." She turned away and dabbed at her eyes.

Tim was shocked. "Should, uh, shouldn't you be in the hospital?"

"No. They wouldn't know where to put me, what floor, what for."

"Do you have a good doctor? Do you trust him? Or her?"

"Yes, several, and yes, him and her. What do I know? I'm sure it'll be diagnosed soon, and then they can treat it and cure it, whatever it is." Her chin crumpled. "Look at me—no, don't. Please turn off the lights. I look a fright."

"Are you in pain?"

"No, not a bit. But I am so deeply, deeply exhausted. That's what's making me weepy. I have never, ever felt so tired. I have so much work to do…"

Tim resisted the urge to hug his aunt. Even in her present state, he felt she would deck him for the gesture. He put his hand out to cover hers and found it ice cold. She pulled it away and tucked it inside the throw.

"I'm so sorry, Aunt Stella. What can I do to help?"

"Nothing. Thanks."

"Are you eating?"

"I don't feel much like eating."

"Well, that's not good. No wonder you're cold and tired: you're probably malnourished. Tell you what: these sweets are not what you need, obviously. I'm going back down to the bakery to get some of their delicious soups and chili, okay? Let me check your refrigerator."

The appliance gleamed brightly, nothing on the shelves to cast a shadow.

"As I suspected. Listen, Aunty, you remind me of the eccentric rich woman who is discovered dead of starvation. They'll blame me for neglecting you, too, if you do. Here, let's get you to the solarium and wrap you up there. Don't lock the door. I'll be right back."

It took half an hour for the short drive and long lineup, but Tim returned with containers of nourishing soups. He filled a mug with some and heated it in the microwave. There was butter in the fridge, so he buttered a slice of bread and took the food to the solarium, where Stella was dozing under the blanket. He noticed that her coffee was half gone, as was the toast, so there was hope yet.

"'Ere yew go, marm," he said in his best below-stairs accent.

"This'll put ya ta roits, sure it will."

"You sound like your mother," Stella said as she struggled to sit up. "Not sure that's a good thing. You're no better at accents than she was."

"Then I'm not sure I should thank you, but you're the only person who would know. Anyway, here's your medicine. Eat up. There's more in the fridge, and you are not to let it get old in there, hear me?"

"Shut up," Stella said, and took a spoonful of the soup. "Mmm, this is good. Thank you, Timothy, this is very kind of you." She looked up at him. "This is between us, please."

"Sure, okay. Who would I tell?"

"Robert."

"You don't want me to tell Robert? Why?"

"I don't want to have to answer a lot of questions. I don't want to appear—"

"What? Weak?"

She nodded.

"Oh, my dear aunt, you must get over yourself. You're in a bad patch right now, and I'm sorry you are—but I'm not sorry *for* you, if that helps. We mortals get sick and injured all the time. We fall down, but we get up, mostly. It's life. Don't try to be Wonder Woman."

Tim poured more coffee, brought a muffin for himself, and sat on the far end of the huge sofa. "If you're okay with this, now, I will tell you about Arnie Cogswell's funeral yesterday."

He challenged himself to make the account interesting, knowing that Stella's politician instincts would kick in unless she was near death herself. He was right. A morbid topic it was, not the best sick-bed chatter, but it had social implications which interested Stella, perhaps even more than Tim. She asked a few questions, even. Then a tiny yawn escaped.

"Time for bed, Aunty. Will you promise me to have chili for supper?"

"Hmm."

"Don't you 'hmm' me. I'm going to check."

"Don't start."

"Tomorrow, after church, after lunch, I will drive here and ring your doorbell. If you do not answer, I will call *all* the emergency services and leave you to sort them out, if you're still alive. Got me? And for God's sake, call me if you take a turn for the worse!"

"Thank you, Timothy. You're very kind."

~

It unnerved Tim to hear Stella express her gratitude like that. It was so unlike her. He liked it, but not the reason for it, either stress or illness. She certainly did look ill. Blood tests and scans? That was frightening.

His mind went directly to cancer, of course, and likely hers had as well. Cancer was the usual bogeyman, but there were a million other possibilities. What did he know? He was a newspaperman, could tell you a lot about that trade. He hadn't even known why he was sleepy in the daytime last month, had to see his doctor to find out that he was lacking the usual doses of caffeine. So, Doctor Brown he was not.

He waited for the cable ferry to pull itself back across the river while he was thinking these things. The attendant waved him on board, and he pulled right up to the heavy iron ramp, and shut the car off. The short ride ended, the ramp was lowered, and the attendant waved him off.

He soon arrived at Lunenburg, where he hoped against hope that he would find the bookstore open. It was, and the clerk was eager to serve him. He ordered a copy of the Holmes tome he had been studying, acknowledging that it would be expensive, shipping would be costly, and it might take a while.

He browsed the shelves, but couldn't concentrate on what he'd like to buy. There was a *Compendium of Easy Herbal Remedies*, but he knew that would never be used by anyone he knew. There were so many books in so many styles and genres.

"Do you need help?" She was the 'Chief Bibliophile', according to her pin.

"I believe I do. I like to read, but nothing too heavy right now. Some light fiction?"

"Fantasy? Science fiction? Western? Mystery?"

"How about one of each?"

He was delighted with these new books, and the clerk was happy with the sales. She promised to call him when his order arrived. He wondered if there would be many more steps before it actually arrived, like the front door order. He had knocked on a locked bookstore door two or three times already, so he hoped he had completed all the 'begin's.

~

While Tim and Robert waited for their Italian supper to be delivered, they appraised a new-to-them Italian *Sabato*. Tim told Robert about his visit with Stella. All of it. Robert could keep his awareness a secret from Stella if he wanted to, but he'd never forgive Tim if Stella became seriously ill and he hadn't been alerted.

"The poor thing," Robert said. "Should we go see her?"

"Seriously? No, not tonight. Let's see if she was actually suffering from malnourishment. There's a good chance. She has zero food in the house. That's just ridiculous. She has Spencer driving her Jag everywhere, and he could easily pick up groceries for her, too. I must see if I can help them do that. I think one of the stores prints shopping lists that you can check off. Would that help? Geez, it feels like I'm planning for my grandmother. I don't like it."

"Hey now, let's not get ahead of ourselves. People don't just curl up and die like autumn leaves; not people like Stella. She will not 'go gentle into that good night.' Give the docs a chance to do the tests. I think your grocery list idea is great. Hey, why don't I dash over and pick up some lists before they close? The stores aren't open tomorrow, so I'd better do it right now. Back in a jif."

He was out the door before Tim could object, and returned with a handful of pre-printed grocery lists right after the delivery guy left. They ate pizza while they caught up with life and death and the wide space between.

February 28: Gossamer threads

Sunday

It was a beautiful morning. The sun rose at a nearly-constant hour in February, but with the bright sun in a clear sky it seemed hours earlier. One could almost hear birds singing in the leafless trees.

While they were putting on their choir gowns in the men's choir room, Spencer sidled up to Tim. "Uh, Tim, how's your aunt?"

"I think she's okay, Spence, thanks for asking. Haven't you seen her lately?"

"Well, you know, she doesn't like me talking about her."

"She doesn't like me talking about her, either. Let's try this: I saw her yesterday. How about you?"

"N-not in person. I've made deliveries for her. Courier service. She opens the garage for me to pick up or deliver stuff. I drove her to a bunch of appointments at—at places."

"She finds you very helpful, Spencer, and I think she will find you even more useful soon. She'll be—she's okay. I think she has a cold. Don't worry."

The minister did pretty well with the sermon topic of 'Lions and Lambs', inspired by the weather lore about March coming in like a lion and going out like a lamb. One could only hope, if lamb-and-lamb wasn't an option.

There were no good choral anthems on the subject of lions, Robert had told the choir weeks ago when he had learned of this topic. On account of the lions' historic habit of eating the singers, no composer had been motivated to put their roars to church music, though he personally regretted this omission. However, they did have "Sheep May Safely Graze" in their library so they had practiced that and they sang it this morning.

> Sheep may safely graze and pasture
> In a watchful Shepherd's sight.
> Those who rule with wisdom guiding
> Bring to hearts a peace abiding
> Bless a land with joy made bright

The lyrics didn't make great sense, but they were translated from German, part of a Bach cantata about the joys of hunting, so the liturgical relevance was likely never solid. It was beautiful music, though, and the tenors and basses actually sang their exposed entrance well.

During the sermon, Tim thought how good it was to see how much Spencer cared about Stella, and he knew that Spencer's livelihood depended on Stella staying alive and active. Life and livelihood seemed to hang on gossamer threads in so many cases. That lovely Lisa might have died if Tim hadn't happened along, and it was sheer happenstance that she got her job back. Well, not entirely. It was Tim's hunches that led him to her workplace, and it was his curiosity that had gotten him involved in any of it. He was glad he hadn't mentioned Wally to the authorities when he'd feared Lisa may have met with abuse.

That reminded him to call Sally, the paramedic, to let her know that if Lisa had been bruised it was because she—no, on second thought, Sally had said she didn't need to know. She must see a ton of lives on gossamer threads in her line of work, and gossamer didn't have much tensile strength. Sally's own well-being could be fragile as gossamer if she kept all these crises in her head. Brave woman.

Then the sermon was over. Tim's thoughts had crowded out the minister's sermons, but he figured insights were good regardless of the source.

~

"I'll dash down to Stella's now," Tim said after lunch.

"I'll come with you."

"No, she expressly said 'no Robert.'"

"I know. That's code language for 'tell Robert to come.'"

"She'll kill me."

"No, she won't. Let's go."

In the car, Robert asked, "What *is* open today, anything?"

"Like a store? I think the pharmacies are open, why?"

"Take me there."

Robert soon returned to the car with a full bag and a wide grin. "Onward, driver, make haste!"

Tim rang Stella's doorbell. When she opened the door, looking slightly better than the day before, Robert popped his head around the corner, said "Hi, beautiful!" and gave Stella his usual air kisses. She was pleased, though only those who knew her well would see the evidence: a slight crinkling around the eyes. She didn't even look at Tim, but kept her eyes on Robert, who was leading this scene.

"Let's go to the kitchen, all right? Sit, darling, we have something to show you. This was Timothy's suggestion, these grocery lists, see? Now, I am going to check off nearly everything on here to get you started, okay? You will get your manservant to get these. Let me see."

He opened all the fancy cupboard doors and pulled out the rolling pantry, which was empty except for a bottle of beets and two cans of beans. He opened the freezer and closed it again. "I see you won't need to order any ice. I thought you had meat pies in here."

"Ate them, I guess," Stella whispered.

"Well sweetheart," Robert gently pinched Stella's cheeks, "that was likely weeks ago. When they're gone you're supposed to get more. They don't grow in there."

Tim was pleased to see a second container of soup had been opened. The chili was still in the fridge. That would be her supper.

Robert sat at the island with Tim and his aunt, both of whom had been following his whirlwind tour of the kitchen. He presented

Stella with the list, on which a number of items had been checked.

"Now don't have a fit, honey, there's nothing here that will perish quickly due to your gross neglect, but surely you can boil, bake, or fry potatoes, can you not?"

Stella nodded meekly. Tim was amazed to see Robert working this magic.

"Make sure your butler brings the list back so you can see what was ordered and get it again the next week, right?"

She nodded.

"Now, did you eat today?"

"A piece of toast for breakfast. Soup for lunch."

"Excellent! Please drink lots of water, too. You have qualified for a dish of this!"

He pulled a quart of ice cream from the pharmacy bag, got three bowls and three spoons, and scooped out a serving for each. "Eat up!"

"Are you still cold, Aunt Stella?"

"A little. Sometimes. Not right now. This is good."

She was allowing herself to behave like a patient, which allowed her to be honest in describing her current state rather than pretending. Magic Robert's work.

"Okay, now, it's too late to try the thermometer, but do you have one in the house?"

"I don't know. Maybe."

"No worries. If you do, stick it under your tongue when you get up in the morning, will you? I think you have a fever. Now, tell me something. How long's it been since that so-called boyfriend of yours took off? A couple of weeks?"

Stella's pale complexion gained a bit of colour. She nodded.

"As I thought. So, here's what you do." He reached in the bag again and brought out a bottle of cranberry juice. "Drink all of this today. There's more in the bag for tomorrow morning. It's marked on the shopping list. There's something else in the bag, a little test for you to take. When you read it, call your doctor and tell her Nurse Bobby said not to look so hard for what's obvious. Okay, love?"

Stella's chin was quivering, so Robert and Tim both turned away quickly.

"Our work here is done, Timothy," Robert said.

Stella hugged them both at the door. One hug in January, another one in February, an excellent trend.

~

Tim was astounded. "What was all that? And what's in the bag you left there?"

"Listen. I work at a university. With university students. They all have sex of all kinds and then they get what you get after you have a lot of careless sex, which can be an array of things up to and including pregnant, which is not the case here. And they break up, and get more things. I see it all the time. And I'm the music teacher! They confess all their sins and sorrows to me. I pity the campus health clinic staff. I've talked to them a number of times, so I know what to look for."

"So what's your diagnosis, Nurse Bobby?"

"An infection of some kind, bladder's my guess. Or mono. My students are a good deal younger than Stella, but the body has the same parts. And she's not drinking, I mean, not even water. There wasn't one water glass taken out of the cupboard that I could see. Typical of someone who is busy, and then too busy. You did the right thing to bring her soup. She's dehydrated, and that's not good for that infection. The cranberry juice will help. The pee test strips I left her will tell the tale."

"Is that all it is? She seemed pretty ill yesterday. I was thinking leukemia or something like that."

"You could be right, of course, God forbid. She could have lots wrong, but my guess is a bladder infection is one of them, and those infections can go very bad, can involve the kidneys, lots of trouble. Sometimes you can smell it, but not always, and not on her today, so that makes it harder to discover. Poor thing."

"I am so glad you came along, Rob. I know she is too."

"Told ya. Now, let's go home and chop some veg. Maybe no

onions. I don't want to see any more tears today."
"Me neither, pal. Me neither."

END

Acknowledgements

I am grateful to

- My highly-skilled First Readers: Judi McDonald, Margaret MacDonald Trites, and Cynthia French. They search my manuscript drafts for what they like, and let me know, kindly and clearly, when it is, or is not, there.
- Moose House Publications for this amazing project.
- MHP Editor Andrew Wetmore, who makes my good stories better.
- The kind readers of *January: Code* who expressed interest in reading more about the life and times of Tim Brown, who is real to us.

About the author

Jan Fancy Hull lives in a log chalet beside a quiet lake in Lunenburg County, Nova Scotia, where she has written non-fiction, poetry, and short and long fiction.

She has pursued various careers, enterprises, and avocations, including radio broadcaster, arts administrator, sailing tours skipper, and employee benefits broker, among others.

In the winter, Jan watches snowflakes fall as she writes. In the warm months, she carves Nova Scotia sandstone and exhibits her sculptures in various venues. She enjoys golfing, and drifting around the lake in a tiny rowboat, but doesn't do enough of either.

There are so many things to do.

Website: janfancyhull.ca
Facebook: Jan Fancy Hull

Sneak peek into *March: Enigma*

Here are two chapters from *March: Enigma*, the third Tim Brown mystery. It should be available in the fall of 2022.

March 2: New Experiences

Tuesday

Tim had mixed feelings about tomorrow's massage experience.

It could be a topic to delve into. He'd never had a massage, didn't really know what it might entail, or where it could lead. That was positive.

But any water-cooler mention of massages had always been accompanied by snickers, usually from men.

Do men get massages, or is it only women? Maybe men are supposed to go to a physiotherapist for aches and strains, not to a spa with pan flute tootling and aromatic candles burning? Nothing about that seems scandalous, though.

He did know that the services performed at the NuYu Spa would be pure and chaste. He just didn't know *how* it worked, how one entered and partook, so to speak.

This was embarrassing. He needed to consult a man who'd had a massage.

That'd be Robert, but he wasn't due in South River until Thursday, in time for choir practice. They rarely phoned each other between times just to chat. Robert was hugely busy with his students, as Tim had been with the newspaper until he gave himself this year away from all that. Now he had more time, or slower time as he preferred to think of it, but he didn't call Robert to pass the time in chit-chat.

But this felt important. Tim didn't even know if he should prepare to be naked, and what if he should?

He called Robert and caught him just out of the shower.

"This is a surprise. Is Stella all right?"

"I'm fine, thanks for asking. Stella's fine, too, or she was expecting to be yesterday morning after she spanked her pharmacist. I haven't called her since. If she's better, she'll bite my head off for asking. If she's dead, we'll find out soon enough. How are you?"

"Yikes! I'm okay, but you sound a bit edgy, Tim. What's up?"

"Sorry, Rob. I'm a bit out of sorts for no reason. The reason I called is that I booked a massage at a little spa in Blockhouse tomorrow."

"Good for you. That'll take your edge off."

"Yeah, well, what I'm calling you about is...you've had massages, right?"

"Certainly. Haven't you?"

"Nope."

"That surprises me. I just assumed you had, somewhere along the way. So what's the question?"

"The question is...what is it like? I mean, what does she do? How should I dress? And undress? And how far?"

"Whaaat?" Robert couldn't hide his amusement. "Oh, you poor bumpkin! You certainly have led a narrow life in so many ways— and I mean that most kindly. Listen. You have nothing to fear. Whoever she is will not want to see any more of your skin than they have to, believe me. You do have to strip to your skivvies, but most of you'll be under a sheet so you won't get chilly. She—did you say she?"

"Yes, she. Melanie."

"Okay. Melanie will uncover whatever part of you she's working on at the time. Then she'll cover that up and go to the next part. She will be discreet. It's not a massage *parlour*, right?"

"Of course not," Tim said, with the vigour of one who had just figured this out a few minutes before.

"Of course not. So, have a shower, wear your good underwear, and enjoy the experience. Tell her where you hurt so she can dig for knots while she makes you feel great all over."

"Okay, that sounds simple. I just—I wondered—do we talk?"

"That's up to her, but she's working, so I doubt it. A little get-to-know-you chat at the beginning, maybe. It's not like going to the hairdresser. They feel they need to talk and cut hair at the same time. They make me nervous, talking with scissors."

"When did you need scissors on your hair?"

The hair on Robert's round head was close-cropped.

"Before you."

"Hmm. Can't see it, but I bet you had cute baby curls."

"Okay now, have we addressed your concerns sufficiently? As I mentioned, I just stepped out of the shower, and I am not dressed as fully as you'll be in the spa."

"Nice image. Of course. Yes. Thanks, Rob. Good to talk with you. See you Thursday."

"I enjoyed it too. Gotta run."

~

Tim felt like Robinson Crusoe. That eighteenth-century fictional character, having been shipwrecked on an uninhabited island, successfully reinvented everything he needed. Tim often felt like a castaway. He didn't know how to do so many things—other than run a community newspaper, of course, which he was pretty good at.

His island wasn't deserted, and the inhabitants weren't cannibals. He might have wished for no observers at all to see him bumble along, but he appreciated company, just as Crusoe did when he found his 'man Friday'. He was grateful for Robert, for his perspectives, his humour, his support. He wouldn't tell anyone about Tim's social innocence.

Was Robert as confident as he seemed to be? Did he have social insecurities? Were there parts of life that he avoided because he had never learned how to "do" them, like riding a bike?

They hadn't ventured down that conversational path in their time together, but Tim thought it would be interesting to go there. He had his own unknowns to contribute to the conversation, and he was developing a curiosity about what other people—successful people, like concert organist and university professor Robert Kirk—knew about things beyond their area of expertise.

These thoughts were leading somewhere. He jotted *Who Knows About What?* in a new notebook labelled MARCH. Perhaps he would open this topic to others, perhaps around a dinner-table. He'd have to pick the guests carefully, of course, eliminating anyone who would confess either too many or too few insecurities. Who would that leave, and how would he know?

He'd discuss that with Robert, as he'd be the chef for that dinner.

March 3: Hands on

Wednesday

He needn't have worried about how to dress, undress, or otherwise behave at the spa. Melanie was a professional. She knew what he needed to know, and when and how to tell him. She put him at ease, so when she knocked to re-enter the small room, he was on the table, on his tummy with his face in the donut-pillow, ready for whatever was coming.

She began at the base of his skull, the top of his spine and the shoulder muscles. Tim immediately wondered why he had waited so long in this life to come for such treatment. Her hands were warm, soft, and strong, and they moved precisely how he wanted them to, even though this had never happened to him before.

His skin, muscles, and bones all wanted this so much, this touch from these kind hands. How had his shoulders supported his head before now? How had the rest of his long skeleton hung down and moved him through life?

He thought about when he was young. His mother had even taken him to the doctor because of his constant complaints that his bones hurt. A blood test and an x-ray confirmed the doctor's early diagnosis—that he was experiencing growing pains. Before then, his mother said, she'd always thought 'growing pains' meant bad behaviour.

Melanie checked in with Tim occasionally, inquiring if he was doing okay.

"Mm-*hmm*," he responded, with longer emphasis on the second syllable each time.

She worked her way to his lower spine. He had strained the muscles and ligaments a few weeks before. When her fingers kneaded the injured area, he said a quiet 'Ow' a few times. It surprised him that it still hurt, and that he had verbalized it.

"Sorry," he mumbled into the donut.

"I don't wonder," Melanie responded. "You did a number on yourself there. Hang on: I'm going to hurt you a little, but it won't harm you. I'll free up some of these knots."

The pain wasn't near unbearable, and didn't last. When it was time for him to turn over, under cover of the flannel sheet she held up as a curtain, his back felt freer than it had for a very long time.

The whole experience astounded him. He felt Melanie's hands on his skin, but it seemed as though she was reaching inside him, finding and releasing tension where he hadn't known there was any. He had never felt such—what was it—pleasure? It wasn't sexual, but he struggled to know what it was. Could intimacy be this professional? Or vice versa?

With few exceptions, she maintained contact with him through the whole process, even when she was leaving one side of the table and walking around his long legs to work on the other side. He found her touch comforting. She removed both hands occasionally to briskly rub massage oil between them, and when she touched him again, the oil and her hands were warm and his skin welcomed them.

She worked through her zones, and they spoke very little, or she spoke and he murmured in response. He barely noticed the new age (or ancient, he wasn't sure) music playing somewhere, but he found it exactly right. He was unfamiliar with sandalwood and other aromatics but he inhaled them now as the scent of healing, far more soothing than the antiseptic odours of hospitals and clinics.

Tim also noticed himself in this setting. How unusual for him to remove all his clothing except his boxers, and his socks until she got to his feet, to lie prone on a table, to have a stranger touch him all over. He felt a warm flow of energy from her hands to his body and then to—where? He felt he was vibrating with that energy.

He observed all this from high up in a corner of the room while his eyes remained closed.

The closest Tim had ever come to such a feeling was sometimes in choir rehearsal, when Robert would ask for the lights to be dimmed. He would lead them in a piece of music, encouraging them to go *into* it. He would have the sensation then of being the singer *and* the music. It was transcendent, and so was this: he became his feelings, yielded to them.

He knew he had been on the table for a long time, and sensed that the session was coming to an end when there was hardly a patch of skin to which she hadn't ministered, with the exception of parts he was grateful she had left private.

He was on his back, the sheet draped over him to keep him warm. She reached under for his right arm, and continued her loving touch right down to his wrist, hand, and fingers.

As she held his hand and expertly manipulated his fingers, an image came to Tim with such an impact that he thought the massage table had collapsed. He jumped, though his eyes remained closed.

Melanie paused, held her grip on his hand and arm for a moment, and then resumed with the left side. A few moments later, she was finished.

"You've been far away, Tim," she said, softly. "Open your eyes and come back to us now."

Melanie placed a tissue in his hand. When he opened his eyes, tears were leaking from their corners, and he dabbed at them.

She helped him sit upright at the edge of the table, wrapped the blanket around him, and rested her hand on his forearm.

"My next client is here now, but I have two rooms, so you just take your time getting dressed. Don't stand up until you feel steady. You've been through a lot here, and I think you'll feel disoriented for a bit."

Tim couldn't speak. He nodded.

Before she opened the door, Melanie said, "After the feeling of being run over by a truck dissipates, I hope you'll feel good, or well, or happy. I'm glad you came and I hope you'll come back. Your back needs more work, but I can fix it. The rest of you needs more work, too, Tim, but you are fearless. We can make you better, together. Blessings. Bye-bye, now."

He managed a weak smile and nodded again.

The door closed quietly behind her, and Tim immediately

missed her presence.

He dressed slowly, feeling like he was in a different body from the one he had walked in with. This one worked remarkably better, he noticed as he bent to put on his shoes.

In the front office, Lisa the receptionist processed his payment and handed him an appointment card.

"Melanie suggests that you come back in about two weeks," she said. "Give us a call. It will be nice to see you here again, Tim."

~

Tim began driving toward South River, but he pulled over on a wide shoulder, put the gearshift in park, and left the engine running.

What day was it? What planet was he on? What had happened back there? Why had there been tears? What did she mean, he'd been far away? What was the "more work" she said he needed, aside from another massage, and how could she tell?

Tim sat there while exhaust swirled around the car, wondering, and then not thinking at all. He didn't know how long he sat there before he shifted into gear again, and slowly drove the rest of the way home.

He was reheating leftovers without much interest when the phone rang. It was Robert.

"Just checking in on you. A first massage can be quite a paradigm-shift. How do you feel?"

"Oh, I'm great, thanks" Tim struggled to make his tongue work. "I felt...it was so...she..."

"I see. Did she work on that spot in your back?"

"Yeah, it helped a lot."

"And the rest of you?"

Tears stung Tim's eyes and he struggled to speak normally.

"I—I have some more work to do, she said." He cleared his throat. "She said, uh, she told me I'm fearless."

"Fearless? Wow. It sounds like she found some nerves that don't show up on body charts. That can happen. She must be good, because you don't let just anybody see your interior, you know. Hang in there, Timo. We can talk tomorrow after choir, or sooner if you need to. I bet you smell like you fell into a bucket of incense, don't you? I love that smell. I must book myself an appointment there sometime when I'm down. You take care now."

The massage had been life-altering, Tim was sure, though he couldn't see how or why yet. The phone call from Robert was, too, in a way; it was so rare, but Rob was always on target.

He discarded the image of Robinson Crusoe. Right now, he felt more like a pin in a bowling alley: sometimes he got knocked down, hard, but then the swishing sweeper-thing pushed him into the Gully of Re-set, and the Whatchacallit From On High picked him up by the hair and stood him on his feet again. It was not a perfect metaphor, but it amused him, and that distracted him from the strikes enough to notice he was hungry after all.

He finished dinner, tidied up in the kitchen, turned out the lights and took a book upstairs, a rare thing because he usually quickly fell asleep reading in bed. When he woke around midnight, he turned off the lamp and returned to a deep sleep.

He woke in the wee hours, so he got up to pee. In the bathroom, he found that he had tears in his eyes again. He couldn't recall having a dream that might have brought them on.

Maybe he had an allergy to the essential oils that Melanie had been using. He hoped not. He liked them, and would regret washing them off in his morning shower.

He returned to bed and, after flipping his pillow over to the dry side, fell back to sleep.

www.ingramcontent.com/pod-product-compliance
Lightning Source LLC
Chambersburg PA
CBHW060913210726
48293CB00006B/2077